Under the Rel

Charles Neufeld

Alpha Editions

This edition published in 2024

ISBN : 9789362510396

Design and Setting By
Alpha Editions
www.alphaedis.com
Email - info@alphaedis.com

Contents

CHAPTER I

A QUARREL AND A FIGHT

The Debating Society of the Königsberg University was sitting. The subject for the occasion was of a trivial nature, but lent itself to keen and heated argument. The whole afternoon had been occupied with the speeches of the minor lights of the society, and now only the two opposing leaders remained to make their closing speeches before the division took place.

Young Osterberg, the leader of the "Ayes," rose to his feet. His remarks were sound and clear, and his arguments, to many, conclusive. After he had occupied the attention of the assembly for nearly twenty minutes, he sat down amidst the plaudits of his own side, to await the speech from the leader of the Opposition.

At that moment a voice, distinctly audible above the buzz of conversation that followed, spoke in a loud, unpleasant tone, evidently intended for the whole room to hear.

"'Tis a pity certain positions are not filled by fellows capable of thinking and arguing logically. Such rot I have never before listened to. Come, Maurice, let us go to the club rooms, we shall find better entertainment there." And the two men rose from their seats and moved towards the door.

Before they reached it the voice of the President stopped them, and in sharp, incisive tones called them to order.

"Such words," he said, "are against the rules of the society and must be withdrawn, or the laws which govern the Association will be enforced and the speaker's name struck off the list of membership."

John Landauer, the man who had uttered the offensive words, turned on hearing the President's mandate. With flashing eyes he glanced in the direction of Osterberg.

"My words may have been untimely as uttered in this room, and for that I apologize; but my opinion of the last speaker, friend Osterberg, remains the same, and what I am not allowed to express here I shall take the earliest opportunity of doing elsewhere."

He turned, and, followed by the youth he had addressed as Maurice, left the room.

An ominous murmur went round the room as the door closed behind them, and an air of suppressed resentment pervaded the place. One and all felt that an insult had been offered to Osterberg, an insult which they knew, since he was a theological student, he would be unable to respond to in the customary manner. However, the expression of the young student's face, usually so kindly, indicated that the altercation had not yet ended.

As soon as the debate was over, a general adjournment to the club followed. Osterberg was one of the first to reach it.

He found Landauer playing billiards with his companion Maurice. Stepping up to him, he eyed him sternly from head to foot.

"Thank you, Landauer, for your opinion of my ability," he said, evidently with difficulty repressing a desire to indulge in personal violence, "it was a plucky remark of yours. Had I been studying for other than the ministry, you would not have dared to give it utterance. Bah! I appreciate a man, but you are a coward!"

Landauer turned fiercely on the speaker.

"Coward? It is not I who am the coward! I do not take shelter under the cloak of the ministry, which forbids duels. You are the coward," he went on, stepping towards him and snatching his cap from his head, "and I challenge you to prove my words false!"

As he spoke he flung the cap on the ground at Osterberg's feet, and defiantly awaited the outcome of his action. The challenge was a customary one amongst the students. The snatching Osterberg's cap from his head was the greatest insult Landauer could have offered him, and the bystanders wondered how it would be received.

For a moment the young theological student stood as if in doubt. His lips twitched with indignation. There was no cowardice in his nature, but he knew the rigorous laws which governed his studies. On the one hand, if he refused to accept the challenge, the stigma of cowardice would stick to him all his life, and on the other, he would have to give up his profession if he should have a scar inflicted under such circumstances. Human nature conquered, and he was about to return insult for insult, when a firm, strong hand was laid on his shoulder.

"One moment," said a voice, in passionless even tones, "I have something to say to our friend here."

The speaker calmly strode up to the bullying Landauer, and, with his open hand, struck him across the face.

"You wish to quarrel? Very well, now is your opportunity. You have insulted not only our friend Osterberg, but the Debating Society of which I am a member. These things cannot go unnoticed. Apparently you selected Osterberg as a butt for your insults, knowing that, from the nature of his studies, he could not retaliate in the usual manner; but such cowardly bullying shall not be passed over, you shall account to me for your caddish behaviour."

The challenge was so startlingly sudden, that Landauer had no answer ready to give, but with rage and mortification expressed in every feature he fumbled in his pocket for a card. At last he drew one out, and with all the bombast he could summon on the spur of the moment, he scribbled the name of a friend upon it, and threw it on the table.

"You shall hear from me to-morrow," he cried, between his teeth.

His opponent smiled as he picked the card up; then, with the same deliberation, he replaced it with one of his own.

"Good," he said. "This is my affair now, and———"

"I'll give you a lesson, Mr Helmar, that you won't have time to forget." And Landauer, flinging his billiard cue on the table, strode from the room.

"Well done, Helmar!" "Good luck to you!" and such-like exclamations of approval filled the room as the door closed behind Landauer. Some of the students, however, blamed Helmar for what they termed his foolhardiness in interfering. But the majority applauded his action, and wished him every success.

Landauer was well known to be an expert swordsman, and had been victorious in several duels. Helmar, on the other hand, was entirely unknown in the use of the weapon, and was naturally pitied by his comrades. But the students admired bravery, especially when in a good cause. In this case they unanimously condemned Landauer's conduct in selecting Osterberg for the object of his assault.

"The fellow's a bully, whatever else he is, and no doubt thought his insult would go unchallenged. But there, the thing's done now, and I do not regret my action in the least. He must get satisfaction from me, if he wants it."

George Helmar was a quiet youth, of studious habits. A young man of seventeen, he had the reputation of being a hard worker, and had none of the quarrelsome spirit such as his adversary possessed. The thin, determined face, with its square jaw and keen grey eyes, the great loose shoulders and powerfully developed limbs might have told more careful observers than his fellow-students that underneath that calm exterior a latent power existed, which Landauer had best not underrate.

He had been brought up in the country, where his father practised medicine. There all his leisure had been spent in manly sports, riding, running, shooting, fencing; all these things he had gone in for as a boy, with the result that the town-bred Landauer, though an expert swordsman, was not, as regards physical training, to be compared with him.

Helmar hoped at some future date to succeed his father in his practice, and to that end had worked hard, using, as a matter of fact, the University recreation rooms and grounds very little. It was, therefore, not strange that his companions should doubt his ability to meet his adversary with any chance of success.

It is often small things that alter the course of a man's life, and so it was with Helmar. What he thought to be but a mere incident in his career turned out to be the cross-roads of his existence.

During the time which elapsed before the duel, he pursued his studies in the same indomitable fashion, considering but little of his chances, assuring himself only of the justness of his cause.

His friend Osterberg, however, was greatly concerned, and passed many sleepless nights weighing the possibilities of what might happen. Although he was to become a clergyman, and duelling was forbidden him, he nevertheless had plenty of fight in him, and many times wished that he could relieve his friend of the self-imposed risk he was taking on his behalf.

Landauer, on the other hand, had too much of the vanity of the bully to cause him any uneasiness. He was confident of his own superiority over Helmar, and discussed his inevitable success wherever opportunity arose.

The day at last arrived, and early in the morning the combatants met at the appointed place. Doctor Hertz was in attendance, and as the two young men stripped and stood grasping the hilts of their swords, he eyed them critically.

Landauer he passed over with a glance, his neat, lithe figure was quite familiar to him, he knew his powers to a fraction, and was perfectly aware that he would give a good account of himself.

With George Helmar it was different. He had never seen him before—it was his first appearance in the duelling world. The doctor's critical glance quickly turned into one of admiration. The tall, loose figure, though perhaps not beautiful in an artistic sense, pleased him greatly. Helmar's back and chest were ribbed with beautifully developed muscles, while his long, sinewy arms hung loosely at his sides, their very pose indicating to his practised eye their perfect suppleness.

The old doctor liked what he saw in the new candidate, and a grim smile played over his face as the word of command was given.

The spot was a solitary one. The common that had been selected was well away from the University, and admirably adapted to an encounter such as this. The trees in the background sheltered the combatants from observation in one direction, but for the rest the common lay open and uninviting, and the chill morning air blowing across it made the onlookers think longingly of their beds.

Notwithstanding this, every eye was riveted on the duellists. No thought of the fact that probably one of the men would be carried lifeless from the spot detracted from their interest in the encounter. They loved a fight, it was their nature; and, rain or snow, wind or hail, they would watch it to the bitter end.

At first the two young men fought cautiously, their heavy sabres flashing and glinting in the morning light as they thrust and parried with lightning rapidity. Later on Landauer seemed inclined to attack, and his blows on Helmar's weapon rang out in quick succession. Acting purely on the defensive, the latter parried the onslaught with an ease that puzzled and angered his opponent, until incautiously he fell into the trap by redoubling his attack. Helmar had reckoned on this. He hoped soon to tire the bully out, and a faint smile passed over his face, as with a head parry he stayed a terrific blow from his fiery antagonist.

Whether it was the smile, or a sense of caution previously unheeded, is doubtful; but Landauer evidently saw his mistake and endeavoured to remedy it by defensive tactics. It was too late. He had already begun to tire, while Helmar was still fresh. Seeing his opportunity, the latter pressed his advantage with the utmost cleverness. Without giving his opponent time to recover, he came at him with a rapidity that fairly astonished everybody, never wasting any power on a stroke which he knew would be parried. Sparks flew from their swords, as with the agility of a swordsman only in the highest stage of training he fought, bearing his opponent back with his lightning thrusts.

It was a fine sight. The whole thing seemed little more than play to him, while his antagonist was already breathing hard and showing signs of fatigue.

In the third round Helmar received a slight wound in the face, and the sight of the blood made the onlookers think that he was tiring too. But they didn't know their man. He had a big reserve of power which, as yet, he had not exerted; but he knew the game was in his own hands, and was prolonging the bully's punishment.

Suddenly Landauer made a ferocious attack, and in doing so for a moment drove the other back. His advantage was but momentary, for in an unguarded moment he had left himself badly open. With no real intention of doing him very serious harm, Helmar lunged out, and his sabre passed down Landauer's right cheek to his left shoulder, and he fell back on the grass with a terribly ugly wound.

The duel was over, and the bully punished. The spectators rushed to express their admiration to the victor and congratulate him on his success, but he would have none of it, and hurriedly went to the assistance of his late foe.

The doctor examined the wound and looked very grave. In response to his inquiries, he told Helmar that he could not yet express an opinion, but the case was serious, and the wounded man must be at once taken to the hospital.

Helmar turned to his friend Osterberg.

"Come," said he, "this place is hateful to me. If I have killed him I shall never forgive myself." He put on his coat and went back to his house.

CHAPTER II

DOWN THE DANUBE

After the duel Helmar endeavoured to return to his studies as before, but it was with a sore heart and a disturbed mind that he applied himself to his "Materia Medica." Each day he anxiously inquired after the wounded man, each night in the quiet of his room he prayed earnestly that Landauer's life might be spared.

Charlie Osterberg was now his constant companion, and tried by every means in his power, but without avail, to cheer his friend and distract his mind from the gloom and despondency that had taken hold of him.

It was on the evening of the fourth day since the duel, young Osterberg, after a visit to the wounded man, returned hastily to George's rooms.

Helmar looked up as his friend entered.

"Well, what news? No, never mind, I read it in your face," he said, as he noticed Charlie's pallor and troubled face. "He is dead?"

Osterberg shook his head.

"Not as bad as that, thank God, but I fear he cannot live. Dr. Hertz was there when I arrived, and before I left, he said the patient was rapidly sinking, and that it was only a question of forty-eight hours; but," he added hurriedly, as he noticed the horrified expression of the listener's face, "he also told me to say to you that, should he die, you will in no way be blamed. You cannot be held responsible. Had you not wounded him, he would probably have killed you."

His friend paid no heed to these consoling words, but, resting his face on his hand, gazed out of the window lost in deep thought.

Receiving no reply, Charlie stepped towards him, and, laying his hand gently on his shoulder, said—

"Cheer up, George, this affair is through no fault of yours. If anybody's, the blame is mine. I should have known better than to have noticed his words, but——" And he broke off with a troubled look in his eyes.

"No, no, Charlie, no blame attaches to you or, for that matter, to me. According to the duelling laws of the country we are in the right—it isn't that. You don't understand."

He paused for a moment, then suddenly looked up into the anxious young face at his side.

"Charlie, are you very keen to remain here and continue your work?"

"I ought to," he replied doubtfully. "My parents have been so good to me and are so anxious that I should do well in my examinations. But why?"

"The thing is as plain as daylight," said Helmar, as if arguing with himself. "I cannot ever face my people again. How would it be possible for me to go to them with blood on my hands? No, a thousand times, no! I am a homicide morally, no matter what the law may countenance. It is a barbarous custom, and one in which I can see no right. Oh! why did he not kill me?" And he turned despairingly to the window.

Osterberg endeavoured to interrupt him, but he turned fiercely on his friend.

"No, do not speak, my mind is made up. My studies are broken, I can never return to them again. My associations are distasteful, and I must get away. I shall go and leave it all. Go where I am not known. Yes, I shall go out into the world with the brand of Cain on me!" And he shook off Charlie's kindly touch, and paced up and down the room.

For a moment or two the silence was only broken by the sound of Helmar's rapid footfalls. Presently Charlie spoke.

"You asked me, just now, if I were anxious to keep on with my work. What did you mean?"

"Nothing, nothing," replied Helmar hurriedly. "I was wrong. What I do in the future must be by myself. I will bring no further trouble on those I love."

Charlie's eyes brightened, and his face broke out into a smile.

"I am going away, too. I realize that there is too much human nature in me for the Church. Why not let us go together? I don't mind where it is, anywhere will do for me. What do you say? Egypt, Japan, India, or America, it's all the same."

Helmar paused in his walk, and looked hard at his young friend.

"Do you mean that, or is it the outcome of what I said?"

"I mean every word. My mind is as fully made up as yours, and, if you will let me, I will throw in my lot with yours. There is but one thing I ask; Mark Arden, my old work companion, wants to go with me, and I have agreed. May he accompany us?"

"Certainly, the more the merrier," replied Helmar, his face lighting up as the prospect of getting away grew brighter. "But we must discuss ways and means. I intend to start to-morrow morning. Money with me is a little flush just now, and to-night I intend to realize on all my books and instruments, which will add a bit more. You and Mark can do the same, and we'll leave for Vienna by the first train in the morning, and then down the Danube on to Constantinople, at which place we can decide our ultimate destination. How does that suit you?"

"Admirably," said Charlie. "I will go and tell Mark." And he turned to leave the room.

"Meet me here at ten to-night, and, in the meantime, sell all your superfluous property, and tell Mark to do the same."

All the final arrangements were settled that night. One pawnshop, at least, did a good trade, and when the three adventurers at last turned into their beds, it was with the knowledge that all the world was before them, with a totally inadequate capital to see them on their way. Health, strength, and inexperience is a grand stimulant to hope, and the three young men only looked on the bright side of the future.

Helmar knew very little of Mark Arden; he had met him a few times with Osterberg, but he had no idea of the man's character. This, however, did not trouble him. In his open-hearted, manly way he trusted to his friend's judgment. In this he was wrong. Osterberg was a simple fellow, believing good of every one, and Mark, with a tact born of a scheming mind, had fostered this trust in him, carefully keeping hidden any of his doings which might open his friend's eyes. His object, so far, was not quite clear even to himself, but when it was settled that they were to journey together, he realized the benefit of what he had done.

He was a peculiar fellow; not absolutely bad, so far as was known, but with a character capable of developing in accordance with whatever surroundings in which he found himself. His main object in life was self. He cared nothing for study, although he was decidedly clever, and he saw in this adventure a means of starting out on a career where his own innate smartness might be given full play, and very likely earn for him a fortune. How he succeeded we shall see.

On the second day Vienna was reached. The excitement of this plunge into the world of adventure was still upon them. Helmar and Osterberg had written to their respective parents explaining what they had done, and giving their reasons for their actions. Mark Arden had carefully abstained from leaving any trace of his whereabouts, he had made up his mind to await developments.

Many suggestions were offered as a means of reaching Constantinople, but Helmar, who was looked upon as the head of the expedition, passed them all by as being of too expensive a nature, and kept to his original plan of securing a boat and doing the journey down the Danube. He argued it was cheaper and more in accordance with the adventurous career they proposed. By this means they would harbour their little stock of money, and as both Mark and

Charlie possessed little more than would carry them to Constantinople, the plan was adopted.

Their object now was to secure a boat, and they at once set about finding a boatman who could supply this need. Mark knew Vienna well, and acted as pilot in their search; but for a long time they were unsuccessful. None of the boatmen wished to sell their craft, and, as hiring was of no use to the adventurers, they had to search elsewhere.

"I think we have interviewed every boatman on the river," said Mark. "The only thing to do now is to visit an old boat-builder I know of in another quarter of the town. He deals in second-hand craft, and is very likely to be able to accommodate us."

"Right you are," said Helmar. "Lead the way, and unless he is a Shylock I dare say we shall be able to strike a bargain with him."

The three friends proceeded at once to the place, and they found the old man busy painting a canoe he had just built. He looked up as they entered, and, recognizing Mark, nodded familiarly.

"Good-morning, Jacob," said Arden. "Nice little craft that. Built to order?"

"Yes," replied the Jew, eyeing his visitors narrowly. "But vat can I do for you?"

"Well, look here," put in Helmar, "we want a small single sail boat. Not a new one—anything will do. We are going for a trip down the river, but in case of accidents we want to buy it. Can you find us one?"

"Ach, mein tear young frients, I have de very ting, but how much vill you pay?"

"We are not particularly flush," said Mark, who was appointed chief haggler. "Where's the boat, and how much do you want for it?"

"De poat is in de water, but I vill hab it prought to de landing-stage for you to zee."

A boatman was sent out to bring in the boat in question, and after a careful scrutiny the trio of adventurers decided it would do, and determined to purchase it, if they could get it at a fair price.

The process of beating the Jew down was no easy task, but Mark seemed quite equal to the wiles of the Israelite, and eventually the bargain was struck, the purchase effected, and the money handed over.

"It's all right enough," said Mark, as they waited whilst the old Jew went to his office to write out the receipt; "the old man is a hard nut to crack, but he's honest, and the boat that he has sold us looks all he has represented it."

Old Jacob soon returned, and the boat was duly handed over.

For the next two or three hours the process of stocking the craft with provisions was gone through, and it was late at night when everything was in readiness for the start. The three companions slept aboard, and at daylight the next morning cast off their moorings and started on their career in the world.

When they said good-bye to Vienna, it was a bright spring morning, and their feelings were in accord with the fresh appearance of the world. No thoughts or anticipations of how their varying fortunes might be marred troubled for one instant their youthful minds. Their hearts were full of hope and the overweening vanity and self-confidence of their years. The East, to them, was paved with gold. Troubles looked like the necessary things to be combatted fearlessly to reach the success that must await them beyond; life, indeed, was one rosy, golden, glorious dream. The stern realities were to come: when their fortitude would be tried, when all that was manly, or otherwise, in them would be brought out, and they would show of what manner of stuff they were made.

The first two or three weeks of the journey passed uneventfully, the wind was in the right direction, and they glided smoothly along the waters of the great and glorious Danube.

Just as the sun was sinking one night towards the end of the third week, they found that the river passed through a dense forest, and decided by way of a change, instead of passing the night in the boat as they had done up till then, to moor her to the bank, and, under a canopy of thick bush, sleep on the bosom of mother earth.

Helmar at once steered for the bank, and the party landed. Drawing the boat up out of the water, they pitched their camp and prepared their evening meal.

When they were seated round their fire, the conversation turned upon their plans for the future.

"We had better decide now," said Helmar, "as to where we shall make for when we reach Constantinople. Let's hear what you have to say, Charlie."

"Whatever you propose will do for me. Mark, here, prefers Japan, but I am not altogether sure that it will be best."

"Oh, yes, it will be," broke in Mark, in decisive tones. "There's a future in Japan second to none. The chance for enterprise is great there, and, besides, if a man has anything in him he can worm himself into Government circles, and that means a fortune."

"Personally I'm in favour of Egypt," said Helmar, quietly. "Japan no doubt is promising enough, but if you only stop to think for a moment, Mark, you will realize that your capital is not sufficient to carry you there." And he eyed the other keenly.

"Of course my capital isn't large, but I understood we were working on a common purse, and you, Helmar, have ample."

"True enough," said Helmar, looking up the stream towards the rosy sunset, "but I am not going to waste it all on travelling. We shall need something to keep us until we get work."

"Oh, very well," said Mark, shrugging his shoulders in a discontented fashion. "Then I suppose as you want us to go to Egypt, that will have to be our destination; but, I can tell you, I didn't expect this sort of thing."

"Perhaps not," replied Helmar, quietly. "But I'm not a fool, and intend going wherever our means will carry us best. Eh, Charlie?" turning to Osterberg.

"You're right, it's no use wasting our capital. Hark! what's that?"

The three men listened intently. There was the sound of voices not far from where they sat.

"By Jove, we must be near a road," said Helmar, as the sound grew louder. "I'm going to reconnoitre."

"No, no, let me go!" said the other two in a breath.

Without waiting for reply they darted off into the bush, and Helmar was left to himself. For some moments he gave himself up to surmising the origin of the sounds he now heard distinctly. As they came nearer he could distinguish the language in which the voices spoke, and with an exclamation of anxiety, he recognized it.

"Gipsies, by Jove! There'll be trouble if they come across those fellows," he muttered. "I must go and find them."

There was reason for his anxiety. In these parts the gipsies were practically brigands, and would rob and even murder without the least compunction. In recognizing the language Helmar had realized a danger for which he had in no wise prepared. He wondered if they had discovered the camping-ground. Suddenly he thought of the fire, and feared the smoke from it might have betrayed their whereabouts. However, in case it had not, he was determined to guard against such a possibility, and immediately poured some water on it.

Looking round, his eye chanced on a heavy branch of a tree, which had been brought in for fire-wood; breaking a substantial limb off it, he quickly trimmed it into a heavy club.

Giving one last look round he slipped off his coat, and, armed with his formidable weapon, darted into the bush, following in the footsteps of his companions as best he could.

CHAPTER III

A SURPRISE AND A REVELATION

Helmar had not proceeded more than fifty yards when his worst fears were realized. He had dodged his way along the tortuous footpath until, nearing an open space, he saw ahead of him his companions surrounded by a small group of dusky, evil-looking men.

"Gipsies!" he exclaimed, and counted six of them, all armed with heavy sticks, and with knives stuck in their belts. Their voices were raised to a high pitch, and, jabbering in infuriated tones, they flourished their weapons in the faces of their two prisoners.

Helmar stood gazing at them for a few seconds. Suddenly he saw one of the men, judging by his size the leader, step up to Mark and make as though to search him. The instant his hand touched him, Mark's fist shot out like lightning, and striking the fellow on the point of the chin, felled him to the ground.

This was the signal for a general *mêlée*. George caught a glimpse of steel as the men closed on their victims, then without waiting for anything further, he gave one ringing cheer, and bounding into the open, brandished his club aloft as he dashed into the struggling mob.

The suddenness of his attack for an instant paralyzed the would-be murderers, and ere they had time to recover, he was laying about him with all the power at his command. In a moment two men fell, and as their heavy sticks slipped from their hands, Mark and Charlie seized them and ranged themselves at Helmar's side.

The fight now waxed furious, the odds were heavily against the adventurers, and the issue looked doubtful. The noise had brought another man on the scene, and Helmar saw that to save themselves he must resort to strategy.

Singling out one man, he attacked him with such agility and force that he gradually beat him back from the rest. The new-comer seeing this, went to the fellow's assistance and endeavoured to stab our hero from behind. George, however, was not to be caught napping. Redoubling his exertions and by constantly dodging he kept his adversaries in front of him, until, at last, he succeeded in dealing the man a terrible blow on his shoulder.

Down he went with a crash, and the other, fearing a similar fate, fled precipitately into the bush. Helmar now turned to see how his companions fared.

The odds here were three to two, and his friends were keeping the men at bay. Without a moment's hesitation, George rushed into the fray, and, setting to work with a will, quickly stretched one of the gipsies out, whereupon the others beat a hasty retreat.

"Quick, boys, make for the river before they come on again! They haven't done with us yet! Follow me!" And he led the way into the path by which he had come.

Mark and Charlie needed no second bidding, but followed as swiftly as their legs could carry them. They were not a moment too soon, for as they disappeared into the bush, the brigands, further reinforced, again appeared on the scene.

It now became a question as to whether they could reach the boat in time to get it into the water before the enemy were upon them. Helmar calculated this as he sped along, and quickly realized that the task would be hopeless. Calling to his friends, he told them to run on and launch the boat, and he would join them as soon as it was accomplished.

"As the leader made an attempt to get over the bough, Helmar swung his heavy club at him." p. 27

"But," said Charlie, "you cannot face them single-handed. Let Mark go to the boat, and I will remain with you."

"No, no, run on for your lives and mine. When the boat is launched, keep her a few yards out from the bank and wait for me. Hurry up; here they come."

Thus exhorted, Mark and Osterberg ran on without further demur, and Helmar followed them until he reached the edge of the camping-ground. Here he seized the bough from which he had broken his club, and flung it across the pathway, and stood waiting the approach of the brigands.

In a moment the leader came up, and, seeing the resolute Helmar awaiting him on the other side of the barrier, he paused. It was only momentary, however, and as the rest of the gipsies joined him, the whole party, now six in number, rushed at the solitary defender.

In that momentary pause, however, Helmar had heard the crunching sound of the boat sliding into the water, followed by the welcome shout of "all right" from his friends. He intended to hold the men at bay for just a few moments longer, so as to give his companions time to get well into the stream. The charge of the gipsies in a body was evidently intended to overwhelm him by numbers. As the leader made an attempt to get over the bough, Helmar swung his heavy club at him, and the fellow fell back. Then, seeing another clear his obstruction to his right, and not having time to defend himself from his attack, he flung his trusty weapon at him and, turning, ran towards the river. Without pausing to see if he was pursued, he plunged headlong into the river, and struck out from the shore.

Everything had worked beautifully. As he came to the surface and looked round, he saw the boat at a safe distance from the shore, and he swam quickly towards it. Reaching it his companions quickly hauled him aboard, and, looking towards the bank, he saw the brigands standing at the water's edge wildly gesticulating and shouting execrations at the top of their voices.

"They seem pretty wild," ventured Osterberg, as the boat quickly widened the distance from the shore, "you just came in the nick of time, George; I believe they intended killing us."

"Yes, you fellows should have waited, instead of rushing off as you did to see who they were. Confound it, I've lost my coat, to say nothing of cooking utensils; however, it's all over now. We've had a lucky escape; I hope it'll be a lesson."

They quickly set sail, and decided to keep on their way all that night rather than risk such another encounter. Mark said little about it, except to bemoan the fact that they would in future have to sleep in the boat, a proceeding which had become particularly distasteful to him.

After this the journey went on without incident. They passed the cataracts in safety and on to Belgrade, at which point they encountered a series of rapids. The river here was shut in by lofty hills on either side, and was strewn with rocky shoals of limestone, crystalline, and granite, so that the greatest care had to be observed in navigating them. After many anxious hours, the last of these was passed and they began to near their journey's end.

Altogether they had been a month in their little craft, and the monotony of it all, in spite of the beautiful scenery and picturesque country through which they passed, was beginning to tell on the voyagers. They were becoming irritable and pettish. Mark Arden had on several occasions made himself particularly disagreeable—airing his views as to the wanton waste of time which their journey had been, in no very measured terms.

"What did you expect?" asked George, on one of these occasions. "Did you think we were going for a picnic? Or did you think some one would pull us along? It's no use complaining now. Look at it in a philosophical light. See what a splendid experience it is for us! It will harden us for what may be in front of us."

"But it's such a dreary journey, no change, no variety, no amusement," grumbled Mark.

"I'll admit it's a bit of a grind," chimed in Charlie. "But what change and variety is got out of it falls to you. You have your own way about provisions, and what is more, you always have the pleasant journey into the villages to obtain them. Besides which, you frequently have the distinction of entertaining the company," he went on, in a jocular way. "For instance, I think it was as good as a play to see you yesterday with your rod, trying to catch our breakfast. If I hadn't been on the look-out, you'd have had George by the eye instead of the fish by the gills."

"You shall try your hand at it to-morrow, and we'll see what a figure you'll cut," he said almost irritably.

George got a little annoyed at this, and did not hesitate to show it.

"I'm sure," he said, "we've given you all the best of it. The whole fact of the matter is, you are discontented already and ought to be back at the University, where you can get everything done for you. I'll tell you what it is, if you are going to make any more fuss, you'd better leave us and go back. I'm sick of it."

"You needn't get in a huff," Mark replied, half apologetically; "a fellow couldn't help feeling the dreariness of this journey. There's nothing but this constant sitting in a boat and drifting down the river."

"Well, what more do you want?" said Charlie. "I'm sure I don't mind. This is a sort of paradise to what we shall probably have to go through."

"I'll tell you what we'll do," said Helmar suddenly; "we are all a bit tired of the river. The next decent town we come to we'll get out and take the train on to Varna. How'll that do?"

His proposal was met with delight by both of his companions, and the surly Mark even cheered up. The thought of getting away from the boat overjoyed him, and he grumbled no more.

Their journey, however, was to end sooner than they expected. They were fast nearing a big town when the wind, which was blowing very hard, suddenly changed its direction. As they rounded a bend in the river, it came down with a rush, and before they could throw their sail over to the other tack the boat capsized, and all three were struggling in the water.

Helmar was the best swimmer, and endeavoured to seize the boat, but it was swept along at such a rapid pace that he was unable to do so, and as he was about to follow it up a cry from Mark recalled him.

Turning, he saw his companion entangled in some of the loose ropes trailing after the boat.

It was with difficulty he extricated him, and by the time he had done so Mark was so exhausted with his struggles that the pursuit of the boat had to be abandoned, and the three made for the shore.

Everything but Helmar's money was lost, and as they sat on the bank, shivering in their wet clothes, they gazed ruefully after the rapidly disappearing boat.

"Well," said Helmar in resigned tones, "you've got your wish, Arden, we must now find another means of conveyance, and in the meantime you will get a chance of stretching your legs."

Arden didn't reply, and the trio got up and walked towards the distant town. Night was already closing in when they reached it, and cold, hungry, and tired, they hurried to the first inn that presented itself.

Their clothes had almost dried on them, and so without bothering to have them put to the fire, they had supper and went to bed. The next morning at Helmar's suggestion they took the train to Varna on the Black Sea, determined, from there, to take ship to Constantinople.

At Varna it became necessary for Helmar to change some of his money into Turkish currency.

"I want you to get this money changed, Mark," said he, when they alighted from the train; "you are better able to do it than I, I do not understand the ways of these money bureaux. There is sure to be one somewhere handy. While you do this, Charlie and I will seek an hotel, and then return here and await you."

He handed Arden some notes as he spoke, carefully counting them out to him lest he should make a mistake.

"The exchequer is getting low," he went on, as he saw his companion pocket them; "that is half of my all, and is just sufficient to see us all three to Constantinople."

"Is it as bad as that?" said Mark, looking keenly at Helmar as he spoke. "It's not a very lively look-out for us. Well, I'll meet you here in a couple of hours' time. I dare say by that time I shall have succeeded in changing them, and you in finding a suitable hotel." And he turned to go.

"Yes, we'll be here in the ticket-office when you return," Helmar called out after him; "don't be longer than you can help."

As soon as he had gone, Charlie Osterberg and Helmar left in search of quarters.

"This is the queerest place I was ever in, Helmar," said Charlie, as they turned into a narrow, unevenly-paved street. "These buildings all look as if they were about to collapse—and don't they look dirty!"

"Eh? What was that you were saying?" replied his companion. "Oh, yes—the houses—'m, I dare say they aren't over-clean. I say, Charlie, I'm half sorry I sent Arden with that money, somehow I wish I'd gone myself."

"Why, what do you mean? He'll change it right enough."

"Oh, yes, he'll change it right enough—but——"

"But what?"

"Oh, nothing. Do you know, I don't care much about him, he's such a grumbler," he broke off lamely.

Nothing more was said, and after a long hunt they at last discovered a hotel suitable to their means. It was a dingy-looking place, but, as Helmar said, "they couldn't live in a palace." Having struck a bargain with the proprietor they returned to the railway station in search of Mark.

The ticket-office seemed quite deserted when they entered. One dim light illuminated the room, and they glanced round for their friend. There was no one there—evidently he had not yet succeeded in his task.

"Let's go and wait outside," said Helmar, "the heat in here is stifling. I expect he's had a more difficult job than we anticipated."

The two friends strolled from the office and sat down on a bench just outside. They had not been there for more than a minute, when a boy, dressed in half-European and half-native costume approached.

"Excellency waits for his friend?" he asked in hesitating tones.

Helmar eyed the youth up and down.

"Well?" he said at last.

"I have paper—what you call letter!"

He handed a dirty envelope to Helmar, and bowing low, waited for the expected *douceur*.

The letter was addressed to Helmar in Mark's handwriting. He tore it open and rapidly scanned the contents.

"The scoundrel!" he cried, and flung the letter to Osterberg.

CHAPTER IV

THE PARTING OF FRIENDS

Charlie picked up the letter and read it out.

"DEAR HELMAR,

"I could not continue the journey as we have been going on. I did not want to rob you of your money, but you gave me the opportunity of borrowing sufficient to take me where I wish to go. At some future date I will return it with interest. Good-bye, and good luck to you. We shall meet again some day.

"MARK ARDEN."

Having read and re-read the brief note, Osterberg silently returned it to his friend. His face wore a troubled expression, and, as soon as Helmar had paid the messenger, he burst out into a torrent of invective.

"The lying scoundrel! Oh, George, I am so sorry I asked to bring him. It is all my fault—and I thought him honest. I can never forgive myself!" And the boy broke off, choking with anger and vexation.

"Never mind him," exclaimed George, placing the letter carefully in his pocket. "Some day, no doubt, we shall find him, and then—well, we shall see! In the meantime, I have still enough, with care, to take us to Egypt, and then we must trust to luck."

They went to their hotel, sadder and wiser youths. The thought of Mark's treachery weighed more heavily on them than either cared to acknowledge. George, with the independence of character essentially his, was the first to throw the unpleasant feeling off. They were sitting in the little room they had rented, their frugal meal finished and thoughts of bed already possessing them. Suddenly Charlie looked over to his friend.

"George, I'm going to stop in Constantinople for some time."

"Why," exclaimed Helmar, "whatever for?"

Charlie paused for a moment before answering.

"It's no use beating about the bush. You have scarcely enough money for yourself, and I've made up my mind that I will not sponge on you. I've thought it all out, and do not think there will be any difficulty in what I intend doing. You know I speak French and English well. My intention is to find employment in one of the banks, or big commercial houses, in Constantinople, and remain there until I have saved sufficient money to join you."

"You'll do no such thing! It was agreed that you should share with me all that I have, and I want you to come. Now, don't be foolish," as Charlie shook his head, "you *must* come!"

"No, old fellow, I will not—at least, not yet. My mind is quite made up, so it is no use your frowning. I shall accept your hospitality as far as Constantinople, and then, for a few weeks, we must part."

Helmar argued and tried to persuade, but all to no purpose; young Osterberg was as determined as he, and, on this particular point, nothing could move him. At length it was decided that they should journey, on the morrow, to Constantinople, whence George should sail at once for Alexandria, leaving his young friend at the Turkish capital.

The following morning they went aboard the little coasting vessel, and were soon on the last stage of their journey together.

On the way the two friends made the acquaintance of a doctor, who, discovering that Helmar was a medical student, took a keen interest in them. The medical man was an English army surgeon, and notwithstanding the difference of nationality his fancy was taken by the young adventurers, and, by the time they reached their destination, he had succeeded in discovering their intentions.

During the voyage Helmar had been very useful to his new friend in assisting him in the case of one of the passengers who had been taken ill, and, in return, Dr. Frank Dixon determined to try and do something for him. One evening they were sitting in the cabin, talking.

"Didn't you say our young friend here," said the doctor, indicating Charlie, "was going to remain in Constantinople if he could find employment?"

"Yes," answered Helmar, with a grimace, "much against my will, that is his intention."

"And a very laudable decision, too. I think it would be a great shame for him to let you spend what little money you have on anything but your own wants. Now, I may be of some help to him. I happen to be an intimate friend of the manager of one of the banks, and can give him a letter to him which, I feel sure, will secure him employment."

"You are awfully kind," broke in Charlie. "If you could do so, without troubling yourself too much, it would save me a good many hardships, but I should never be able to thank you sufficiently."

"Tut-tut," said the doctor, smiling at the eager young face before him, "it is nothing; besides, why should I not help you? I like your independent spirit, and feel sure you will not betray my confidence in you. Let me see, to-morrow we shall arrive. I'll tell you what to do. Array yourself in your best, and I will write the letter to-night and give it you before we land. I hope it may bring you the luck you deserve. As for you, Helmar," he went on, turning to the other, "you go on to Egypt. It will not be long before I am there too; we are bound therefore to meet, and then perhaps I may be of use to *you*. And now, good-night. I am going to turn in."

The friends wished their benefactor good-night, and retired to their berths.

In the morning they drew into the dock. The doctor, true to his promise, furnished Osterberg with a letter to the bank, to which place he at once proceeded. Helmar accompanied him to see how he fared.

Their luck was in, the letter secured Charlie a berth as corresponding clerk, and Helmar, satisfied with his friend's success, went at once to the shipping office and took his passage to Alexandria.

The boat started at three in the afternoon, and so the two friends spent their time in obtaining some new clothes for Osterberg, and generally fitting him to enter upon his clerical duties. As the time approached for Helmar's departure they made their way to the quay.

"I cannot say how long I shall stay in Alexandria, Charlie," said Helmar, "but I shall let you know of my movements. In the meantime, letters addressed to the Post Office will find me."

The warning bell rang, and George hurriedly shook his companion by the hand.

"I shall not be long in following you, old chap," said Charlie, pressing his friend's hand. "Give me a few weeks, or even a month or two, just long enough to get a little money together, and I'll be with you. Good-bye, and good luck."

Helmar ran up the gangway. Reaching the deck, he turned and waved his hat while the moorings were cast off. Charlie stood watching the receding boat until it was out of sight.

"There goes the man who has thrown up everything for me," he muttered, with a pained expression in his eyes. "I don't think he'll ever regret it. The greatest object of my life shall be to repay him tenfold!" And he turned away into the town.

George Helmar did not pace the deck, as most modern heroes do, for his passage was steerage, and there was very little deck for him to promenade. Just at first he was low-spirited, he felt the loneliness of his own company, everything seemed different without the bright companionship of his friend beside him. He felt keenly leaving Europe, and all the associations of the land of his birth. He was going to a country of which he knew nothing; he was about to face adventures, the outcome of which it would be impossible to anticipate. He might do well for himself, or on the contrary he might be a failure. All these things passed through his mind in the first few moments of depression that followed his departure, as he found himself cooped up in the unpleasant quarters of the steerage passengers.

He was a man of strong determination, however, and quickly threw off his despondent mood, and busied himself with plans for the future. He pictured no glorious El Dorado in the country to which he was journeying—he was much too sensible. He was aware that he would have to work, and work hard, for whatever he was to make.

One fact he had not passed idly by. He knew that trouble was brewing in Egypt; what it was he was not in a position to know. He had heard, vaguely, that at any moment fighting was likely to occur, and, if so, no doubt he would be in its midst; the very word "War" held out a world of hope to his adventurous spirit. In such times, he knew, there were no end of opportunities for the bold spirit, and, such being the case, he had no intention of letting any such chances pass unheeded.

Thoughts of his father and others he had left behind frequently recurred to him, and he wondered what they would say of his doings. At last he decided to write to all those whom his departure had affected, and tell them everything as it had occurred. This done, he felt more at his ease, and he gave himself up to the enjoyment of the lovely sea air as the vessel sped through the smooth, blue waters of the Mediterranean.

At last land was sighted, and in a short time Helmar put his foot on Egyptian soil.

The quay was thronged with a motley, dirty crew, evidently gathered there to await the arrival of the boat. The air was filled with the yelling and chattering of Arabs and negroes. The crowd was composed of all sorts of porters, hawkers offering their cheap wares for sale at exorbitant prices, dirty donkey boys with their wretched "mokes" looking even more starved and miserable than their owners. The dresses were of many kinds, and in a great variety of colours, from a dingy white to a bright scarlet. Close-fitting gowns and tunics, long, highly-coloured flowing robes, turbans, or semi-European clothing, with the usual Turkish fez, were scattered about in great profusion, and Helmar was glad to jostle his way through them to rest his eyes from the dazzling mixture. The many different tongues that caught his ear, as he made his way through the crowd, confused him terribly. Greek, Italian, French, English, Arabic, Turkish, and Persian, all shouting at once, as it seemed to him, jarred on his nerves, and he wondered if this pandemonium went on all over the town.

Making his way from the docks, he wandered about from place to place in search of quarters.

Failing to find what he wanted, he looked about for some likely-looking Europeans to whom he could appeal for guidance. He was chary of his countrymen abroad, and it was some time before he came across the man he desired.

He was recommended to a certain Greek's house, and, after what seemed an interminable day, he found to his satisfaction that here he could make himself more or less comfortable.

The next morning he set about finding work of some sort. He wandered about from street to street, gradually becoming more and more keenly interested in all he saw. First the inhabitants, then the buildings, attracted his attention. He watched the movements of the picturesque Egyptians, and was so taken with what he saw that, unconsciously, he found himself following them. This brought him again into the lower quarters of the town. The streets in this neighbourhood, whatever their redeeming charm, were certainly not to be recommended from any hygienic point of view, the smell being so bad that he quickly lost his interest in the wily native and hurriedly retraced his steps. Reaching the great square, the "Place des Consuls," with its masterful statue in the centre, he realized that the day was wearing on, and, instead of looking for work, he had been "doing" the city as a sightseer.

"This will not do," he thought. "I cannot spend the whole day without result, my cash will soon give out. Cairo seems to my mind to be the place I want, this is too near the sea. Ah, yes, Cairo, Cairo!" he went on aloud, "that surely would suit my purpose better. Why not go there at once, while I have money enough to pay my way?"

Once the thought possessed him it quickly became a fixed intention, and he hurried back to his room. Here he settled with the Greek, and then left at once for the railway station.

The express was about to start, so purchasing a ticket he got aboard, and in a few moments was on his way to Cairo.

CHAPTER V

HELMAR TO THE RESCUE

The third-class carriage in which George took his place was not the comfortable, up-to-date compartment to be found on European railways. At first glance it appeared to be more like a cattle-truck than anything else, except that it lacked the white-washed walls and healthy smell of such places.

The "pen," as he designated it, was filled with a contingent of all classes of people, Egyptians predominating. The majority were squatting on their haunches on the floor, regardless of those who wished to move about, in an attitude reminding one for all the world of the "Dusky Red Man" of America holding a "pow-wow."

Apparently this was the class principally catered for by the railway company, for George had observed before entering the train that the greater number of the carriages were labelled "third." In place of windows, these fearful and wonderful structures possessed iron bars placed horizontally along each side, still further likening them to cattle-vans.

Amidst such cheerless surroundings Helmar slunk into a corner, whence he could observe the country through which the train passed. After leaving Alexandria the scenery became so interesting that he forgot the condition of the cars, forgot the whining crowd of mendicants, women and children, traders, etc., who were his fellow-passengers; he even forgot the noisome smell of the place, so taken up was he with the curious and novel scenes presented to his wondering gaze.

The train sped past countless small villages, with their miniature dwellings around which gambolled little black, naked Egyptians, whose life apparently was a frolicsome pleasure. The larger towns, such as Kafr Dowar, Damanhour, Tarrâneh, El Wardan, with their monuments and minarets, presented the aspect of busy cities. Then on again, with the Nile on one side and the desert stretching further away on the other. As the journey neared its end the Arabian mountains came into view, whilst on the right, over the muddy banks of the river and across the plains, he saw the everlasting Pyramids.

In this way he passed the weary hours of the journey, until at length he saw in the distance the Mokhattam hills, at the foot of which nestled the great Cairo he was bound for.

His feelings when he first set foot in the city were mainly of intense relief at leaving the unwholesome car he had been travelling in; then, as he gazed admiringly at the Oriental buildings around him, they changed to those of satisfaction that he had reached the spot at last, where there was a reasonable possibility of making a start in his career for fortune. He looked upon the idea that had first induced him to leave Alexandria as an inspiration.

He was not long in finding quarters, rough, it is true, but compatible with the means he was now reduced to. What little money still remained to him he calculated might, with care, last him a week, and, if he did not find work, at the end of that time he would be absolutely penniless.

These conditions having occupied his attention for a time, he set about his quest for work at once. He had but vague ideas of how to conduct his search, but instinct told him that his best tactics would be to discover merchants of his own nationality, and try them first.

With this object he walked about, carefully observing every business house he came across. His wanderings took him through the broad streets of the mediæval quarter and along the principal boulevards until he reached the main street. Here he found what he sought—the European shops.

He was not long before he came upon a German bookseller's, and, with his customary rapid decision, he entered and asked for the manager. The clerk to whom he addressed himself led the way to an inner office, where our hero was confronted with a little fat, bristly man, with a keen though kindly face of undoubted Teutonic type. Without pausing to consider his words, he plunged into the object of his visit.

"I have just come from Europe, sir, and want work. Can you assist me?"

"That depends," he answered quickly. "What can you do? Where do you come from, and what recommendations have you?"

"I have no calling but that of medicine," replied Helmar with a sinking heart. "And I come from the Königsberg University. As for recommendations, I have none."

"Um! Not much to apply for work with," grunted the little man. "But tell me," he went on, "you are a countryman of mine, and, if possible, I should like to help you. Why did you come out here?"

Helmar then told him his whole story, disguising nothing; even going so far as to tell him who his father was. The little bookseller listened patiently to all he had to say, and at the conclusion of his narrative rose from his chair and came towards him.

"Your story seems to me a straight one, and you appear to be an open-hearted young man. I'll see what I can do for you. You say you speak and write English and French?"

"Yes," replied George anxiously, "tolerably well."

The man left his office for a few moments.

Presently he returned. "I have a large catalogue to make out, which requires a knowledge of two or three languages. It will take three weeks or more to compile. If you like to undertake it, it will be a means of keeping you until you can find something better. We are not quite ready to start yet, but present yourself here the day after to-morrow, and you can begin your duties. How will that suit you?"

George gratefully accepted the offer, and left the shop delighted with his good fortune.

As he hurried along towards his quarters, it seemed to him that he was walking on air. His wildest anticipations had been more than realized. He had never for one moment expected that his first effort could have possibly met with such success, and he wanted to laugh aloud. He knew nothing of catalogue-making, but no doubt, he thought, it required but a little common-sense, and he felt he possessed that. At any rate he had undertaken it, and would go through with it now.

On the appointed day George started his new task, and found it not only easy but congenial work. The many books in various languages attracted him further than their covers and titles, and he filled up all the odd and spare moments he could afford in studying many of them, particularly the Arabic ones. And so the days passed. In the evenings he wandered about the neighbourhood as far as Boulak, admiring the palaces of the Khedives, and watching the steamboats and dahabîehs arrive and depart for the Nile. At times he would stray further afield to the great Pyramids, and stand motionless with astonishment before their towering stone wonders. His first sight of the sun setting behind them, casting a golden-reddish glow all around, amazed and allured him so much that he made frequent visits to the same spot at the same hours.

But he wanted to see as much as he could during the next few days, for he could not tell what would happen after his catalogue was done. He therefore visited the regions of every-day commercial life; the carpet bazaars decorated with their Oriental manufactures of all colours; the Khan Khalili, wherein the Persian, Spanish, Jewish, and Turkish merchants offer for sale their stock of jewels, silks, brass-work, etc.; the silver bazaar, where the finest filigree work is pressed upon prospective buyers. He brushed shoulders with shoe-sellers, the pistachio-sellers, and the water-carriers, who assure all who choose to listen that theirs is "Water sweet as honey! Water from the spring!" and in a commanding voice invite you to "Drink, O faithful! The wind is hot, and the way long!" but not without the necessary piastres first.

During these few days George saw and learnt a good deal of Cairo, but he had not learnt quite sufficient of its manners and streets.

The day came when the catalogue business was finished, and his employer promised to find him some other occupation on the morrow. George was quite pleased with himself, and started off for another of his rambles.

For a while he was quite heedless of the direction he was taking, busily building castles in the air as fast as his thoughts would allow him; but he was brought to earth with a run as the fact dawned upon him suddenly that for the first time he had lost his way. He was in the densest part of the native quarter.

The evening was rapidly closing in, and he looked about for some one to direct him. Not a European face could he see anywhere. The street in which he found himself was filled with a chattering mob of natives, the houses formed one continuous line of small, poky stalls, where evil-looking Egyptians, Turks, and Arabs were offering their worthless stock for sale.

Hurrying along, he wandered through a labyrinth of streets, all more or less similar, until he became so confused that in despair he appealed to one of the native vendors.

His efforts to discover his whereabouts from this man were futile. The Egyptian was unable to understand him, and the fellow's jargon was quite unintelligible to Helmar. In desperation he continued his way; the prospect of spending the night in wandering through the city being anything but pleasant to him. Night was fast closing in, and he was apparently a long distance from his destination.

Suddenly, as he turned into an almost deserted street, he saw ahead of him a man dressed in European costume, and he increased his pace to overtake him.

To his annoyance, just as he was about to come up with him, the stranger turned into a squalid house, and Helmar was left to rail at his ill luck outside.

Realizing that there was nothing to be gained by going on, he thought he might as well wait in the hopes of the man coming out shortly. He was really feeling very uneasy; the neighbourhood was filthy, and the quietness of the street depressed him.

Sauntering quietly up the street, his attention was unexpectedly drawn to the figure of an Arab emerging from a house on the opposite side. It was now growing dark, and Helmar was quite unable to distinguish the fellow's face; but his furtive movements made him a little curious, and his interest in the man became riveted. He saw the Arab looking sharply along the street from end to end, and, apparently satisfied with his survey, quickly draw back into the shadow of the doorway. Helmar's curiosity now grew keener, and so engrossed was he for the time in the man's stealthy movements that he forgot the real object of his waiting. Consequently he failed to observe that the European had come out of the house he had a few minutes previously entered. Suddenly the figure of a crouching Arab darted from the shadow and walked swiftly and silently up the street.

Looking up the road in the same direction, Helmar was astonished to see the European he had been waiting for hurrying along at a rapid pace, fast disappearing in the gloom of the deserted slum.

The street, except for the two men in front of him, was now quite deserted, and our hero quickened his pace for fear of losing sight of his quarry.

The native had crossed the road, and was now running along with silent footsteps some distance ahead of him. Suddenly, as the fellow passed under the light of a dingy lamp, Helmar caught the glint of a long curved knife he was carrying in his hand.

"Hallo!" he muttered, "there's crime afoot!" and dodging on to the sandy road he hurried on. The European in front was walking leisurely along, totally unconscious of any danger that might be threatening him.

George began to fear something serious was about to happen. The stealthy footsteps of the Arab, his long knife, the pace with which he was overtaking the man ahead, looked decidedly unpleasant.

Ten yards only separated one from the other, while thirty or more separated the Arab from George. Could he get sufficiently near to warn the stranger?

Despite the roughness of the road, Helmar slipped his shoes from his feet and hurried along with all possible speed. A couple of yards only now separated the two men in front of him, and George had yet a few yards to go before he could come up with them.

He was about to shout a warning when something seemed to attract the European's attention. Turning, he came suddenly to a standstill, and the pursuing Arab charged into him. For an instant the gleaming knife poised in the air, but, ere it had time to fall on its intended victim, George reached the struggling pair, and, with the swiftness of a hawk, he seized the upraised arm in an iron grip. Exerting his great strength to its utmost, he gave one terrific wrench and the would-be assassin was forced to his knees, while his shining blade fell clattering to the ground.

Helmar's assistance was only just in time; another moment and the assassin would have accomplished his work. The freed stranger turned at once to aid his preserver. He saw the native struggling to release himself from George's terrible hold, and feared lest the man should escape. There was no need, however, George held the fellow with the greatest ease.

"Steady! Hold that end a minute.... That's it. Now tie it tight ... pull ... hard. Good. I think we've got him safely this time—the villain!"

These and other ejaculations were the only words passed between the two men as they secured their prisoner with the folds of his own sash. When this was accomplished, the stranger turned to Helmar and held out his hand.

"You have saved my life, sir," he exclaimed, in English. "I cannot thank you sufficiently, but it is best not to remain here. If you will still further assist me in conveying this man to the police quarters, we shall then have time to become acquainted."

As he finished speaking, he looked round sharply as if expecting a fresh attack from another quarter. George noticed his glance and looked inquiringly at him.

"You do not understand," went on the stranger, in answer to the look; "this attack is part of a plot—there are others. Come!"

Without demur, George assisted in dragging the unwilling prisoner along, and in a few minutes they reached the police head-quarters. Here they disposed of the Arab, and turned into a private room.

Helmar was struck with the air of authority his companion displayed as soon as the police station was reached, and, consequently, was not surprised when he introduced himself.

"My name is Inspector Childs, chief of the detective department of Cairo. Who may I have the pleasure of thanking for my preservation?"

George gave his name, and the two men shook hands again.

"It seems to me the most providential thing that you should have been in that neighbourhood to-night," said the inspector, eyeing the young man keenly. "But perhaps you are a stranger in the city, and perhaps you do not realize the danger of walking in the native quarter, after dark, just now."

"You are right; I did not know there was the least danger. The fact is, I am a stranger in the country, having come direct from Germany for the purpose of earning a living. I had really lost my way, and was following you to ask for guidance. I have been here but a few days."

"Ah, a living, eh!" said the inspector, repeating his words musingly. "Then I presume you have got nothing definite on hand just now." Suddenly he seemed to rouse himself. "You have rendered me the greatest possible service this evening; I shall be glad to help you in some way. Have you any particular profession or choice in the means of earning the living you speak of?"

"None whatever. I have been doing a small job, but that is finished now—in fact, I was returning from my place of employment when I saw you. The work was nothing very great, but I was glad of it as a start, and have been promised some further temporary employment by the same man."

"If you are not bound to him I can offer you something perhaps a little more profitable with the police staff here. Of course the progress you make will depend on yourself."

"I should be glad to accept anything that offers me a future. The work that I have been doing has only been given me to keep me going until I can find something better. If you think me capable and can offer me something more permanent, I should be delighted. What would my duties consist of, and when would they begin?"

"Your work would begin at once, and it would consist of general police duties; as for your capabilities, your exhibition of resource and action to-night is quite sufficient recommendation. What do you say?"

"You are very kind. I shall not hesitate to accept any position you consider me fitted for. I will write to the bookseller to-morrow and tell him."

The inspector paused for a moment, tapping his desk with his knuckle, as if endeavouring to make up his mind to what use he could put George.

"I have a very ticklish affair on to-night—an affair of so much risk that I hardly like to ask you to take part in it as a start. But if you care to," he went on thoughtfully, "I am quite willing to take you with me, although I quite meant going alone. But you must decide at once."

"Make your mind easy," exclaimed George, his eyes glistening at the prospect of adventure. "Whatever it is, if you think I can be of assistance, I am with you."

The inspector eyed the keen, eager face with approval.

"So be it, then! Here, put this in your pocket," he said, handing him a revolver. "We will start at once."

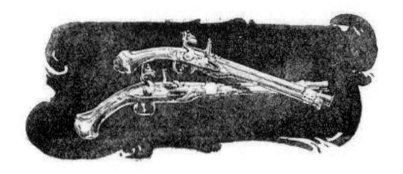

CHAPTER VI

A TIGHT CORNER

Following his new friend, George left the office. The spirit of adventure was fully upon him, and with his hand in his coat pocket, he gripped the weapon the inspector had given him, speculating in his mind as to what was the object of their night's work, and how their expedition would result. Evidently it was an affair of importance from the hesitation of the officer to enlist his services; instinctively he felt there was danger ahead.

Their direction again lay towards the low quarter of the city, and Helmar noted the familiarity and ease with which his guide wound his way through all the lanes, blind alleys, and courts that had so confused and puzzled him.

"I had better explain to you," said the inspector, after a few moments' silence, as they threaded their way along the narrow, dirty, evil-smelling streets, "what we are about to do. Being a stranger in the country, you probably are not aware that for some time past, meetings of a revolutionary character have been going on in nearly all the towns in Egypt. The fountain head of this movement is as yet undiscovered, as also is the ultimate object. Of one thing the authorities are assured, and that is, there is some terrible secret danger threatening the country, and the duty of our department is to watch, and, if possible, stop the work of this organization."

"Of what are the authorities afraid?" asked Helmar, as he listened with keen interest to his companion's explanations.

"I can't quite say. My own opinion is a native rising. There are several big Pashas the Government would not trust as far as they can see, and, for my part, I think nothing is more likely than that one of these should head a rebellion against the power of the Khedive."

"I see; and our work to-night is in connection with one of these meetings?"

"Exactly. The meeting is to be held at one of the lowest dives in the city, and its locality I have only to-night discovered; in fact, that was the business I was engaged upon when your timely aid saved my life."

"I see," exclaimed George; "but that attempt on you shows that these people are aware of your movements. The probabilities are that even now we are being watched."

"Precisely; notwithstanding the silence and deserted appearance of these streets, I have no doubt that a lynx eye has been upon us from the moment we left the station. The object of our journey is to discover, if possible, whether the meeting takes place, and, if so, who passes in or out of the building. Our danger is in being discovered. Should their sentries or spies find us out, we shall probably have a rough time."

A grim smile spread itself over the inspector's keen face as he finished speaking, and he looked at Helmar to observe the effect of his words.

"Well, if it comes to a fight, I have little doubt that we can give a good account of ourselves," he replied. "For my part nothing would give me greater pleasure than to try conclusions with some of the cowardly assassins."

"No doubt you will have your wish. It is the duty of a police-officer not to avoid trouble if he finds it."

They were now nearing the outskirts of the town. The streets were wider and cleaner, long, open spaces stretched between the houses, and the reeking atmosphere of the native quarter gave place to the fresh air of the open country. There was no moon to guide them, and they had long since got beyond the limit of the city lighting.

Suddenly, in the middle of one of these long, open spaces, the officer caught hold of his companion's arm, and stopped in an attitude of keen attention.

"Not a word!" he whispered, after a momentary pause. "We are followed. Come, drop down here, under this bush, and don't move till you see what I do. Shush!"

The pair lay down and pushed themselves as far under the bush as possible. Here they were within reach of the foot-walk they had been travelling, and yet entirely screened from observation.

So far George's untrained ear had discovered nothing, and he marvelled at his companion's sharpness, but before they had been there a minute, he heard the soft patter-patter of bare feet coming along the path. The officer squeezed his arm to impress silence upon him, and then, raising himself, he tucked his feet under him ready for a spring. The footsteps came nearer and nearer.

George felt a quiver of excitement pass all over him as he waited; every nerve was strained to its utmost tension, and it was with difficulty he repressed the desire to jump out of his hiding-place.

The footsteps were now nearing at a run, evidently the spy thought he had lost his quarry, and was anxious to see what had become of them.

Suddenly the figure loomed up in the darkness, and just as it came abreast of the bush, the officer bounded from his place of concealment. Before the man could so much as cry out he had gripped him by the throat, and brought him down to the ground.

George was hardly a moment behind his chief.

"Quick, gag him with his turban!" said Childs. "There is no time to lose."

While the inspector held the man, Helmar unwound the turban and bound it round the fellow's mouth. Then cutting the spare end off, he secured his hands behind him. The man's sash was useful in binding his feet, and, thus trussed, they threw him under the bush.

"I calculated on this," said the officer. "Had we not secured this fellow, the meeting would have been warned, and we should probably never have escaped with our lives. Come along, he is safe for a while, and we can now continue our journey without fear of observation."

"But," said Helmar, "how is it that this nigger came to follow us—who put him on your track?"

"Ah, I see you don't understand. There are spies all over the town, and the police movements are watched. I, in particular, never leave the office but I am followed by one of these thieving, murdering Arabs."

The inspector now altered his direction, and they returned towards the town. In a few minutes they approached a dingy-looking house standing well back from the road. The place stood in its own grounds, and over the door was a sign which George failed to understand. At first glance there appeared to be no indication of occupation—the house was in complete darkness.

Before they came up to it, the officer made a *détour* and reached the ground at the back.

"That is the house," said he in a whisper. "It is one of the most infamous gambling hells in the city. You can see no lights because all the shutters are closed, and no doubt there are blankets over them; but—holloa, there's a light shining through that window!" he went on, pointing to one that had just come into view as they reached the garden.

The two men now climbed over the fence, and, dropping into the shrubs on the other side, cautiously neared the building. Telling George to remain where he was, the inspector crawled right up to the window, through the shutters of which a stream of light poured.

Watching him eagerly, George saw him place his hand on the sill and peer through the crack. The moments slipped by, and his eye remained glued to the crack. Suddenly there was a rustle in the bush close by. It passed unnoticed, for George had eyes and ears for nothing but what his chief was doing. Again there was a rustle, this time more pronounced. Still it remained unnoticed.

The inspector suddenly left the window, and the next moment rejoined his companion.

"Well?" whispered Helmar, anxiously. "What news?"

The inspector's face was very grave, and his tones, as he answered, were full of import.

"The best—or rather, the worst. I recognized two people there, one a trusted member of the official staff, and the other a man who has been suspected for a long time. We had better get back—there is nothing more to be done to-night, I have seen all I wish to. To-morrow—we'll wait until to-morrow."

As he finished speaking, he turned sharply round and peered into the scrubbly bush behind them.

"What is it?" asked Helmar, his hand slipping to his revolver unconsciously.

"Did you hear anything?" asked his companion. "By Jove, there's some one on our track. Come along, we'll get out while we have a whole skin."

Leading the way out of the shrubs they made for the fence. The night was particularly dark, and the air was so still that the light sound of their footsteps became ominously loud. The inspector was convinced that there was some one in the garden watching them, and their only chance of safety was by taking to the open instead of returning as they came, through the scrub. At last the fence was reached.

"Up you get, youngster!" whispered Childs. "Look well before you drop on the other side."

George sprang on to the top and looked over. At that moment he heard a terrible cry behind him. Glancing round, he was just in time to see the glint of a long keen blade, and the next instant the inspector fall to the ground with a groan.

Without a moment's hesitation, George dropped from the fence to his assistance. He drew his revolver, and, just as a hideous great black wretch rushed at him, he fired point-blank. Down fell the man across the fallen officer, and then, as if by magic, half-a-dozen wild-looking figures appeared all round him.

There was no mistaking their intention. With a yell of fury they rushed on him. Helmar was as cool as if anything but his life depended upon the issue. As the nearest of the Arabs approached, he dropped him with another shot, then turning with an astonishing quickness of the eye brought another to his knees. It was, however, his last shot, for, as the man fell, his knife which had been upraised, struck him on the wrist, lacerating it terribly; his revolver fell from his nerveless grasp, and he was at the mercy of his antagonists.

For a moment or two he struggled furiously with the remaining three, but the contest was too uneven. The assailants were armed with long, keen knives, and Helmar had now nothing with which to defend himself.

"Just as a hideous black wretch rushed at him, he fired point-blank."
p. 66

In those moments he realized the futility of his efforts, but he meant to sell his life dearly, and struck out with his left to such purpose that for a second the savages drew back. It was, however, but a momentary lull, and with a combined rush they overwhelmed him.

For one brief moment he struggled fiercely, then he saw one of his assailants raise a long narrow blade—the next instant it fell, and, with a sickening sensation, it struck him in the shoulder. He struggled to release himself, and then, without a single cry, sank to the ground.

The sound of the firing and the cries of his assailants had roused the neighbourhood, and just as the murderers were about to finish their work a crowd approached, and they precipitately fled. It was a mixed and villainous crew that first reached the spot after the departure of the murderers, mainly consisting of natives; but there was a sprinkling of Europeans of doubtful repute, and they quickly gathered round the two inanimate bodies.

CHAPTER VII

A GOOD SAMARITAN

When Helmar woke again to consciousness, it was with no idea either of the lapse of time or any recollections of what had occurred to him in the meantime. Beyond being able to turn his head slowly from side to side, he was unable to move, and a terrible feeling of lassitude and weakness nipped all inclination in that direction.

The room in which he found himself was squalid and gloomy, and, as his dull, inquiring gaze wandered over his surroundings, he endeavoured to realize where he was. The effort was more than he was equal to, and, closing his eyes, he relapsed into a calm, dreamless sleep.

In that first dawn of consciousness he had failed to see the silent figure at his bedside—a figure which, had his gaze rested upon it, would probably have troubled his weakened mind and stayed his peaceful slumber.

The moment his eyes closed, the figure silently rose and glided noiselessly from the room. Presently it returned with a glass containing a steaming potion. Setting it down, it bent over the bed and gazed long and earnestly at the sleeper. A look of satisfaction came over its grim and wrinkled face as it resumed its vigil at the bedside.

When next the sick man awoke, a tiny lamp was shedding its dim rays over the dingy apartment. This time the figure at once approached the sufferer and held the glass to his lips. Too weak to resist or even care what was happening, he silently drank. The blood instantly coursed more rapidly through his body, and he felt refreshed and stronger. Watching the look of intelligence come into his eyes, the figure put the glass down and spoke to him in excellent French.

"You feel better now?" she asked.

"Yes," he replied in a faint voice, as though trying to recollect something. "I have been ill, haven't I?"

"Very ill," was the response.

"Who are you?" he asked, after a pause, "and where am I?"

"I am Mariam Abagi," she answered quickly, "and you are in a house at Gizeh. I am what you call a Syrian Arab. But do not worry—you are too ill yet to think or talk; wait until you are better," and she silently left the room.

For a moment or two Helmar tried to understand and recall something of what had happened, but all seemed so dim and misty that he had to give it up, and at last, becoming drowsy again, fell asleep.

Mariam Abagi was a woman of unusual character for her caste. She was married to a German who was disliked and suspected by the natives. They looked upon him as a spy, a traitor come from Europe for some evil purpose, and eventually did away with him. Mariam was a really good woman, and resented the deed bitterly. Naoum, her son, never saw his father, but inherited some of his good business qualities, and all his mother's kindness of heart. So when he had found Helmar in distress after the affair with the inspector, he instinctively went to his aid, and, finding him still alive, did not hesitate to take him to Mariam at once. On discovering Helmar's nationality, and learning how he too had fallen foul of the treacherous natives, she showed great regard for him, which gradually developed into strong affection, and her kindness knew no bounds. Her son shared the feelings of his mother, and the two, as will be seen, proved to be great benefactors to Helmar.

During the next few days he made more rapid progress toward recovery. Each time he saw the patient nurse, he endeavoured to extract from her the meaning of the position in which he found himself, but without success— she would tell him nothing. He began to get a hazy recollection of a fight, but how it came about, and with whom, he could not recall.

What puzzled him most was this old woman. She was tall and gaunt, of the Arab type, and her face was lined and wrinkled to such an extent that it was impossible to tell whether its expression was kindly or otherwise. When his strength grew and things became clearer to his mental vision, he determined to have an explanation.

Late one evening as the woman came in with the lamp, he broached the subject.

"Mariam," he said abruptly, as she was about to leave the room, "come here. I am strong now, and I want to talk to you. Now tell me all about it. How did I get into this plight? And how came I into this house?"

She eyed him keenly for a moment, then walking over to the bed sat down beside it.

"My son brought you here; you were wounded in a fight with Arabs in Cairo."

"Ah, yes," he said thoughtfully. "There was a meeting and we went to stop it. I remember something of it now. Where is the police inspector?"

"Dead."

"Dead?"

"Yes, dead," she repeated.

George did not answer. He was thinking hard. At last he spoke again.

"Am I not in Cairo, then?" he asked in astonishment.

"No, you are in Gizeh, a little distance from the city. Cairo is in such a state of tumult at the present time, it would be impossible to keep you in hiding there after the part you took with the police. So my son brought you here to me for safety."

"How long have I been here?" he asked.

"Since that affair with the police officer," Mariam answered.

"Yes," said George, after another long pause, "I can see it all now; we were set upon. But how did your son find me?"

"He was with the crowd who went round at the noise of the fighting. The people thought you were killed, and so left you. But my son, Naoum, he loves not people of this country, and he saw you were not of them, so he stayed and discovered you were still alive. He is a good man is Naoum, and a dutiful son; he knows my feelings towards your countrymen, and he brought you to me here. I love the men of Europe, therefore I help you. Mariam Abagi does not love all and would not help many, but you are young to die."

As she finished speaking, a troubled expression passed over her parchment-like face, and she sat munching her lips, blinking at the flickering light. Helmar sighed and shifted his position uneasily. The keen black eyes were turned on him at once.

"But I can never repay you," he said. "You don't understand; I am a stranger—I have no money."

The old woman's eyes flashed in a moment, but fortunately she was in such a position that he could not see them.

"I require no money," she said, sharply. "I have enough for my wants. I do not this for gain," and her jaws shut with a snap.

George saw that he had made a mistake and endeavoured to remedy it, but only plunged the further into the mire.

"Yes, yes, I know, you are very good, but I cannot let you do this for me without——"

"Peace! You mean well, I know, but I will not listen. Your troubles are not yet over. It will be sufficient reward to me that you get away from this place without being killed."

"How do you mean?" he asked, failing to grasp the woman's meaning.

"Ah, I forgot, you do not know. The country is now in a critical position, and Arabi Pasha is at the head of the army. The excited and corrupted citizens are stirring up strife, and menacing all the Europeans and any one else who had, or is supposed to have had, any connection with the hated government, and Arabi has nearly lost power over the mob. It is kept secret that you are here, and so you are safe for the present! But I do not know how long this safety will last. I have some power, and my son is powerful too, but that may not avail us long, and then you will have to fly. Have no fear, however, I shall watch, and, at the first warning of danger, will provide for you."

After this Mariam would answer no more questions, and left him to ponder over what she had said. He could hardly realize the full purport of all she had told him. This then was the danger Inspector Childs had spoken of; this then was the result of those meetings the police had been watching, the one they had endeavoured to spy upon. In his weakened state the idea of it all set his brain in a whirl, and his thoughts became confused. The one thing that seemed to strike him more forcibly than the rest was, how on earth was he to escape?

The days dragged slowly by, and he soon reached the convalescent stage. The wound he had received in his shoulder quickly healed under Mariam's treatment, and it became only a question of time for the recovery of his strength. He saw no one but the old woman who personally attended to all his wants. The son she spoke of did not show himself, although on several occasions he had heard a man's voice in another room.

Once or twice Mariam had spoken of her power, and gave him to understand that she did not require money; the squalor of her room made this seem rather enigmatical to the sick man, but he knew such people were sometimes eccentric in their mode of living, and this might possibly account for his surroundings. However, it was no affair of his, she had been an angel of goodness to him, and he had no right to pry into her private affairs.

Helmar was young, and his great vitality stood him in good stead; the moment his wound healed his strength began to come back rapidly, and with returning health he felt it incumbent upon him to suggest that he should relieve the faithful Mariam of the trouble he was causing her. Knowing the old woman's peculiarities, he was a little afraid to broach the subject, but his duty lay so plainly before him that, despite his feelings, he decided to speak his mind.

One evening, after a day of chafing at his inactivity, the opportunity came. She had brought in some food, and their conversation soon turned upon the terrible state of the country.

"I don't want you to think me ungrateful for your kindness, Mariam," he said, hesitatingly, "but I am now so far recovered and so strong that I feel I must no longer trespass on your goodness."

A grim smile played over her withered old face.

"And whither would you go? Death may await you outside these doors."

"Perhaps that is so," said George, doubtfully, "but I must take my chance."

"I like the young man for his spirit," said the old woman more to herself than her companion. "It is right, but he is a good youth and must not die—life is dear to me, then how much more so to him. Listen," she went on in unmistakable tones of command, "my son does big trade on the river. He owns many nuggars and dahabîehs which carry wheat and produce down to Alexandria. If you could reach that city in safety, you would find means of leaving the country in a ship."

"But I don't understand; how am I to reach Alexandria?"

"My son will hide you on board one of his boats, and in that way you can escape. Your danger will be great, for although my son is known all along the river, your life will surely pay the forfeit if by any chance you should be discovered."

It was a case of "Hobson's choice." Helmar was glad to accept any means of escape, and eagerly fell in with all the old woman had to say. Bearing out her character for beneficence, Mariam was as good as her word, and arranged all the details for his departure.

The first time Helmar put on his clothes he discovered, to his great delight, the money he had earned at the bookseller's was still in his pocket. This was a surprise, for he had naturally concluded it had been stolen. He now pressed Mariam to take it. But she would have none.

"You'll require that, and more, yourself," she said. So Helmar let the matter drop.

He was unfeignedly sorry to part with his protectress. A sort of filial affection had grown up in him for this woman, and when she came in for the last time, bringing her son with her, George felt that he was about to leave his best friend. On her part, the old woman seemed no less affected, and but for the presence of her son, she would undoubtedly have broken down altogether.

The man in whose guardianship Mariam was about to trust her patient was a powerfully-built fellow of forty. He possessed a strong, honest face of a similar cast to his mother's, although perhaps a shade paler. He was dressed in the ordinary Egyptian garb, and, as his mother presented him, he advanced with outstretched hand and gripped Helmar's in a manner as hearty as it was honest.

"The night is dark, Mussiu," he said, "we must not delay. For the moment the place is quiet, but the riotousness of the people is liable to break out at any moment, and, unless the greatest caution is used, we may be discovered and challenged. Come, let us start, for it is some distance to the river!"

Helmar turned to his nurse. He was deeply affected at parting with the old soul.

"Good-bye, Mariam," he exclaimed. "I can never thank you for all you have done for me. I shall never forget it. Some day perhaps you will allow me to repay you."

"Do not talk of thanks. I like it not. You will be a second son to me. Take these," she went on, handing him his revolver and a long knife of Egyptian make, "they may be of use to you. I shall watch for you always, and some day we shall meet again. Farewell!"

Without another word she turned and left the room.

Naoum stood looking on with a stolid face, and, as his mother departed, led the way to another door, and the two men left the house.

To anybody of a less courageous spirit the position Helmar found himself placed in would have been appalling. With little money, with hardly recovered health, only these two people whom he could count his friends in a now hostile country—all these things combined to make his position one of the greatest insecurity and danger. Instead of doubting the outcome of it all, however, he rather gloried in the situation, and did not trouble himself in the least as to the future. He felt more than ever the keen enjoyment of the roving, happy-go-lucky existence he had elected to follow. The simple effect of stretching his legs as he walked beside his companion inspired in him a keen feeling of appreciation of life, and a grim determination to follow to the end his adventurous career.

"How far is it now?" he asked, as they swung along through the slummy quarters.

"Quarter of a mile," was the laconic reply.

"Wish it was more," said George, "it's a treat to be walking again."

"I dare say it is, but we may find it's all too long before we reach the quay. Come along down here," he went on, turning into what looked like a blind court, "we must take all the most deserted streets and listen well, and look well ahead for sounds of trouble. The last two weeks have been terrible times."

"And what does Arabi hope to gain by all this?" asked George.

"The country and his own glorification. He hopes to destroy the Khedive's power and rule, and has adopted 'Egypt for the Egyptians' as his war-cry."

"He must be foolish. The European powers will never allow it. It can only end in one way, and he will be the one to pay for it."

"Yes, I know he will be punished, but there it is, and in the meantime the country is in a fearful state of alarm."

They were nearing the river, and Helmar relapsed into silence as they wound their way through the narrow streets. On every side the tumble-down appearance of the buildings made their walk more solitary and dismal. The smell, as they approached the river, became more pronounced, and made him wonder how any one could live there at all.

His guide seemed heedless of everything but his anxiety to reach their destination. At every corner and turning he paused to listen for any danger signal. Helmar, on the contrary, seemed quite to ignore his danger, and walked along indifferently, observing everything and comparing all with his recollections of the night when he had traversed a similar part in Cairo before he was wounded.

At last the quay was reached. The river was covered with all sorts of odd craft, and George gazed with astonished eyes at the scene before him. The moon was just rising, and the great golden globe shone over the river, causing the boats of varying build to cast weird and fantastic shadows on the water.

The guide pointed to two great cumbersome vessels near the other side of the river. They were built on the barge principle, with sail booms fore and aft like the Chinese river boats. These were the dahabîehs, one of which was to carry them down to Alexandria. As they reached the water's edge, Naoum gave a peculiar low whistle, and a boat suddenly shot out from the vessel's side, propelled by a solitary occupant.

The boat had hardly appeared when four men dashed out from the shadow and ran on to the shore towards the fugitives. They were dressed in uniform of the Khedive's army. As the fellows caught sight of Helmar's white face, they set up a shout which was immediately answered in various directions. The boat was rapidly nearing their side of the river. Naoum drew his pistol, and Helmar his revolver.

As soon as the men saw this they drew back, and two of them ran off, shouting as they went.

"The moment the boat reaches us," said Naoum in agitated tones, "you must jump in instantly. They have gone for assistance, and if they return before we get off, it means—murder."

The two Arabs left to watch our friends were evidently afraid to attack, and drew back to a respectful distance, eyeing the fugitives furtively. As they caught sight of the boat, now rapidly approaching, they set up another warning howl, and crept forward as though about to attack.

Their cry was answered by the sound of hurrying feet, and just as the boat touched the shore and Helmar and his guide had jumped in, about a dozen men rushed towards them. The sight of their escaping prey so enraged the Arabs that they opened fire at once.

Naoum and the waterman plied vigorously at the oars, and the boat skimmed over the water, while a hail of bullets struck the water around them.

They were not a moment too soon, and even then the chances were largely against them.

"Down with you," cried Naoum, addressing Helmar, "or they'll hit you! I'll pull the boat!"

"Not I," replied George, scornfully. "Do you think I'm going to take shelter while you are exposed to their fire? No, no, pull away, and I'll look after the tiller."

The distance that separated them from the shore was rapidly widening, and the danger lessened.

"I don't think, so long as they aim at us, that they can do much damage," said Naoum, smiling calmly. "Egyptians are not noted for their accurate marksmanship."

Helmar laughed a boyish, ringing laugh, as he listened to his companion's words. The spirit of adventure was upon him, and he was in a seventh heaven of delight as the whizzing bullets sped harmlessly by.

When in mid-stream, the current rapidly took them down to the silent vessel, and a few moments later they reached it and climbed aboard, while the baffled rebels slunk off into the shadow of the quay. The boat was quickly hauled up, moorings cast off, and the dahabîeh began to glide down the sluggish river.

CHAPTER VIII

AN ENCOUNTER ON THE NILE

"Thus far we have escaped," said Naoum, as the two men stood on the rough untidy dahabîeh, gazing at the slowly receding town. "They will probably not attempt to follow us, but I don't, for one moment, think our troubles are over. We must keep a sharp look-out along the banks for the rebels."

"You think then we shall come across them again?" asked George, glancing keenly at the speaker.

"I don't only think—I feel sure. Alexandria will be in a worse state than Cairo, and it is certain the river will be watched carefully. We must anchor in the day-time and travel at night, that is our only hope."

The man's quiet words in no way deceived Helmar, he realized that there was great danger ahead, and it would require all their fortitude and resource to cope with it. This knowledge, rather than damping his spirits, tended to raise them, and he looked forward with keen anticipation to what the future might have in store for him.

The old dahabîeh was a dreary old craft, in a dirty and ruinous condition. It was carrying a heavy load of grain, and this made the journey so slow that, by sunrise, they were still within a distant view of Cairo.

Daylight entirely changed the aspect of their surroundings. The weird beauty of the moonlight on the water had led George to anticipate a glorious scene when morning broke, but disappointment awaited him. The banks of the river were low and uninviting; as for the beautiful tropical jungle he had expected to find, there was none to be seen—nothing out of the common, but the broad, muddy banks.

The heat was at its utmost, and the scourge of the Delta, the épizootie, had done its dread work. Annually this plague among the beasts plays havoc with the Nile, its surroundings and inhabitants. As the animals die of the disease, they are either left lying about on the banks to rot, decay, and pollute the air with devastating microbes, or are thrown into the water. It is then the hot sun does its work, and both the atmosphere and water become putrid.

All down the river from Cairo, George kept coming across the carcases of either buffaloes or oxen, and when they did not actually meet his eye, his nose detected their close proximity.

Life during the time was monotonous to a degree. In daylight when at anchor, the intense heat and smell caused sleep to be abandoned as far as Helmar was concerned. The watermen seemed able to put up with both, and stretched themselves out under any shelter, and slept as soundly on the bare planks as if they were on a feather bed.

Helmar and Naoum mainly occupied themselves with keeping watch, and as soon as the sun sank, the former took an hour or two's sleep.

Sometimes the monotony would be relieved by watching the natives making use of their river. Little parties could be seen in the distance washing their clothes; others cleaning or bathing what cattle they had; occasionally far away could be seen a collection of shiny, ebony-looking human beings taking a dip in the green, slimy, insanitary water and afterwards drinking it.

In this way most of the journey was accomplished. So far they had come across no sign of the rebels, and George began to think they had escaped them altogether. Naoum was not so sanguine, in fact he saw a greater danger ahead than even he had anticipated at first.

"You can't see as I do," he said one evening, as George and he sat watching the setting sun; "the fact that we have not as yet come across them indicates nothing. The nearer we get to our destination the keener will be Arabi's watch on the river for fugitives."

"Yes, but there is just a possibility that we have passed them on our way without having seen them," said George optimistically.

"Yes, that may be so," replied his companion doubtfully. "Allah only knows what we shall do if Alexandria is occupied by them. There is but one course open to you as far as I can see. When we get into the Mahmoudieh Canal, you will have to hide amongst the grain; and if you ever reach Alexandria in safety, take my advice and get out of the country at once."

Helmar did not reply, he was thinking hard. He had just arrived in the country in the hopes of making a fortune. So far he had only met with trouble— trouble that first threatened to wipe him out of existence, and now tried to force him to return home.

The first he had escaped by what seemed to him a miracle, and the second, which he was just about to face, offered no alternative of escape than by the same means. The idea of flying before this danger was absolutely repugnant to him. If he were to die, why not meet his death boldly, instead of escaping by running away? It was absurd and cowardly to return home at the first sign of danger! How they would laugh at him! What would his father think? What would all say?—no, he had come to this country of his own choice, and whatever the consequences, he would stay. His good fortune had so far pulled him through—he would still trust to it.

"Well," he said at last, "I shall be guided by circumstances. We shall see how things turn out, but it seems rough on you to take this venture on my behalf."

There was a nice light breeze after sundown, and the vessel was slipping along at, for her, a very good speed. Naoum sat smoking and gazing at the banks as they passed by; George gave himself up to reflections.

The man at the tiller moved to and fro with the regularity of clockwork, altering the tack as the wind chopped and changed about. The rest of the crew were squatting about the deck in various attitudes of perfect laziness. The splash of the water at the bow of the boat had insidiously attracted George's attention, and he found himself humming a tune to the time of the lapping stream.

Suddenly Naoum turned with an exclamation. George looked at his companion, his tune gone from his mind, and all thoughts absorbed into a keen excitement. They were rounding a sharp bend, and Naoum's attention was fixed on the outer bank.

"What is it?" asked George, in tones of suppressed excitement.

Naoum turned sharply to him and waved his arm in the direction of the cabin. "Quick, below for your life! If your face is seen you are doomed."

It was too late. Just as George was about to dive below, there was a sharp report followed by the "plosh" of a bullet, as it dropped into the water just a few yards ahead of the vessel.

"Duck down under the bulwarks," said Naoum hurriedly, "they can't have seen you yet. The bank is lined with rebels," he went on, gazing hard through the gathering darkness. "Allah! but they mean to bring us to book!"

As he spoke there was a heavy rattle of musketry, and bullets flew in all directions around them. The crew sat huddled together in a place of safety, terror written in every line of their brown faces. Naoum alone seemed impervious to the danger, and watched every movement of the men on the bank.

"What shall we do?" asked George, with a set, determined look on his face that made his question seem superfluous. "We won't surrender," he added in emphatic tones.

"We'll run for it," was the quiet answer. "Their guns can't do us much harm. They couldn't hit a mountain."

George peered over the side at the bank.

"Hallo! what are they doing? Looks as if they were launching boats."

Naoum watched their actions keenly, and his face took on a slightly anxious expression as he realized the truth of George's statement.

"They *are* launching boats, but what for?" he said, as if asking himself the question. Then a thought seemed to suddenly strike him. "I have it—yes, that's it."

"What is it?" asked George, as Naoum walked towards the cabin.

Without answering he disappeared, and a moment later returned with several rifles. These he served out to his men with a supply of cartridges. He then harangued them in Arabic, which George was only partly able to understand, but when he had finished, he observed the fellows line up under the bulwarks and load their rifles.

"What's your idea?" asked George, as soon as Naoum had finished.

"These rebels are going to follow us, and I have no doubt they will overtake us. Then will come a tough time," replied Naoum.

"Ah! I understand. They mean to capture us if possible."

"Yes. That is what they intend, and we shall stand a poor chance if they come up with us."

"We'll not give in at any rate, but make a bold stand and give them a taste of what we are made of first," said George.

Naoum and George now went together to the stern of the boat and watched anxiously the pursuing rebels, who after their first volley from the shore had wasted no more powder, apparently content to wait until they came up with their prey. They filled two boats, and George thought that, given a fair and even chance, they could easily be overpowered. They were still some distance in the rear, and had so far gained nothing on the fugitives. But it was very apparent they were making a great effort, and presently it became evident they were slowly but surely gaining upon the dahabîeh.

The men were posted all round the vessel, prepared to fire on either boat the moment it came within range.

"Now, boys," cried out George, forgetful of the Arabs' language, "when they are within rifle shot, take a steady aim. Remember we have no ammunition to waste."

Naoum was also busy with his men, giving them instructions and placing them in positions.

The boats were slowly getting nearer and nearer, and presently the rattle of the rebels' rifles rang out, but the bullets falling short of Naoum's vessel, they quickly ceased firing.

"Don't fire until their shots come nearer," said Naoum quietly. "As soon as they show us we are within range of their rifles it will be time enough for us to reply."

"Presently the firing re-commenced, and Naoum gave orders to attack." p. 90

Presently the firing re-commenced with a fearful fusillade, and Naoum gave orders to attack. Nearer and nearer came the rebels, and more fierce became the firing. George was on one side of the vessel and Naoum on the other encouraging the men in their defence.

The rebels' ranks were thinning fast, and George began to hope they would give in. They were still three to one, however, and if they should once get aboard the dahabîeh the defenders' chance would be a very poor one.

They were but a few yards off and ceased firing. Evidently they had spent all their ammunition, and were going to attempt to board the vessel and capture it with a hand-to-hand fight.

While they were yet watching, one of the boats drew near to the vessel's side, and the next moment a head appeared above the bulwarks of the dahabîeh, quickly followed by another and another.

This was the signal Naoum's men waited for, and without further delay they set to work with a will, pitching the struggling rebels back into the water and taking pot shots at them afterwards as if they were ducks.

The struggle, however, had only just begun; as fast as the defenders beat the assailants off more came on. Whilst the *mêlée* was in progress the defenders had not seen the other boats come alongside, and the reinforcements they brought. All along the side of the dahabîeh the Arabs were clambering up like so many ants, and though the advantage was still with Naoum, the outcome looked doubtful. The crew were hard put to it.

Helmar worked indefatigably with his rifle used as a club; everywhere he darted, dealing terrible blows as the dusky creatures showed themselves, but despite his efforts they seemed to be in overwhelming numbers.

At last they gained a foothold on the deck, and the firing ceased altogether. It became a struggle to the death, man against man. It was here the crew showed their superiority over their enemies, and slowly but surely began to drive them back.

Suddenly George saw three men pressing Naoum sorely. He himself had just succeeded in throwing off his own assailant; with a bound he went to his friend's rescue. He arrived only just in time, the men were in the act of knifing him.

Without a thought, he rained blow after blow with his clubbed rifle on the would-be assassins, and they went down like ninepins; then, turning to where the crew were fighting, he saw to his delight that they had driven the foe back over the bulwarks, while the deck lay covered with damaged rebels. Naoum's men had fought like demons, and their devotion to their master touched Helmar—it would have been so much easier for them to have sold him.

In a few more moments the rebels were driven off, dropping over the side into the water, without thinking as to the whereabouts of the boats so long as they got safely out of the hornet's nest they had fallen into.

As the last of them disappeared, Helmar fell rather than sat down on the deck, breathing hard.

"That was a close call," he panted. "If they'd held on a bit longer, I was completely done. Poof! I've had enough for one day."

Naoum was taking pot shots at the boats as they dodged about, picking up the men who had fallen into the water. He paused at his companion's words.

"Yes, Allah is good, we are now out of danger and have no more to fear."

The rifles were collected and put away, and the dahabîeh resumed its calm appearance as it glided lazily onwards.

The following morning it entered the Mahmoudieh Canal, which runs direct to Alexandria. After his late experience, George realized what the appearance of a white face on board might mean to his protector, and for the rest of the journey kept out of sight.

CHAPTER IX

THE REIGN OF TERROR IN ALEXANDRIA

After what had happened, Helmar was prepared for almost anything when he actually arrived at Alexandria.

For some time past everybody had been possessed of the feeling that something serious was about to happen. Arabi Pasha and his co-conspirator, Mahmoud Sami, had caused sedition to be preached amongst the native soldiers and police, and amassed together so large a following that his party had become masters of the situation. His firm conviction that the Khedive's rule and the power of the Europeans could be easily overthrown, got so instilled into the souls of the populace they could restrain their hot-blooded feelings no longer, and on an ever-memorable day in June 1882, broke out in one of the bloodiest riots of modern times.

The first indication of what was to take place occurred one afternoon, when the chief streets of the city were suddenly awakened from their tranquillity by the shouts and yells of hundreds of natives.

"Down with the Christians," some cried; others, "Death to the unbelievers!" And they rushed about madly in different parts of the town, ultimately joining forces when the riot became general.

Europeans were beaten with "nabouts," knocked down and trampled on; shots were fired, the soldiers charged, and the police helped to make the butchery more complete. Shops and houses were attacked and pillaged, the proprietors being taken out and massacred in cold blood, and, after all valuables had been taken from them, their bodies thrown into the bye-streets. In one of these streets were found three bodies of Europeans. One was stabbed through the heart, another had bullet-holes in his head, whilst the head of the third was almost severed from the trunk, and the body divested of nearly all its clothes. The mob evidently felt confident that their actions were approved, for they paraded the streets with their stolen goods and clothes with an air of glory and bravado. One soldier was seen to sit on the curbstone and change his own garments for the new stolen ones he had just acquired.

The riff-raff of the crowd consisted of the lowest class of Arabs of the city. They fortified themselves with club-like weapons, felled their victims with them, and after stripping their bodies, cast them into the sea. Most diabolical deeds and acts were perpetrated, and the Arabic cry, coming almost spontaneously from the infuriated crowd, of, "Oh, Moslems! Kill him! Kill the Christian!" rent the air whenever a European appeared. One poor merchant was dragged from his carriage and bayoneted on the spot, whilst not many yards away a German, who had appealed to a soldier for protection, was responded to with a shot which penetrated his face. At the gate of the town the guard on duty was seen to draw his sword and strike a man twice, splitting his skull with the first stroke, and severing his head from his body with the second.

These are but a tithe of the instances of the brutality displayed by the rioters which history chronicles, and which went on incessantly all day, during which time hundreds met their death at the hands of this maddened, murderous crew. Arabi was appealed to, to put a stop to the riot. To show the hold he had over the people, it is only necessary to say that at his given word the tramping, yelling, and shouting ceased almost as quickly as it had begun.

For days after the place remained littered with the bodies of the massacred, and the spectacle, together with the appearance of the shops and houses that had been attacked, made Alexandria look like a town after a siege. Shops were shut and barred, windows barricaded with iron shutters, and the only persons about the streets were Arab soldiers.

Fugitives were removed by train, the people crowding on the roofs and steps; ships laden with the English set off as quickly as possible for Malta.

Outside the harbour was drawn up the French and English fleet.

It was at this period that the dahabîeh, with George Helmar carefully kept from view, arrived outside the town almost unnoticed. The occupants of the place were too busily engaged to pay much attention to the addition of one vessel to the already large number idling about the canal. Besides, this was a trading boat and owned by a well-known native.

When the night-time approached Naoum suggested to George that he might venture up and take a view of the situation.

"It seems to me suspiciously quiet," said Naoum, as he stood beside George, eyeing the shore with a keen glance. "Can't say I like it."

"Yes, it is quiet, but do you see those shops are barricaded at the end of the streets leading down to the water?"

"Um—I don't like the look of that. There's been mischief."

"What's that smoke over there?" exclaimed George, hurriedly. "Why, it's a fire, and look—look at those shattered houses, and—hallo, there's a gang of murderous-looking soldiers—we are too late!"

Naoum did not answer. He was watching all the things his companion had drawn his attention to. There was no doubt in his mind now—the place was evidently in the rebels' hands, the process of sacking was going on. He turned to George.

"Well?" he said inquiringly. "You daren't go ashore."

"What, then, am I to do? I can't trespass on your good-nature any longer, and, besides, my presence here is a constant source of danger to you. No, I *must* chance it. I can't stay here."

He spoke with determination, and Naoum was not slow to appreciate the sentiments that prompted him; yet he would not see him deliberately plunge into the deadly danger that awaited him ashore.

"As I said, you can't land, friend Helmar. Allah has guided your steps to me, and you will have to throw in your lot on this boat until we can find a safe means for your escape. Come, you are a good man, say, will you stay? Sooner or later things will calm down and then———"

"No, no, Naoum, you have done so much for me already, I cannot let you risk more. My mind is made up, I will forge my own way ahead now."

"There is no need to talk of risk, or of what I have done," he replied, with a kind look into the resolute face beside him; "I ask for no greater pleasure than that you stay here."

Helmar only shook his head. It seemed to him that his duty lay plainly before him—he must no longer jeopardize this man's safety. He was well and strong again now, and must fight his own battles. Inclination made him wish to remain, but he must go.

Seeing his charge's mind was made up, Naoum, with the philosophy of the East, attempted no further persuasion, and resigned himself to the inevitable.

"When, then, will you leave?" he asked.

"As soon as you will help me to land," George answered at once. "Do not think me ungrateful, Naoum—I am only doing my duty."

"The boat shall be brought along the shore when you like," he replied, turning away, "but I should advise you to await darkness; remember your face is still white."

Accepting his friend's advice, Helmar decided to wait until the sun had gone down and then seek shelter in some small drinking saloon where doubtless he might meet other refugees. He had still the money on him which he had in his pocket at the time he was wounded, and this would pay for his immediate wants.

As darkness came on, the boat was pulled for the landing-stage. All along the river silence reigned, but from the distant parts of the city they could hear many sounds grating discordantly on the still night air. That little trip to the shore was, to the occupants of the boat, impressive to a degree. Neither knew what the future was to bring forth, both realized that danger was on all sides, and each one felt that he was parting from a friend, tried as only those who have fought side by side for one another are tried.

The younger man fully appreciated the risks this stranger had run for his sake, and a feeling possessed him that though duty demanded the parting, still, in a measure, it seemed like desertion.

Naoum on the other hand admired the spirit which prompted George's decision, and though he regretted bitterly the loss of so brave and good a companion, would not have had it otherwise.

The landing-stage reached, Helmar sprang ashore, and, with a hearty grip of the hand and a quiet "good-bye and good luck," they parted. Each felt he knew the other's thoughts, and, if good wishes could help them, there was no doubt their lives would be prosperous and happy.

"Allah is good. I shall see the boy again," thought Naoum.

Left to himself, George primed his revolver, put it in his belt ready to hand, and then made his way from the water's edge to explore the city.

It was some moments before he decided which way to go. In every street the houses were barricaded, and along the water front they were quite deserted. At last he decided to venture up a little dark alley to the left. He selected this particular one on account of its obscurity.

From the vessel he had seen a stray party of Arabi's soldiery, and he had no fancy for running the risk of encountering them by taking one of the larger thoroughfares.

How dark and quiet it seemed, not a sign of life was to be seen anywhere. In the distance he could still hear the discordant cries from other parts of the town and sometimes the discharge of fire-arms, but here—here in the lowest quarter of the city, where crime and low life usually prevailed, everything was silent as the grave.

George stepped cautiously along, his ears strained to catch the least suspicious sound, his eyes peering on every side to catch a glimpse of light through some stray chink in the closed and shuttered windows—but none presented itself.

After he had traversed the street without discovering anything to alarm him, he breathed more freely and turned into another, stretching his legs in a brisk walk instead of keeping to his furtive, silent glide.

This street, like the last, appeared to be deserted, but the houses showed signs of rough treatment; windows were broken, doors smashed, mounds of plaster, brick, and wood lay scattered about, evidences of the wanton work of the looting hordes that had no doubt recently visited it.

As he neared the end of this unwholesome, wretched place, he fancied he saw the faint flicker of a light from one of the windows, and he hurriedly made his way towards it.

His senses had not deceived him, the house was inhabited—but by whom? He paused outside and looked up at the window. The light was gone, but the sound of voices inside cheered his heart. He stood for a moment listening. At first he could not make out the language that was being spoken, but after a while, as his ear became accustomed to the confused tongues, he detected one voice speaking in his own language.

His heart beat high with hope, and he strained his ear against the wood-work of the walls. There evidently were many persons inside and of mixed nationality. This gave him his cue; if all these people of different tongues were gathered together in one house it could only mean one thing—refugees.

Without speculating further he tapped on the shuttered window of the ground floor, and waited. Immediately the voices inside ceased. He tapped again, louder than before. A moment after, the shutter of the window above was cautiously opened, and against the dim light of the sky he saw a head protruded.

The night was so dark he could not make out whether the head was that of a white man or not, but he inclined to the latter belief, and summoning all his best Arabic, he asked for shelter for the night.

"I have money to pay," he added, "but have nowhere to sleep."

There was a grunt as the head was withdrawn and another face appeared in its place. There was no mistaking it this time, it was distinctly white, and when a voice came in English—

"Who are you and what do you want?" Helmar's heart gave an instinctive leap for joy.

"These are queer times," the speaker went on, "and I do not care to do business with every passing stranger."

"I am a German," replied Helmar in the same language, "and am a stranger just come to the city from Cairo. I do not know what has happened here, but the town seems to be full of trouble. I must find somewhere to sleep."

The tones of his voice evidently calmed the stranger's fears, for he replied in much milder tones—

"Are you alone?"

"Quite," replied Helmar.

"Very well then, wait a moment," and the head disappeared and he heard footsteps descending the stairs.

The next moment the door was cautiously opened, and the burly figure of a man stood in the dark uninviting passage.

"Quick, come in," he said in hurried tones, "there *is* trouble about, and we don't want more; this house is supposed to be deserted."

George stepped in quickly, and the door was closed behind him. The man bolted and barred it as though the place was in a state of siege.

"Step this way," he said, evidently relieved at having got him safely in and the door secured.

Helmar followed the man to the end of the passage, where, flinging open another door, his host ushered him into a well-lighted room.

"Ladies and gentlemen," he said, "another guest. I hope there is no objection?"

At the sight of the new-comer several men rose from their seats and looked earnestly at him. The room in which Helmar found himself was part of the bar of one of the many cheap cafés of this neighbourhood. It was filled by a number of men and women of all nationalities, seated at various small tables scattered round the room. The room itself was innocent of all attempts at decoration; the walls showed its dirty plaster, the rough floor was sanded, and the worn and cheerless tables and benches were polished with the dirt of ages. The atmosphere reeked with the smell of tobacco and coffee, and, as he stepped in, bowing to the assembled company, Helmar could not help feeling a strong desire to open a window.

After their scrutiny, the occupants, one by one, resumed their seats, and George felt that they were mutely asking him for an explanation. As fugitives they were naturally suspicious of strangers, and he was about to speak, when he saw a slight figure step from an obscure corner.

In a moment his eyes glistened, and an exclamation rose to his lips as he almost jumped forward and grasped the hand of his old chum Osterberg.

CHAPTER X

THE MEETING OF FRIENDS

George was simply thunderstruck. It seemed almost miraculous that he should meet his bosom friend in such a place and under such circumstances. The two stared at each other in perfect astonishment for some moments, still clasping hands.

"Well, of all the wonders," George exclaimed, after they had expressed sufficient surprise and finished their greetings, "who would have expected this? But why are you here, and why all this mystery?"

"But surely you know, George! You know what has happened?" said Osterberg.

"I know nothing more than that Arabi is leading a rebellion against the Khedive's rule, with the object of deposing him, and that Cairo is becoming impossible to residents in consequence. I suppose Alexandria, from the look of the streets I came through, is in even a worse plight. But tell me about it."

"That's putting it mildly. We've had one of the most inhuman riots here imaginable. The Seditionists have been pillaging the town and massacring all Europeans who came in their way. I only came here a week ago, and now, like all the occupants of this house, am hiding, waiting for an opportunity to get away in safety. It's frightful, it's terrible. Heaven only knows how many people have been massacred."

"I didn't know it was as bad as that. You must have all been terror-stricken," replied George. "But let us come and have a quiet talk. How marvellous I should have chosen this place above all others to seek refuge in!"

The two young men sat and talked in the background, Helmar first giving an account of all that had happened to him, which was punctuated with exclamations of surprise from Osterberg as George recounted his adventures.

Osterberg, after parting with his friend at Constantinople, obtained work in the bank and gave great satisfaction to his employer. One day the latter called him in and told him there was a vacancy in the branch at Alexandria, and offered it to Osterberg. He accepted with alacrity and arrived in the town but a few days before the riots took place.

"And here I am taking refuge like the others, with the proprietor of this café," he wound up. "Not quite so eventful a time as yours, George, is it?"

"And what are we going to do now? Do you think we are safe for any length of time? Surely they must attack us in due course?" said George.

"I think we shall be unmolested for a while," replied Osterberg. "The place was visited early by the rabble soldiery and they took all that was worth taking, so now I don't suppose they will bother us."

That night was one of the worst Helmar had ever experienced; the only beds that could be scrambled together were used by the women-folk, and the men slept on the floor, benches, and tables. Fortunately blankets were not needed, as the heat was intense, but the benches were rickety and the sand on the floor worked into the sleepers' clothes. Altogether the plight of the refugees was miserable.

Helmar was unfeignedly delighted to meet his friend once more, and this compensated largely for the woeful condition in which he found himself. Osterberg, as he said, had now endured it for three days and so didn't mind the imprisonment; but with George it was different, and he had yet to get used to it.

The next two days were passed in this miserable captivity. Helmar chafed at the confinement, but was forced to put up with it. He often thought of leaving and trusting to good luck in the outside world, but Osterberg was always at his side, ready to point out the madness of such a proceeding.

At last the welcome news came that Arabi, probably tired of his soldiers' wanton slaughter, had issued a proclamation that every European must leave the city within a certain time or abide by the consequences.

This was news indeed, and the whites flocked in hundreds to the ships in the harbour. So great was the crush that Helmar and Osterberg were only just able to secure a passage in the last one to leave. They determined to go to Port Said and there apply to the British authorities for assistance. What they were to do after that, fate should decide; both able-bodied men, they had no doubt that they could make themselves useful. Helmar's idea, now that he could speak a little Arabic, was to try to become an interpreter.

It was a dreary journey to Port Said, but they reached it in safety and proceeded immediately to the British Consul. Helmar was to be spokesman and explain the object of their visit. After some delay, they were told an interview would be granted in about half-an-hour's time. Leaving the office, they strolled about in order to kill time.

"We *are* in luck," said George, as they walked arm-in-arm. "I wonder what will happen."

"Being Germans, possibly we shall be sent about our business," said Osterberg, "and after all, it's only to be expected."

"I don't think so," replied his friend; "you don't know these people. I'll bet something will be done for us."

At this moment he caught sight, through the window, of a man dressed in European clothes crossing the square. The figure was so familiar that he paused and looked again.

"By Jove! If I'm not very much mistaken, that's our old friend the doctor we met on the boat going to Constantinople!"

Osterberg looked across at the man approaching.

"You are right. It is he," he exclaimed, and they both made straight for the doctor.

"Ah, my friends, we meet sooner than we anticipated. I am delighted to see you, but am sorry for your plight. But come," he went on, shaking hands heartily, "this is no place to talk, we will go to my quarters."

Helmar and his friend followed the doctor to his rooms.

"So you managed to escape from Alexandria?" said Doctor Dixon, as he leant back in his chair after listening to the young men's story. "Well, considering all things, you are lucky. Arabi Pasha, or his followers, are about the most inhuman devils I ever came across. And to think Arabi was one of the Khedive's most trusted ministers! Well, well, we live and learn!"

"Now the point comes, what are we to do?" said George. "This rebellion has robbed us of our means of living, and we are simply thrown on the world without resource—at least without money. We have been to see the consul, but cannot do so for half-an-hour."

The doctor laughed. George felt angry at this outburst of merriment at their troubles, and his face showed it.

"There, there, my lad," said the officer, becoming serious, "I was not laughing at your troubles, but the way you put them. Now I dare say we can do something for you. You say you speak Arabic. Well," as George nodded in assent, "I'll see the consul and try to use my influence with him in getting you a job as interpreter. How'll that do?"

"Excellently," replied our hero, beaming with delight; "but how about Osterberg?"

"Ah, well, we'll look after him. He has his bank to go to, and I don't suppose for a moment Arabi will be allowed to remain in Alexandria for long. In fact, news came through this morning that the British warships were bombarding the place already, and if that is so, the blue-jackets will soon clear the town of the rabble. In the meantime provision will be made for him."

Osterberg thanked him for his kind words, and the trio fell to discussing their journey from Varna to Constantinople.

"By the way," said the doctor, "didn't you say that another fellow left the University with you? He played you a scurvy trick or something—didn't you say?"

"Yes, you mean Mark Arden," said Helmar quickly.

"Was that his name? You didn't tell me before. Strange———"

"Why, what do you mean?" asked both young men in a breath.

"Oh, it's nothing. Only some weeks ago a young German of that name came here and he was found some employment. I forget exactly what. Anyhow the fellow misbehaved himself—stole some money or something and was imprisoned. There was a frightful scene when sentence was passed on him. He swore revenge for what he called 'the insulting treatment,' was taken away to the cells, and three days afterwards escaped."

"What was he like?" asked George.

The doctor described him. There was no doubt about it, it was certainly Mark.

"The scoundrel," said Helmar, bitterly, "to think he should disgrace himself in such a manner! Has anything been heard of him since?"

"No, we found no trace at all, and I shouldn't be surprised if he made his way into the rebel camp. But come, we must get to business. Osterberg can remain here until we return."

Helmar followed his friend over to the consul's office. The doctor left him for a moment outside while he interviewed the arbitrator of his fate.

Whilst waiting the result, Helmar could not help thinking of the perfidious Mark. What a viper he had been, and how quickly he had again fallen across his path! One thing was certain, if ever Helmar met him again, he would extort from him the money he had stolen, and denounce him for the rascal he was.

His reflections were cut short by the door being thrown open and a sharp summons for him to enter.

George found himself in a bare-looking office. The only furniture consisted of a desk, one or two hard, uncomfortable chairs, and a long, wooden bench. For decoration the wall was covered with innumerable paper files and maps. He had no time for inspection. He was standing in front of the desk, seated at which was a slight man. He was partially bald, and his face matched his hair—it was brick-dust colour. His features were small, though clear and sharply cut, while his eyes were jet black and keenly penetrating. The doctor was standing beside him, and the pair eyed the young man as he stepped forward.

"German," said the man, without taking his eyes from Helmar's face. "Any relatives in the country?"

"No, sir," replied George without hesitation.

"Want work, eh? Um," and he bit the end of his pen; "you speak Arabic, Dr. Dixon tells me?"

"Yes, sir."

"How much do you know?" he asked in that language.

George replied in the same tongue, and the rest of the conversation was carried on in it.

"Well, I can't promise you anything now at once, but Dr. Dixon recommends you highly, so that if we require any one, I have no doubt you will suit. You speak Arabic well for a man only a few months in the country."

"I speak English and French as well, sir," broke in Helmar, "and——"

"Yes, yes, I have no doubt—that will do. You will hear from me as soon as it is possible."

The doctor smiled at the way the interview was closed, but George simply expressed his thanks and walked out. Presently the doctor joined him, and the two walked back to the quarters.

"Well, what do you think of him?" asked the doctor.

"Who? The consul? A smart-looking man."

"A little abrupt, eh?"

"Yes, but all business men are more or less like that. If he finds me something to do, it *will* be a relief, and anyway I can never thank you sufficiently for what you have done. It is strange, I always seem to be under obligations. First Mariam, then Naoum, and now you."

"Never mind that, my boy, every one must start in life, and to get that start one has to be under obligations to some one, if it's only your parents. Now about quarters? I'll arrange that you have a spare room with your friend in my house, and you must be my guests until something turns up. No, no more thanks, you've done quite enough in that line already."

In a few hours the two friends, Osterberg and George, were installed in the doctor's house. He was a bachelor, and his place was comfortably arranged. Everything he had he placed at their disposal, and for the next three or four days they thoroughly enjoyed themselves. At last the summons George had awaited came. After the doctor had finished his hospital duties he returned home with the announcement.

"Our fleet has bombarded Alexandria, and the blue-jackets have landed," he cried, as he stepped into the sitting-room. "You, Osterberg, will be able to return to your bank, and you, Helmar, the consul is going to send to the general commanding the forces there as an interpreter. Everything will be arranged here, you will be engaged at a certain salary before you go, and I believe you leave to-night."

The news was so good and had come so suddenly that neither of the young men knew what to say, they were so overjoyed. At length their feelings burst out in a torrent of thanks, from which the kindly doctor took refuge by leaving the room.

CHAPTER XI

A MYSTERIOUS MESSENGER

Everything turned out as the doctor had said, and at seven o'clock they bade good-bye to their friend and protector, and left for the transport.

They had three hours to spare before the boat left, and to fill in the time they went for a walk round the port.

"It seems to me the most marvellous thing, the way in which we have fallen on our feet," said George, as they walked slowly along. "No one can doubt but that a Higher Power guides our footsteps. The miraculous escapes I have so far had teach me this, if I had needed any teaching."

"Yes, and the providential way we have been brought together astonishes me still more," answered his companion. "Let us turn down here, it will take us out of the town; we have plenty of time. I don't suppose either of us will have much opportunity for pleasure after this. I say, isn't Dr. Dixon a brick?"

"Rather! I only wish I was going to see more of him."

They had turned into a quiet street, which rapidly brought them to the outskirts of the town. The houses on either side stood right up to the pavement, and appeared to be of the better class. This portion of Port Said was much more picturesque than the parts of Cairo and Alexandria to which our hero was used, and he remarked upon it.

As they neared the end of the street, an Arab turned into it, from one of the many bye-ways, and came quickly towards them. He was a picturesque-looking man, dressed in his native garb. His dusky polished skin shone in the evening light, and he hurried along with a light, easy, swaying stride, his every movement displaying the athletic qualities that his robes tended to hide. As he approached the two friends, his watchful black eyes glanced quickly up and down the street, and then, apparently satisfied with what he saw, rested with a keen, penetrating look upon Helmar.

Without slackening his pace for a moment, or giving the least indication of his intention, he suddenly held out his hand and a piece of paper fluttered at our hero's feet, and the fellow passed swiftly on.

The whole thing was done so suddenly, that neither of the friends had time to say a word before the man had passed; and when, after picking up the paper, they looked round for him, he had disappeared as quickly as he had come.

George gazed at his companion, holding the missive in his hand, and burst out laughing.

"What a queer chap! If it weren't that he touched me as he passed, and I felt that he was flesh and blood, I should be inclined to think he was a ghost. I wonder what he is up to?"

"Examine the paper. Doubtless that will enlighten us," said the practical Osterberg. "If I'm not mistaken, this is some game, in which we are wanted to participate."

George examined the paper, turning it over and over wonderingly. It was a dirty envelope, of the cheaper kind, sealed down and addressed to him.

"The mystery deepens. It's from some one who knows me, evidently. The writing seems familiar, too. I wonder——"

"Confound it, man, open it!" broke in his impatient companion. "You are right about the handwriting. It *is* familiar."

Helmar tore the envelope open, and examined the contents. It was a brief note, signed by Mark Arden.

The two read the contents eagerly.

"DEAR GEORGE,

"I have just found out you are in the town. For certain reasons, I cannot meet you in public; but, if you will meet me at the last Mosque outside the town, on the lake's edge (any one can direct you), in half-an-hour, I shall be glad to return you the money I borrowed at Varna.

"Yours   ever,

"MARK."

As they finished reading this extraordinary epistle, the two young men silently looked at one another. Osterberg was the first to break the silence.

"Well, of all the unadulterated cheek I ever heard of, this beats everything! I suppose he's going to pay you out of what he stole from the barracks. What are you going to do about it?"

Helmar looked long at the paper before replying. He was trying to find out what lay hidden under these lines. Somehow, he could not bring himself to believe in their genuineness. There was a deeply suspicious air about the whole thing, not the least being the delivery of the note. At last he appeared to make up his mind.

"We'll see it through. If there is any trickery, I dare say we can hold our own. Will you come?"

"Rather!" cried his friend. "But have we time?"

Helmar looked at his watch. It still wanted two hours to the time he must be aboard the transport, and he had no doubt the quay could be reached in time.

"Oh, yes, heaps of time! We'd better find out where this particular Mosque is. We'll ask the first person we meet."

At this moment an elderly Arab came along from behind, as if in answer to his expressed intention, and Helmar stopped him, and inquired the way. The old fellow grinned, showing a row of perfect white teeth, which, in a man of his apparent years, astonished the companions.

"It is not far," he said, in a peculiar, grating voice, "and I am going that way myself. It will take but a few minutes."

Osterberg looked inquiringly at George.

"All right, come along. You lead the way, old man," said Helmar, "and we will follow."

Helmar slipped his hand in his coat pocket to make sure his revolver was there, and, having satisfied himself on the point, hurried along behind the Arab, talking and laughing with his friend, as if he had not the slightest doubt but that everything was fair and above-board.

The limit of the town was reached, and they passed along the sandy road until they came to some gardens. Here they turned off, and soon found themselves in a lonely, obscure sort of disused brick-field surrounded by some tumble-down hovels. At this spot their guide suddenly stopped.

"That is the Mosque, in the distance," he said, and without waiting for reply, hurried off at a pace that belied his age.

"I believe there's some trickery," said Osterberg. "I half wish we hadn't come. What's to be done?"

"That old man has brought us to this spot for a purpose," said Helmar. "Why didn't he leave us at the gardens?" A dark look came into his eyes as he spoke. "Well, we'll give Mr. Mark ten minutes to turn up," he went on. "After that, we'll go."

The two young men stood for a minute or two, kicking their heels about, and, at last, Osterberg got so impatient that he suddenly burst out——

"Come on, don't let us wait here, let us get back to the quay. This is some beastly hoax. The place is as silent as the grave—it gives me the creeps."

"I said we would give him ten minutes, and we will do so," said George, determinedly. "I'm not going until the time has elapsed. Hallo!" as he caught sight of a figure approaching, "here comes somebody. Perhaps it's Mark."

His surmise proved correct. Mark came quickly up, and held out his hand. He was dressed in Egyptian costume, and with his dark complexion and black eyes might easily have passed as a native.

"Ah! Helmar, and you, Osterberg!" he said. "I am glad to see you." Then, as neither took the proffered hand, he drew back. "Why, what's up? Aren't you going to shake hands?"

"You said in your note," exclaimed our hero, impatiently, "that you wanted to return the money you owe me. Where is it?"

"Ah, that's it!" answered Mark, with apparent relief. "Well, if you'll come into this house I'll give it you. Oh, it's all right!" as Helmar did not offer to move, "there's not a soul about besides ourselves. Come along."

"But why can't you pay me here? I have no time to fool about, and must get back to the quay in time to catch the boat."

"I know—at least, that is—all right," said Mark, seeing that he had made a mistake. "But you don't understand. This is where I have to live."

"Since you robbed those who helped you here, eh?" said George, contemptuously.

"I see you have heard of that, then," replied Mark, with a smile. "But really I had no intention of stealing, I only borrowed it as I borrowed it from you, and am equally as ready to return it as I am yours."

"Why don't you do so, then?" said Helmar, a little mollified at the man's open words. "Look here, Mark, I don't want to say hard things, but if you're not a knave you are a fool, and the sooner you pull yourself together and live a decent life, the better!"

"Oh, don't preach, Helmar!" cried Arden impatiently. "Allow me to do as I think fit. Now, will you come and get that money, or must I, on account of some silly notion of yours, go and fetch it? Of course, if you will not, then——"

"All right, lead the way," said Helmar, "I'll follow."

Arden led the way to a tumble-down, two-storied building, and the trio entered. It was dark inside.

"You'd better follow me pretty closely," said their guide, "the floor is none too sound, and you may have a tumble if you don't."

The two friends followed close up to their guide, and as they turned into a room, Osterberg fancied he heard a sound proceed from it. As nothing further alarmed him, he put it down to his straining nerves. As soon as they were inside, the door closed sharply behind them, and the ominous click of the lock made them both start. Helmar was about to say something, when Mark anticipated him.

"Hold on while I strike a light. The beastly wind has blown the door to."

This was such palpable nonsense that George expostulated.

"There isn't a breath of wind, man. Hurry up with the light!"

Arden fumbled with some matches for a moment, and then a light was struck.

"'Trapped, by Heavens!' shouted Helmar." p. 124

"Trapped, by Heavens!" shouted Helmar, as the light revealed the room filled with armed Arabs.

"Yes, as you say—trapped!" said Arden, with a leer on his dark face. "You are the fool, Helmar, not I. But see here, I am on business. Not of my own, but that of the person who employs me."

Helmar was gazing at their surroundings and calculating the chances of escape. As far as he could see, there were at least a dozen fierce-looking Arabs standing in a ring round the walls, and the only mode of egress was a broken window and the door. The door was securely locked, but the window was not only broken, but the wall below it was in decay and looked as if one heavy blow against it would bring the whole thing down—it seemed to be only held up by a couple of wooden props set up from the floor on either side of the window.

He had no time for any careful survey, for Arden, observing his wandering gaze, exclaimed—

"It's no use, you can't escape. At a word from me these Arabs will kill you. Now, listen to what I have to say. As you know, Arabi is in open rebellion. I am employed by him. I am going round the country endeavouring to secure European recruits. He knows that he has practically only the British to deal with, and he wants to get as many Europeans as he can on his side. Now, in bringing you here, I am really doing you a good turn," he went on, with cool effrontery. "I am helping you to a far better position and infinitely more money than you will have with the British authorities. If you will join us you will be made an officer in his army, at a big salary, and you will be liberated at once; if you refuse—well, these men have their orders and you will never leave this place alive."

"So you would be a murderer as well as a thief!" cried George, with flashing eyes. "I will not talk about ingratitude to such a cur as you. You probably do not understand the word. I have this day signed to assist the British authorities to the utmost of my power, and——"

"Yes, I am quite aware of it," interrupted the villain. "Your movements have been watched from the moment you arrived in Port Said; but come—your answer. I have no time to waste."

Arden was holding the light in his hand. It was a small oil lamp, with uncovered flame. As he finished speaking, he held it out towards our hero, peering into his face. With a bound like a panther, George darted forward and seized the spluttering light. Giving one powerful twist, he wrenched it from the villain's hand, and, turning it upside down, a huge flame flashed out all over it. He dashed it to the ground and the burning oil ran over the floor, catching light to the pieces of worn-out mats scattered about, and in less time than it takes to write, the rotten boards flared up. Helmar, seeing what had happened, backed himself to the wall, dragging his companion with him.

His movements had been so rapid that even Arden's usual presence of mind had failed him; but, as he saw the flame burst from the flooring, he shouted to the Arabs to seize their prisoners.

He had, however, calculated without his host. The house was so rotten and dry that the flames spread with great rapidity, and the Arabs, in terror of their lives, made for the door. Seeing this, almost blinded by the smoke, Helmar and Osterberg dashed to the window, and, tearing away the two supports, sprang on to the sill. The supports gone, the weight of their bodies finished the work that time had begun, and with a terrible crash the wall gave way, and the companions fell with it. Springing to their feet, quite unhurt, they found themselves out in the open, and ran off at top speed in the direction of the town.

They were not a moment too soon, for Arden, at the head of the Arabs who had escaped by the door, came round the corner and followed in hot pursuit.

It was almost dark, but George remembered the direction from which they had approached the desolate house, and with unerring judgment led the way as fast as his legs could carry him.

Osterberg followed his fleet-footed friend, keeping pace with difficulty, and they soon reached the boundary of the gardens.

"Which way now?" panted Osterberg, as the dim outline of trees loomed through the darkness.

"Follow me," cried George in answer, as without a moment's hesitation he turned a sharp corner.

Each felt rather than knew that the swift-footed Arabs were coming ever nearer, and that their only means of salvation lay in strategy. For this reason George preferred the gardens to the open roads. Since Arabi's rising, Europeans had taken to staying in their houses at night, rather than run any risk of a stab in the dark, so that there was little hope of meeting any one who could help them in the open thoroughfare. The gardens appealed to Helmar on account of their dense foliage and excellent cover. In case the worst should come to the worst, they would at least afford them shelter, and he hoped against hope that by this means he could give their enemies the slip.

The patter of feet behind them had now grown louder and perfectly distinct, and at times Helmar even fancied he could hear the heavy breathing of the pursuers.

Darting like a brace of hares through the labyrinth of paths, the two young men kept on. Their pace was terrific, but the sound of feet was still not far behind them.

"George," panted Osterberg, as he drew up alongside his friend, "we can't keep this up. Can't we take the scrub and hide?"

"Not yet, not yet, keep going, we shall find a place soon."

Just then a light appeared among the trees to their right, and inspired with fresh hope they renewed their exertions, searching vainly for a path by which to reach it. Suddenly an idea struck George.

"Never mind the light. Here, take this path to the left. Arden and his Arabs are sure to think we have made for that light in the hopes of assistance."

Without hesitation they turned to the left, and in a few minutes came to an open gate in the boundary fence. For a second they paused to listen and recover their wind.

"You were right, George," whispered his companion, "I cannot hear the footsteps, they have gone in the other direction. Come along, let's hurry. Do you know where we are?"

"Haven't the faintest notion," was the comforting reply.

"Well then, I suppose we must trust to luck. Which way?" he asked, as they stepped into the dusty road.

George glanced quickly up and down. He saw some twinkling lights to the right.

"There we are, that's the town," and the two set off again at a run.

The lights became clearer and more numerous as they hurried along, and at last Helmar stopped running.

"I think we are safe now. Listen!"

The companions strained their ears to catch the slightest sound from behind, but they could hear nothing.

"Thank goodness, they have lost us. I don't think we need fear further pursuit," said George. "Now, I wonder if we are in time to catch our boat." Fearing to strike a match to look at the time, they hurried on towards the town, and in a few minutes reached the outskirts. With hurried pace they made for the landing-stage, and reached it a few minutes before the gangway was about to be hauled aboard the transport.

"A narrow shave in more ways than one," said Helmar, as they stepped on deck. "Come, we must report ourselves to the captain. I don't think we had better say anything about what has happened."

Osterberg agreed, and the two young men reported themselves at once.

CHAPTER XII

THE NEW OCCUPATION

The ironclad that bore Helmar and his young friend to Alexandria also carried a great number of refugees, all bound for their homes in Europe. The time passed so pleasantly, that when their destination came into view, it was with feelings of regret that the young men prepared to disembark.

As the docks loomed up, the evidences of the bombardment became distinctly visible. How different everything seemed now, from the peaceful business-like appearance the place presented when Helmar first landed on those self-same docks! The great heavy ironclads lay at anchor all around, silent and harmless enough to look at, but, withal, a mighty latent power protecting the shattered city. On shore the destruction seemed terrible; forts in all directions could be seen, battered and tumbled heaps of debris, a ghastly tribute to England's mighty naval power. Buildings that had been before all full of life and bustling activity were nothing but charred ruins.

Altogether, the picture that presented itself, as the vessel slowly forged towards the shore, was one of appalling significance, and as George and Osterberg took in the terrible details, neither could help a feeling of regret at the necessity of such things.

"It seems so terrible," said Osterberg, with a sigh, "to think that, for the sake of one great villain, all this destruction should have taken place."

"Yes, but you must not forget that if it hadn't, probably there would not be a single European left alive in the city," answered the practical Helmar. "Personally I glory in a power that is so quick to avenge, and only regret that it did not come in time to prevent the terrible massacres of the hound Arabi. 'Egypt for the Egyptians' is no excuse for such wanton destruction of human life. If I am any judge there'll be a terrible reckoning for that gentleman and his satellites in the near future. England is roused now, and some one will have to answer for it."

Helmar was an enthusiast. He admired and believed in the English as a race, and gloried, in a broad-minded way, in their mighty power. Since he had left his own country, the English he had met had, at once, held out a helping hand to him, and there was no thought in his mind but of gratitude towards them.

"We will not say 'Good-bye,'" said George, as the young men shook hands on the quay. "Some day I expect we shall come together again. Your life is, apparently, to be of a more peaceful nature than mine, and perhaps it is as well; but still, these are troublous times, and one never can tell what may occur to bring us together. *Au revoir*, and good luck."

Osterberg replied in a similar strain, concluding with the fatherly advice, "Do not put your head into too many traps," then hastened off to seek his bank, or, at any rate, what might still remain of it.

Although not an enlisted man, Helmar was now, more or less, bound down by the same rules as governed the marines. There were many restrictions put upon him, and his associations were entirely of a martial description. He was, of course, billeted with the sailors, who only numbered some four hundred, and his duties consisted mainly of attending the orderly room in his capacity of interpreter. To a man of his energy and brains, this soon became simply intolerable, and he quickly determined to find other and more exciting means of occupying his time.

Directly British forces landed from the ironclads, Arabi and his soldiery abandoned the city and took up their position at Kafr Dowar, a few miles to the south. A city patrol was quickly organized, consisting of blue-jackets and soldiers, and, in order to keep his mind and body employed, Helmar obtained permission to join these parties when he was not otherwise occupied.

After the bombardment had ceased and before they evacuated the city, the rebels set light to hundreds of buildings, using petroleum, the better to work their fell purpose. The damage done in the European quarters was terrific, and many of the streets had become simply impassable, fallen ruins and dead and charred bodies in most instances blocking the way. All buildings that had escaped the incendiaries were looted from top to bottom, and not a vestige of anything valuable was left by the rabble.

There was plenty of work, therefore, to be done in the city for some time to come. Notwithstanding the fact that the place was now in the hands of the British, acts of incendiarism were still being perpetrated at intervals. Natives who had remained in the town were the chief offenders, and it was a task of great difficulty for the patrols to stop the wanton destruction.

One evening an alarm was given, and the patrol, which Helmar chanced to be with, was ordered to the spot. The conflagration was near one of the city gates, and, as the little party approached, a mob of Bedouins was seen hovering round, evidently with the intention of looting.

The officer in charge of the patrol gave the order for his men to conceal themselves, and the whole party waited developments. Avoiding the fire the Bedouins entered another house, creeping cautiously to avoid detection. The watchers realized at once what was on; the fire had been started to distract attention from them, and, meanwhile, they were looting to their hearts' content. There were about twenty of the ragged creatures, and, as the last one entered the building, the patrol dashed in after them.

There was a short, sharp fight, and then the would-be looters endeavoured to escape, but the trap was perfect, and, with one or two exceptions, the whole party were captured, taken to the Market Square and shot.

Such incidents were of frequent occurrence, and often the native police were the offenders; no mercy was shown, however; those found guilty of pillaging only were flogged, while incendiaries were shot.

Helmar found his knowledge of Arabic brought plenty of work. The residents and shop-owners required much help, and, in many instances, permission was granted to erect makeshift places in the public thoroughfares to carry on business.

Destitute native families had to be provided for, homeless orphans and widowed mothers to be looked after. All these required people like Helmar to deal with them, and he found that his knowledge of their language brought him into constant demand.

As often as not, his task was an unpleasant one. A fight, a tussle, a battle fair and square wouldn't have troubled him in the least, but when his work demanded the witnessing of prisoners being shot or flogged, he often felt, although he knew they deserved it, an absolute loathing for his duty. However, he was not always required for these things, and when they came, they were soon over, and, in the midst of all the bustle, he quickly forgot his momentary weakness.

On one occasion only did his feelings get the better of him.

A row of prisoners were lying down on their stomachs, moaning in the courtyards, awaiting their punishment; men of all nationalities and ages, varying from fifteen to seventy. Each was, in turn, tied to the pillar with his back bared, and received so many strokes from the cat at the hands of a marine, whilst the officer in command counted each blow, as it fell on the lacerated back. As the skin gradually turned red, blue, and then swelled, and the shrieks and yells of the victim filled the air, Helmar uttered a suppressed groan and turned his head, but he could not leave the courtyard. A fine specimen of an Arab had attracted his attention, and he wondered how he would submit to the treatment. His curiosity was soon satisfied. The man was led up to the wall and securely tied, then, setting his teeth, took his punishment without flinching or the utterance of a word. Whilst the marines were untying him, George saw that the man was almost fainting, and, as he tottered away, he went to his assistance and supported him to the doorway. Here he offered him a tin of water, but, to his utter astonishment, the man refused it.

"No, no," and the man waved the refreshing liquid away. Then he explained in broken accents that it was a month of fasting, when no good Moslem either drinks, eats, or smokes between sunrise and sunset.

Helmar was deeply impressed with the man's faith, which was strong enough to deny himself in his extremity for the sake of his religion.

The rigorous manner in which crime was punished soon had its effect, and matters began to calm down inside the town.

Incendiarism and robbery gradually ceased, citizens began to breathe more freely, and business revived.

Helmar's occupation now began to grow more monotonous, and he looked about for something fresh. He found there was much work to be done in repairing the fortifications and building fresh ones. In this work native labour was largely requisitioned, and George saw an opportunity of employment in dealing with the workers. He soon obtained work here in a post of some slight importance, and, in a short time, proved himself so capable that the officers and those in authority began to notice him.

Rumour had it that Arabi at Kafr Dowar was preparing to attack the town, and in consequence the authorities prepared to receive him. A large number of soldiers, blue-jackets, and marines with Gatling guns were landed, and the resources of the town were taxed to the utmost. Night and day the work of fortification went on, and guns were mounted at many points on the southern parts of the town.

In this instance rumour was correct, and the rebel Pasha began to show fight. A contingent of his mounted infantry was known to be somewhere in the district of Ramleh water-works, so two regiments of mounted men were sent out in the direction to disperse them. They met, and a fierce but short encounter ensued, and the Egyptians fled towards Ramleh for reinforcements. This necessitated the dispatch of artillery and more troops to protect the place. On arriving there they found the ridge along the canal occupied by the enemy, and the water-works in danger. It soon became patent to the officer in command that the hill which commanded the position must be strongly held, and big guns mounted there. To this end he communicated with the town, and considerable delay was caused.

It was at this time that Helmar received the order to join the forces at Ramleh. He had just turned into his blankets after a sixteen-hours day's work, and he felt that the much-needed rest was well earned. He was just dozing off to sleep, when a head was put through the doorway and a voice called him—

"Helmar!"

George was on his feet in an instant.

"Yes!" he answered, recognizing the voice of an engineer.

"You are wanted at once by the Colonel. Hurry up!"

George did not wait an instant. He had lain down to sleep in his clothes, so putting on his helmet he ran out towards the Commander's quarters. In a few moments he found himself in the presence of his chief.

"Helmar, I want you to join the officer in charge at Ramleh. The attack, I believe, is expected to be centred on that point at daylight, and there the defences are very incomplete. This is a case of emergency, or I should not send for you, for I am aware you have been at work for more than sixteen hours. However, you will take your gang to the point at once and render all the assistance possible. That will do!"

The prospect, to most men, would not have been alluring, but to Helmar it was one of unmixed pleasure. True, he could have done with some sleep, but the hope of being in the thick of the fight on the morrow dwarfed into insignificance his desire for rest.

In a short time he had aroused his blackies, and grumbling at being disturbed, they marched with their picks and shovels in the direction of the point to be defended.

The enemy was still keeping up a desultory fire, and the solemn "boom" of their heavy guns could now and then be heard, while the hiss of the flying shell grated harshly on the still night air. The blackies were used to this sort of thing, and marched along as unconcernedly as if it were the natural state of things, only now and then would be heard a remark as a shell came a little nearer than usual.

The spot was reached, and in a few minutes Helmar was superintending the throwing up of trenches. Approaching an officer in charge of a party of sappers close to him, he fell into conversation.

"They expect an attack here at daylight?" he said, by way of greeting.

"Yes, Arabi has found our weak spot, and the General has information of his intention. We shall give them a warm reception, but the trouble is, we have no guns of any kind mounted yet."

"Well, what do you think will happen?"

"Can't say, I'm sure," replied the officer, looking towards the east. "I believe at the first streak of daylight they are going to try to mount some of the naval guns on that steep hill the other side of the railway. I don't quite see how it is to be done under fire."

Helmar looked over at the hill in question. Well might the officer doubt the ability of the troops to mount the guns under fire. The hill was very steep and open, not a fraction of cover on it anywhere. Every man on the work would be exposed to the enemy's fire. The task looked a hopeless one.

"Yes, you're right," he said at last, "it will be a tough job. How do they propose to go about it?"

"Set the blackies to haul them up," was the laconic reply.

Helmar did not answer. The first streaks of daylight were already appearing, and his work was nearly completed. Already the fighting men of the camp were on the move and about to occupy the trenches. As the daylight began to broaden, he saw that the work of hauling the guns up on to the hill had begun. Shortly after, the fighting line occupied his trenches, and his gang were dismissed and sent back to their quarters. His work was completed, and he made his way towards the hill. Already Arabi's men had advanced to the attack, and firing had started at all points. It was quickly evident that the information was correct, and this portion of the town was to receive the main attack, for a terrific fusillade was opened by the enemy's artillery.

The noise soon became deafening, the enemy's heavy guns being answered by the few small ones that the British had been able to get into position during the night. There was no doubt that, until the heavy naval batteries were got into position, it would go hard with the defending forces.

Helmar hurried along in face of the terrific fire, totally heedless of the danger he was running, until he reached the railway.

Hurrying on with the greatest possible speed, he reached the base of the hill, where he stood watching the efforts of the men. It was frightful work, the great heavy guns moved ever so slowly, and to George the outlook seemed hopeless.

He had not noticed the officer in charge standing close by him, but as a sergeant ran up to receive some order his attention was attracted, and he recognized a Captain of Engineers to whom he had been of use several times since his arrival in Alexandria.

The officer looked very much concerned about something as he stood there directing the sergeant. At the very moment the man went off to do the bidding of his superior, the officer turned and caught sight of George standing there. Beckoning him to his side, he asked—

"Is not your name Helmar?"

"Yes, sir," replied George.

"What are you doing now?" demanded the officer.

"I have just finished the trenches, sir; my men have gone back and I was about to follow, when I stopped to watch the hauling up of those guns," said George.

"Ah! Those guns are giving much trouble. But I have just hit upon an idea which will save time and labour, and you are the very man I want to help carry it out. Come with me for a few minutes and I will give you the necessary instructions."

George followed the officer promptly.

CHAPTER XIII

HELMAR PROVES HIS METAL

As George followed the officer he wondered what the plan was and in what manner his services could be of use in its execution. So far his occupations had been many and various, and, being willing and prepared to do any mortal thing, he felt no anxiety about the task he was to have next.

Having reached the spot where the operations were going on, the officer, addressing Helmar, said—

"Unless we get those guns into position quickly, there is no telling what may happen. The situation is getting very serious, but if I can carry out my plan successfully there will be nothing to fear. It is necessary, however, to have a trustworthy and fearless man for the job, for he will not only have a hard task but will be in a warm corner."

"Give me your orders, sir, and I will do my best to carry them out," said George, without hesitation.

"Well, it will take a long time to get the guns up by manual labour," said his companion meditatively, "and it seems to me that we might easily adopt another means. Now," he went on, in decisive tones, "there are plenty of ropes and wire cables, and my suggestion is, we fix two blocks, one on the top of the hill and the other on the railway line opposite to it, and then, fastening a cable to the gun and passing it through the pulleys, secure it to a locomotive and—the thing is done."

The officer looked at George for a moment, wondering if he grasped the situation clearly. The plan was of such a simple nature that he could not fail to do so.

"Do you understand what I mean?" asked the officer.

"Perfectly," replied George, "it seems to me a splendid plan."

"Good!" exclaimed the officer. "Now, I want you to undertake the securing of the block on the hill." Then turning to the men, he called out, "Cease hauling there! Sergeant," he went on, "send in word at once to dispatch a locomotive down the line to us with the least possible delay."

The work assigned to George was of great importance and of great danger. The enemy had already trained their heavy guns on to the hill, and it was only their bad gunnery that made it possible for the officer's plan to be carried out. In every direction shells were flying, bursting overhead, on either side, short, and far over the city, till the air was filled with flying fragments of metal; every moment was a constant threat, a constant danger to the little party of blue-jackets at the foot of the hill.

Without waiting for further orders, Helmar, with the assistance of one or two of the eager sailors, selected an iron block of great strength, some necessary tools and ropes, and began the ascent.

The first part of the climb was a little sheltered, but, as they proceeded, the shells hurtled away over their heads in rapid succession, and as the hissing missiles sped on their way, the men involuntarily ducked their heads as though to avoid them. The devoted little party had barely a hundred and fifty yards to go to reach the summit, but every foot of the way they knew they would be exposed to this murderous fire.

The battle was raging all along the south of the city, a dense cloud of smoke covering the land like a pall, hiding the glaring light of the sun and making the atmosphere more densely oppressive than ever. The little party toiled wearily up the hill, the perspiration pouring off them as they struggled beneath their iron burdens, prepared to do or die. Helmar led the way, and never for a moment paused, although the weight of the heavy block was almost unbearable. He thought nothing of the flying shells, nothing of the death he was facing at every step, only of reaching the top and securing the pulley. A few more yards and the journey would be over.

"Come on, lads, only another step or two!" he cried, gasping for breath in the parching air.

"Ay, ay," came the answer in various tones.

At last the top was reached. The sight now became fearful; the bursting shells, ploughing up the ground on all sides, were enough to strike terror into any one's heart. The blue-jackets, used to facing fire of all kinds, simply laughed and joked as they pointed out the inaccuracy of the firing.

"Them savages 'ad better go back to their bows and arrers," exclaimed one of the men, as he saw a shell pitch about half-way short of the hill. "Blowed if they could 'it an 'aystack, the black divils!"

His companions laughed, and it did all hands good. Notwithstanding their indomitable pluck, the nervous strain was great, and the laugh relieved them. The hill-top was very bare, and, as George glanced round for a means of securing the pulley, he began to think that after all he had no easy task. The only possible means of securing it was to drive strong poles deep and firmly into the earth, and then fix the pulleys to them.

As Helmar stood examining the spot, a splinter of one of the shells struck the earth close to him, and glancing off, whizzed past within an inch of his face. Springing back, he turned to a man near him.

"That was a close call," he said.

"Ay, and it might ha' been closer," was the solemn reply.

There was no time to be lost, Helmar had made up his mind, and gave his instructions to the men. Taking a crowbar, about seven feet long, they drove it into the earth until there was little more than two feet of it remaining above ground. Just as this was finished, a shell pitched and burst barely twenty yards from them, and the whole party narrowly escaped death. The explosion tore up the ground until it looked as if a plough had recently passed over it.

For fear the crowbar should not be firm enough to hold the weight of the gun, Helmar now fixed a stay to it and secured it to the ground; then collecting all the loose, heavy stones around, had them rolled into position so as to prevent the stake from drawing.

The hill was now becoming too hot to hold them; the Arabs, bent on dislodging them, continued their fire with greater accuracy, until it became so deadly that the rest of the work had to be done lying down.

The process of fastening the iron block to the crowbar was comparatively easy, and yet it was during this operation that the first casualty happened. George was lashing the wire rope round the stanchion, with the assistance of one of the men, when, without a cry or a moan, his companion fell back on the ground, shot clean through the chest. Helmar was terribly shocked, but continued his work, the man's place being at once filled by one of the others, and so the task was completed.

"If that doesn't hold, nothing will," exclaimed George, ducking involuntarily, as a shot passed over his head. "Come on, boys, we'd better go back. No, on second thoughts, go you down and haul up the cable, I'll remain here and take care of him," pointing to the dying sailor.

Without a word, the men darted off, and Helmar was left alone.

While waiting for the return of his comrades, he laid the dying man in a comfortable position, nursing his head on his lap. This was the first time Helmar had been under fire. His anticipation of it had been somewhat unnerving, but when he found himself in the midst of the hail of lead and iron, his spirits had at once risen and he felt a wild longing to shout defiance at the distant Arabs.

He could see nothing of the enemy through the dense canopy of smoke, but, from his elevated position, he could see the line of the city defences quite plainly. The garrison troops on all sides seemed to be gaining ground, only at this one point did it seem that nothing was being done. Suddenly he saw the locomotive dash out from the town and run swiftly down the line towards him, and, at the same time, the cheery "heave-ho" of the tars broke on his ear as they hauled the cable up the hill.

The next minute the pilot rope was passed through the block and the men ran off with it towards the railway, while George remained to guide the hawser into its place when it came up.

The whole operation did not last more than a few minutes; he saw the men reach the railway, pass the rope through the pulley there, and then secure it to the waiting engine.

The officer now came up and joined Helmar.

"You have done well, my lad," he cried. "Do you think the stanchion will hold the weight of the heavy guns?"

"I hope so, sir," answered Helmar, eyeing the crowbar narrowly.

"Very well, I'll give the order to heave in the slack. We'll see."

"At last the gun reached the top." p. 151

He then gave the signal, and the engine began to steam slowly back to the town. The guide rope hauled taut, and then began to pass rapidly through the blocks. The hawser began to ascend. Up it came, lumbering along like a great snake until the block was reached. The officer signalled, and the engine came to a standstill. George passed the great steel rope safely through the pulley, and the work went on until the hawser had passed the second block on the railway. The engine then came back, and as soon as the great cable was secured to it, it started again for the town. The work had started in real earnest.

All this time the enemy's fire was kept up incessantly, the locomotive being an object for their gunners to try their skill. But for the Arabs' atrocious practice, the naval guns would never have been got into position; as it was, whilst Helmar and the officer stood looking on, the gun began slowly to ascend.

With a lynx eye, George watched the straining crowbar, fearful that it should draw and his work prove unavailing. It held, and, assisted by the men below, the heavy burden was steadily hauled up.

At last the gun reached the top, and Helmar breathed a sigh of relief as he saw it wheeled off to its position. After this, the other guns were fetched up in a similar manner, and in less than half-an-hour the whole battery opened fire on the enemy. The naval brigade's practice quickly silenced the enemy's guns, and long before sundown Arabi and his hordes were in full retreat.

As soon as his share in the work was over, George quietly slipped away and retired, thinking no more about it, content to leave the issue of the day in other more capable hands, while he took his well-earned rest. It did not occur to him that he had done anything wonderful, and therefore great was his surprise when, towards sundown, he was again rudely awakened by a loud voice telling him to get up.

"Be sharp, too; the Colonel wants you."

Somewhat flustered by this peremptory order, George hurried out and followed the orderly until he reached a house on the outskirts. Here the man paused.

"You're not very smart-looking," he said, eyeing Helmar's non-military appearance with a glance of contempt.

"I can't help that," said George. "You said, 'come at once,' so I came. It's no use finding fault with my appearance now, you should have thought of that before."

"All right, I don't want any cheek, only when you go before the Colonel you are supposed to look smart. Just remember, young fellar, it's an honour to speak to the chief."

"Oh, is it?" said George, tired of the man's patronage. "Well, if you'll lead the way, I shall be obliged, for it is no honour to speak to you."

Muttering something derogatory to Helmar's nationality, the man led the way into the house.

In a few minutes Helmar stood in front of the Colonel in charge. In the room several other officers were standing round, amongst whom he recognized the Captain whom he had assisted with the guns. The latter smiled on him as he entered.

"I am told," said the Colonel, looking up at Helmar, "that it was due to your gallant conduct to-day, my man, that the guns were got into position so rapidly. It seems that, under a very heavy fire, you went to the top of the hill on which they were to be posted, and fixed up the hauling gear. These reports are very satisfactory to me. You are engaged as an interpreter at present. I shall endeavour to find you a position the better to show your capabilities. I compliment you heartily on what you have done."

When Helmar got outside he could scarcely refrain from shouting for joy. The very first engagement he had been in, it seemed, he had distinguished himself and received the Colonel's congratulations. It seemed too good to be true. And yet the Colonel had said it himself. "Bah!" he muttered, "I did no more than the others did—yes, but very likely they got praised too."

He anxiously hurried back, wondering what the morrow would bring forth. Evidently luck was coming his way.

CHAPTER XIV

THE REGIMENTAL COOK

The sun had long risen when George awoke from his heavy, dreamless slumber. Tired nature had at last demanded and received her share of the healing balm of sleep. The day had been exciting, and eventful; and though the nervous strain had been great, it was long before his busy brain allowed him to get to sleep. When it did, however, it was hours before his body was sufficiently refreshed to begin the new day.

The sun was pouring down with scorching intensity when he sprang from his blankets; the heat of the atmosphere was like that of an oven, and he flung back the fastenings of the doorway and plunged his head into a bucket of water that stood ready to hand. Thoroughly refreshed and cooled with his dip, he set out in search of breakfast, his thoughts running wild over the events of the preceding day, as he made his way down the lines towards the cook-house.

As he hurried along he was astonished at the number of men who paused in their work to take notice of him. As a matter of fact, he was scarcely known to any one, except the officers with whom he came into contact in his work, and yet he was greeted like an old friend by nearly every one he came across. It was some time before he began to realize that, in some way, the events of yesterday had brought this about.

Reaching the cook-house, he plunged into the subject of breakfast. Had the cook anything to eat?

"Anything to eat?" replied that worthy. "Well, rather. Always got something for you, Mr. Helmar!" his greasy face smiling with a look of pride at the man who had so distinguished himself on the hill yesterday.

"I'm beastly hungry, and am afraid I'm a bit late," said George apologetically. "But I was so tired that I overslept myself."

"Late? Not a bit of it—leastways, not for you. Here y'are, I been a-savin' this for you," and the benevolent-looking "slushy" dived into an oven and produced a piece of steak and some onions on a tin plate.

George accepted this mark of extreme favour with the greatest pleasure. The steak smelt savoury, although, by the looks of it, he thought it would have done credit to a shoemaker's shop; but he fell to with such a healthy appetite that the cook was still further pleased.

"'Ere, 'av a drop o' my kauffee," he said, holding out a pannikin of the steaming liquid; "there's a goodish 'stick' in it," he added, with a knowing wink.

George accepted it without demur. He did not care for brandy, but he felt that he was under an obligation to the man and would not hurt his feelings by refusing what the soldiers considered a priceless treasure.

While George was discussing his solid breakfast the cook looked on, chattering away about the doings of yesterday, avoiding with soldier-like tact Helmar's share in the proceedings; but just as the meal was over and he was about to depart, he said—

"S'pose you won't be 'avin' many more meals along o' us?"

"What do you mean?" asked George, in surprise.

The man smiled and looked knowing.

"Orficers' mess grub better'n we do, yer know," he replied, winking with the whole side of his face.

"Yes, I dare say they do, but that's got nothing to do with it," said George.

"Ho, 'asn't it! They tells me as you are a-goin' to be made a horsifer."

Our hero laughed, and the man looked offended.

"No, no, that's wrong. You know, I'm not English, they can't do that— besides, there's no reason for it."

"Well, now, I never thought o' that," replied the cook, somewhat crestfallen. "But they're a-goin' to do somethin' for yer; everybody's a-talkin' about 'ow you got them guns up the 'ill, and I sez, right yer are, I sez, 'e's a chap as deserves to git hon."

George was quite confused at the man's praise, and, to avoid more of it, said good-bye and left the kitchen. What he had heard had opened his eyes. Now he knew the meaning of his morning's greetings from the strangers he had passed. Apparently he was looked upon as a sort of hero—well, he hoped they would find him something to do to prove their belief in him.

Cutting across the parade ground towards the office, where his duties as interpreter required him, he was met by an orderly sergeant.

"Mornin', Mr. Helmar. I was just coming to look for you. You're wanted at the office. I think," he went on, impressively, "there's a little trip on hand and you are to go on it."

"Good! Do you know what it is, and where to?"

"Can't say, I'm sure. They keep these things very quiet. The Adjutant's inside," he went on, "you'd better go in."

Helmar stepped in. A group of officers, standing round a desk, turned as he entered.

"Ah," said one who was sitting at the table with a chart spread in front of him, "I want you to hold yourself in readiness to accompany Captain Forsyth, this evening, on a patrol towards Kafr Dowar. You will act as interpreter. The commanding officer has selected you, as the work to be done will entail considerable risk, and we require a reliable man. Further instructions will be given you by Captain Forsyth. The patrol starts at sundown. You can go now and get ready."

"Very good, sir," replied George, and turned to leave. One of the officers followed, and, as they got outside, joined him.

"Your orders are not very explicit, Helmar," said he, "and probably convey but little to you. Of course, I dare say you know that after yesterday's engagement Arabi has retreated to Kafr Dowar. It is believed he has some thousands gathered under his banner, but we want to be sure. We are going out to gather all information possible, in which work you will be of great assistance to me."

"You, then, are Captain Forsyth?" asked George, at once.

"Yes, I asked that you might accompany me, for I do not care to trust to the native interpreters, and, besides," with a smile, "I am glad to have a man who not only can fight, but is also a man of resource."

"I don't know the country, sir," answered Helmar doubtfully, "and, under the circumstances, that seems to me to be a vital point. Arabi's men are pretty smart, and no doubt there will be many traps to avoid."

"I have taken all that into consideration. As far as the country is concerned, I will answer for that, and the traps—well, we must be as shrewd as the enemy."

"I am only too glad of the chance," said Helmar, afraid lest, in offering objections, the officer should think he did not want to go, "and if it comes to a tight corner, I will give the best account of myself possible."

"That's all right, then," said Captain Forsyth. "And now you had better go and get ready. I am going to let you use one of my own horses instead of a trooper; a blanket on the saddle is all that you can carry, except, of course, a day or two's rations in your wallet in case of accidents. You can get your arms from the quartermaster."

The officer returned to the room, and Helmar hurried off to secure all that he needed.

There was but little difficulty; evidently orders had been given beforehand, for his equipments were laid out and waiting for him. In an hour's time he had collected together everything he required, and the rest of the day was his own.

His spirits were at the highest possible pitch, and the thoughts of the luck which was following him made him feel ready to undertake the most daring enterprises. He blessed the engineer officer who had given him the opportunity with the guns the day before. The drudgery of ganging natives in the trenches seemed as if it had now gone for ever, and he was about to embark on responsible work, or, at least, work that would give him scope to prove his mettle. The more he thought of it, the more castles he built of rising to a big position, until, at last, realizing the absurdity of his dreams, he brought himself back to the practical side of his duty.

Late in the afternoon, about an hour before sundown, he again visited his friend the cook. He found that worthy looking as benevolently greasy as ever, and ready to offer him all the resources of his larder.

"I thought I'd come and get my tea now, cook, I've got to go out on patrol at sundown. I'm afraid I'm a beastly nuisance."

"Nuisance? No, o' course not. I ain't one o' them blokes as grumble cause a feller's 'ungry. Wot d'yer say to a bit o' cold meat and some tea to start with?"

"Splendid. I haven't had any dinner, I had breakfast so late, so we'll make up for it now."

"An' where are yer goin', if it's a fair question?" asked his companion.

"Well, I don't know that I ought to say. Still, I wasn't told to keep it quiet, so I suppose it doesn't matter. It seems old Arabi has retired to Kafr Dowar and is going to make a stand there. We're going to gather information. I don't suppose there'll be much excitement."

"Um," replied the cook, placing a pile of toast and dripping in front of his visitor. "I wouldn't mind bettin' a day's pay you git all the fun yer want afore yer git back."

"Why, what makes you think that?" asked George, amused at the man's tone of conviction.

"Yer don't know them horsifers like I do; I ain't been in service all these years for nothin'. I tell yer, if there wasn't no danger they'd a sent one o' them blessed blacks to interpit instead o' you. They knows you've got the grit, so they sends you, and it's odds yer don't come back with a 'ole skin."

George knew the man's words were not meant unkindly, although they were something of a raven's croaking; however, with undamped ardour, he attacked the pile of greasy toast and waited for his host to continue.

"I ain't got no opinion o' them all-fired Gypies!" he went on, as Helmar did not reply. "They're that treacherous as never, and if they gits 'old o' yer it means murder. Now, my advice is, an' I've 'ad twenty year experience as a soldier ov 'er Majesty Queen Victoria—the greatest soverin o' the day— askin' yer pardon, as yer a Doycher—wot I says is, bayonit 'em, an' when yer done it see as they ain't alive arter. If yer don't, yer a goner."

The good-natured cook had worked himself up to such a pitch of excitement as he laid the law down to our hero, that the latter was seriously afraid of apoplexy, and when the old fellow had finished, it was with difficulty he refrained from bursting out into a roar of laughter. However, keeping a straight face, he took a long pull at the pannikin of tea, and prepared to leave.

"I've no doubt you are right, cook, and I shan't forget your advice. Well, good-bye, see you again some day."

"Good-bye, Mr. Helmar," replied the cook, again beaming with good-nature and fat. "Good luck to you; don't forgit there's allers a drop o' good kauffee 'ere," and he turned to his work with a chuckle.

Helmar hurried back to his quarters, and calling the chief nigger of his gang up, sent him to Captain Forsyth's quarters for the horse. While he was gone George busied himself with looking to his saddle. Presently, the fellow returned with a fine upstanding, raw-boned, dark brown horse. The animal looked all fire and mettle, and as George cast his eye over it, he registered a mental vow to thank the officer for his generosity.

"You go to Kafr Dowar?" asked the nigger, as he held the horse for George to saddle him.

"What's it to do with you where I'm going?" he asked sharply. "Mind your own business."

"Be not angry with thy servant," said the man with a furtive glance, which he quickly averted as he caught Helmar's eye. "I but thought. Arabi is there."

"How do you know?" asked George quickly.

"I hear," was the evasive reply. Then, seeing the dissatisfied look on Helmar's face, he tried to ingratiate himself. "The horse is good, he will travel fast," he went on, with a glance of admiration at the animal.

For a moment Helmar was thrown off his guard.

"Yes, and it will take Arabi all his time to catch him, if we should come across him."

"Then you go to Kafr Dowar," said the man, with a grin.

George, seeing his mistake, was about to reply, when he saw the patrol getting ready, so, without further parley, he mounted his horse and rode towards them.

CHAPTER XV

ON PATROL

It was with very mixed feelings that Helmar rode over to the patrol. Of late he had come to regard all Egyptians with suspicion, and, in fact, the entire native population. As regards the so-called "loyal" blackies, he looked upon them as mercenaries, giving their loyalty for gain to the stronger side; being more enlightened than others, they realized that Arabi's rebellion could not possibly survive any serious opposition, and that in the end England was bound to crush it—hence their loyalty! Of course, it was well known that their ranks were crowded with spies—this was only natural—and he felt certain, though unable to prove it, that the man who had just spoken to him was one of these.

As he rode up and joined the little party of horsemen, he was in two minds about speaking to Captain Forsyth of the man's suspicious behaviour; but, in the rush of moving off, he had no opportunity, and with the bustle and interest of his new work, the incident entirely slipped from his mind. It was not till later on that every word of that conversation was brought vividly back to him.

"All right, Captain Forsyth," said the Adjutant, after inspecting the patrol; "you can move off. Good-bye, and good luck to you!"

The order to march was given, and the little party of twelve people slowly filed from the lines.

The beautiful cool of the evening after the sweltering heat of the day was refreshing to all, man and beast alike; the men laughed and chatted, the horses snorted, threw their heads up and proudly showed their mettle as the slow "walk march" was quickly changed into a canter.

The camp was gradually left behind in the distance, and long ere night set in, Alexandria, with its domes and spires, was lost in the haze of the evening, and the bare, level, open country surrounded them on all sides.

Their road lay in the direction of Kafr Dowar, distant about twenty miles to the south-east. For some time after leaving the city the railway was followed, until they arrived at the neck of land that separates the lakes Mariut and Abukir, then, leaving the road entirely, Captain Forsyth edged away from the railway and skirted along the south-west bank of Lake Abukir.

Not very far out of the city, the officer dropped back to the rear where George was riding.

"I'm going to divide the party, Helmar," he said, "and I want you to ride with me. We will travel on the west side of the railway, and shall probably meet stray Arabs in that direction, from whom we can obtain information. It will be imperative to keep a sharp look-out."

"Yes," replied Helmar, "so far we do not know if Arabi has left Kafr Dowar or not. Anyway, if he has, I expect he still has a large force there."

A flanking party was then sent out to the east. The main body, consisting of six men, were to continue the road direct for Kafr Dowar, while Captain Forsyth himself, a trooper named Brian, and George took the western flank.

Helmar and his companions soon reached and crossed the railway, and, pressing on, the main body was quickly lost to view, and the work of scouring the country began in earnest.

Helmar was very quick to learn his duties. A sort of instinct kept all his nerves and senses strained, detecting anything that might furnish information, and, although night had closed in, he found he was able to distinguish many things that he would not have thought possible in such darkness.

Their course lay across country, and the officer kept on the right track by the aid of the brilliant light of the stars. He pointed out the manner in which it was done to Helmar, who marvelled at the simplicity of it all, and wondered how it was he had never thought to try it before.

For some miles the journey was quite uneventful, and Captain Forsyth began to think that the Arabs had really retired beyond Kafr Dowar, even perhaps to Damanhour.

"There doesn't seem to be a sign of the enemy anywhere," said he. "We must be within six miles of their reputed camp now, and we haven't even seen a light. It seems very strange."

"Personally," replied George, "I think it's suspicious. These Gypsies are very foxy; there are some about, or I'm much mistaken. You don't catch a man like Arabi retiring all his troops without leaving a strong rear-guard somewhere behind. What about that rise over there?" he went on, pointing to the dim outline of a hill in the distance. "I thought I saw the flash of a light there just now, but it might have been only fancy."

Captain Forsyth pulled his horse up for a moment and looked keenly in the direction indicated; but, as nothing appeared, the journey was resumed. A little further on, he suddenly exclaimed under his breath and whispered, "Wait a minute!" while he sprang from his horse.

George felt a breath of excitement as he watched the officer's movements. The trooper Brian had come up alongside him.

"Faith, seems to me there's some one on the move ahead of us. Can't you hear the sound of horses' hoofs, sir?"

Helmar listened. At first he could hear nothing but the sighing of the evening breeze as it rustled over the open plains; but gradually he became aware of other sounds blending with it. He listened intently, and the sounds became more distinct, but still so dim that they seemed very far off.

"Yes, I think you are right, Brian, but they are a long way off. They seem to me more to the left and in the direction of the patrol."

"That's so," replied the Irishman, "and, sure, it's to be hoped the sergeant is aware of 'em."

Just then the officer re-mounted his horse.

"Well, sir, do you think it's anything coming our way?"

"No," he replied, "not our way, but it's a party of horsemen, and they seem to be going straight for our main patrol. Brian, you and Helmar remain here; don't advance. I am going to join the sergeant's party. If you hear the sound of fire-arms from that direction, you two will join us at once; and if not, in twenty minutes from now strike a light and I shall rejoin you. Don't make any mistake. Helmar, I shall leave you in charge."

While the officer was speaking, George gave all his attention to the sounds approaching, and his restless eyes scanned the darkness all round. What he had thought to be coming from the east now sounded to be from the west.

"Very good, sir," he replied, as Forsyth finished speaking. "But it strikes me you are either wrong about the direction of the sounds, or there are others coming towards us from the west."

The officer listened, but he remained convinced that what he had heard came from the direction he had said.

"No, I am right," he said, at last. "There is no sound to the west. Don't forget your instructions," and he turned his horse and disappeared in the darkness, the clatter of his horse's feet soon becoming deadened by the heavy sand.

"You're right, Mr. Helmar, and he's wrong, though it wasn't for me to say so," said Brian, in tones of firm conviction. "As the officer disappeared, did you notice how quickly the sound of his horse's hoofs died away?"

"Yes," replied Helmar. "But what has that to do with it?"

"Simple enough," replied the other; "he's forgotten about the wind. There isn't too much, it's true, but what there is is coming from the west, and consequently the sound travels with it. Now, you listen. You can't hear a sound of him now."

It was as the Irishman said. Strain as they would, there was not a sound to be heard from his retreating horse.

"You're right," said George, at last, "and the other sound is still to be heard, which means——"

"Which means that some one is approaching us from the west, and the sound is travelling with the wind. Before he gets back we'll have trouble on our hands, or I'm—I'm—a Dutchman," he finished up in his broad Irish brogue.

Although Helmar was determined and courageous, he was a novice at the art of war, and was ready to adopt any plan that appealed to his common-sense when danger threatened, so he consulted his companion.

"Assuming that we are right, what plan do you suggest?" he asked, eyeing the Irishman keenly.

"Well, it's hard to say what's best. Sure, I'm right on for a fight, but we must first locate how many are coming, and p'raps after all they may be friendlies, though I wouldn't give much for the chance."

"Neither would I," replied George, laughing. "Well, I'll tell you what I propose; we'll just lay low and be guided by circumstances, and, in the meantime, look to our arms."

The two men's revolvers were loaded, and the magazine of their rifles full; after they had examined them carefully they sat in solemn silence, with every nerve strained to its highest tension for the slightest suspicious sound.

Every moment increased their certainty of the approach of horsemen, although at a slow pace, for the sounds were infinitely more distinct.

"They're coming, right enough," said Brian abruptly in a whisper. "I caught the sound of voices just now, and by jabers it seems to me they're Gypies."

This was a surmise of the Irishman's imagination, for as yet Helmar had heard no voice; but still the sounds came nearer.

"Another two minutes and it'll be time to give the signal to Captain Forsyth," said Helmar, feeling over the face of his watch.

"Eh? And bring a hornet's nest about us!" exclaimed the Irishman in disgust. "But there, it's military orders, and I suppose they must be obeyed, whatever the consequences."

"It seems to me all wrong anyhow," replied Helmar; "I don't think he ought to have given such an order. A scout has no business to give signals like that, or even to carry matches, but I suppose it's got to be done. Get your pistol out and be ready while I strike a light."

A grunt from the Irishman signified assent, and, a moment after, Helmar struck a match. Simultaneously as the match flared up, there was a howl from the west, and the two watchers heard the galloping of horses from that direction, while from the eastward they heard a loud "whoop" from Captain Forsyth, who almost instantly dashed up.

"Quick, for your lives, men," he cried, "we are surrounded. There's a party of the enemy in hot pursuit of me. We must turn back and try to outflank them and join the rest of the patrol. Come on!"

Leading the way, he turned his horse and the three men galloped off.

"It's no go, cap'n," cried Brian, whose horse had leapt into the lead and was trying to bolt. "There's a party coming straight for us. Let's make a stand and give 'em a taste of our lead."

"On, man, on for your life! They're coming in all directions," he shouted back. "That match did it."

They turned their horses in another direction, but as they did so a rattle of musketry met them, and a hail of bullets flew over and around them.

"Pull up," said Forsyth, in quiet tones, "the game's up, we must make a fight for it."

Another volley whistled about them, and Brian's horse was hit and fell to the ground.

"Are you hurt?" cried Helmar, dismounting to his assistance.

"Not a bit," replied the fallen man cheerily, springing to his feet.

The officer jumped off his horse, and the three men stood ready to sell their lives as dearly as possible. They were none too soon, for, in the darkness, the enemy, riding at full gallop, were almost on top of them before they could pull up. The moment they were near enough to see, they poured another murderous volley into the devoted little party, and the Irishman fell with a bullet through his chest. In reply, the Captain and our hero blazed away with their rifles into the cluster of horsemen.

Suddenly a voice rang out above the noise of the cracking rifles, and the Arabs ceased fire; then clear and strong came in unmistakable European tones—

"Surrender, you English, or you die!"

In an instant Helmar recognized the voice—it was Arden's. Rage filled him as he thought that once more he was in the power of this man, and he made up his mind to fire his last cartridge before he gave in. He raised his rifle to his shoulder, but Forsyth stayed him.

"It's no use. He has got us foul. Alive we may escape, but with fifty to one against us, it is suicide." Then raising his voice to a shout, he cried, "We surrender!"

The words were hardly out of his mouth when, with a terrific shout, a volley was poured into the unprepared Arabs, and a frightful *mêlée* ensued as the rest of the patrol, headed by the sergeant, charged to the rescue.

In the confusion Forsyth and Helmar sprang on to their horses—Brian was beyond their help—and galloped towards their friends. The darkness was so intense that the two men immediately got separated. Helmar unconsciously altered his direction and immediately fell in with a party of horsemen galloping off. Thinking it to be the patrol, he joined them, and raced away. His horse was very fresh and quickly forged ahead into the midst of his companions, when, to his dismay, he discovered his mistake—he was in the midst of the flying enemy.

With an exclamation of horror he endeavoured to pull up, but this attracted attention, and the men beside him, turning, saw his white face and shouted to their leader. George raised his revolver, but ere he could pull the trigger it was knocked from his hand and he was defenceless.

The Arabs now closed all around him—there was no possibility of escape. One man had seized his horse's bridle, and he was forced to gallop on whether he liked it or not. He threw back his head and shouted, thinking his friends might still be within hearing, but a blow on the mouth with the butt end of a pistol silenced him, and bursting with rage and mortification he had to gallop on.

His feelings were terrible; to be captured in this childish manner was too disgusting for words—and by Arden too! He railed bitterly at losing the Captain in the darkness.

"If I had only had sense enough to stick close to him," he thought to himself, "I should have been all right, instead of again being in the power of this treacherous Mark. There'll be precious little mercy for me this time, and when we get to his camp, I expect he'll have me hanged."

Then the thought struck him that as yet Mark, if he was with the party, had not seen him, and he felt inclined, notwithstanding the exigencies of his position, to laugh at the surprise it would cause that worthy when he became aware of who his prisoner chanced to be.

They were ascending a hill, and on the top of it George could see a number of lights twinkling and bobbing about through the fringe of bush that covered it. His captors gave him but little time to speculate as to the place they were nearing, for not for one instant did they slacken their speed as they ascended the steep slopes. Helmar knew by the pace of the journey that he could not be far from Kafr Dowar, but he had never heard that it was on a hill, and besides, the railway passed through it. This latter thought convinced him that this place must be only some patrolling station of the rebels, and he felt sorry for himself that such was the case; he would probably be in the power of Arden or some subordinate, either of whom might, as likely as not, order him to be beheaded for the amusement of the crowd.

These thoughts were not very comforting, and he was glad to put them from him for others of a less morbid character, as he entered the low scrubby bush in which the camp was pitched.

No word had passed between him and his captors from the moment they had become aware of his presence amongst them. This ominous silence had struck him at first as curious, but realizing a few of the peculiarities of the "Gypies," he took this for one of them and refrained from breaking it.

He was still in doubt as to whether Arden was with them, or whether this was another party altogether, but, whichever way it was, he meant to keep to himself the fact that he could understand Arabic, and trusted that his knowledge of their language might help him to escape, or at least save his skin.

On the whole, after the first shock of his capture was over, he began to think that his fate might have been very much worse; he might have been with poor Brian lying dead on the sandy plain, a prey for the vultures who would swarm in dozens over his carcase at daylight; or he might only have been wounded, when to be left out in the scorching rays of the sun would have been ten times worse.

With reflections such as these he endeavoured to comfort himself, and, as he entered the rebels' encampment, he felt he was ready to face anything that was likely to happen.

Passing by a row of mud huts, the party drew up outside one bigger than the rest.

Helmar was jealously guarded by two of the soldiers armed with rifles and pistols, while a confabulation was being held by the rest. They were talking some yards away, and so many tongues were going at once that it was impossible for him to make out what was said.

At last, however, they evidently came to a decision, and at a word he was led off, with his horse, to a hut where his guards told him in Arabic to dismount.

George was prepared for something like this, and remained where he was, pretending that he did not understand. Immediately the men, taking the bait, conveyed their meaning by signs, and he instantly dismounted. He was then led into the hut, and the moment after the soldiers left him, closing and barring the door behind them.

A A

CHAPTER XVI

WE MEET AGAIN

The place in which George found himself so roughly thrust was pitch dark. He vainly turned from side to side to discover, if possible, what his surroundings were, but he could see nothing. The ominous "clumping" of the bars as the rebel soldiers put them in place, warned him that they had no idea of giving him any opportunity of escape, and he must be content for a while at least to remain where he was and make the best of things. He listened for the sound of retreating footsteps, but, hearing none, concluded that the two men had been told off to mount guard over him, thus making his captivity doubly secure.

Waiting for a moment or two, to get accustomed to the darkness, he proceeded to feel his way about, in the hopes of finding something on which to sit and rest; but, after hesitatingly moving round the walls, he came to the conclusion that the hut was bare of all furniture, and if he wished for rest he must sit on the ground. Being somewhat philosophical, this he did, leaning his back against the wall, and gave himself up to formulating a plan of campaign. This was no easy matter; he had but the vaguest ideas what his fate was to be, and therefore it was impossible to know what was the best line of action to adopt.

The one thing he feared was that there was no sufficiently powerful rebel here to protect him from the barbarity of the half-wild soldiery; and if this were so, his life, when daylight came, would not be worth twopence. If Mark Arden happened to be in command he might possibly attempt to save him for a worse fate than even the one he had already pictured; of the two, he would sooner face the soldiers, for then his end would be swift, and he could at least face it like a man.

His thoughts brought him so little comfort, so little hope, that at last he put them from him altogether, and, in spite of all his danger, in spite of all this discomfort, he curled himself up and slept the sound refreshing sleep of a tired man. Once more he was back in Germany, once more amongst the students of the University; the Debating Society was in full swing, and he was again enacting that little drama in the club-rooms. Somehow Arabi was mixed up with it all, encouraging him to help his friend from the bullying Landauer, smiling brightly on him as he uttered the scathing words preceding his challenge. Suddenly in the midst of it all there came a terrific peal of thunder, and he awoke with a start, to hear the bars being removed from his prison-door and to see the bright sunlight streaming in through cracks in both roof and wall of the cranky hut.

He rubbed his eyes for a moment to make sure he was not still dreaming, then, as the door was flung open and the dirty face of a ragged, half-dressed soldier appeared, he recollected everything, and sprang to his feet in anticipation of rough treatment.

Critically scanning the man who stood before him, George could not be certain if it was the same fellow who had thrust him in there the night before. He was not long left in doubt, for he was addressed in the broken English common to natives used to mixing with Europeans, and George knew at once that this was a fresh jailer.

"The officer will speak with the Englishman," he said with a grin.

"And how do you propose to drag me from here if I do not choose to go?" p. 181

"Oh," replied George in the same language, "and what does he want with me? Who is this officer? Why can't he come to me?" he went on in defiant tones.

"You are prisoner, and the officer he not come to prisoners. You are to die soon," was the comforting reply.

"Yes, and who is going to kill me? You?" with fine contempt in his tones, eyeing the insignificant wretch up and down.

"I come not here to talk with the dog of a Christian. If you will not come with me, I must take you, for the Pasha will not wait. Come!"

Helmar burst out into a loud laugh. The thought of this dirty little Egyptian taking him anywhere against his will was too much for him; notwithstanding the exigencies of the situation he resolved to tease him.

"And how do you propose to drag me from here if I do not choose to go?"

The little man's eyes glittered, and his hand rested on a revolver in his belt. He saw that the "dog of a Christian" was laughing at him, and he did not like it.

"My orders are to bring you; if you will not come alive, then——" and he drew his revolver and levelled it at George's head.

Thinking he had gone far enough, and realizing that the wretch was in earnest, George stopped laughing.

"All right, lead the way, I'll go with you. But you might give me something to eat; I haven't touched food since yesterday afternoon and am hungry."

"You not need food much longer," replied the man with a grim smile, as he led the way out into the scorching sunlight.

"Evidently," thought George, "they don't intend to waste time with me. But, by Jupiter! I'll make a fight for it when the time comes!"

The place he was in was a small encampment of mud huts scattered about amongst a scrubbly low bush. A number of rebel soldiers were to be seen in various attitudes of laziness, all smoking or chewing. As George passed along with his guide they eyed him with much disfavour, without moving from their particular position of ease, and if looks could kill, he would never have reached the officer's hut alive.

"What place is this?" he asked, more interested in his surroundings than in his fate. "Is it Kafr Dowar?"

The man shook his head and refused to answer. Not yet satisfied, George tried again.

"How far is this from Alexandria?"

This time the answer came short, sharp, and in deep tones of hatred.

"Too far for the Christian ever to return."

"How these wretches do hate Europeans," thought he, as he trudged along beside the man and began to think more seriously of what was in store for him.

A few yards further on they stopped outside the same hut where they halted the night before. The guard knocked at the door, which was instantly opened, and two soldiers barred the way. George's guard at once explained, and the two men fell back, leaving them free to enter.

The guide led the way. The room was dark, and as far as Helmar could see at first glance, it as devoid of windows and in almost as ruinous a condition as his prison. He saw in one swift glance an untidy bed, covered with brown blankets, occupying one side of the room, and then his attention was riveted on a man dressed in Egyptian costume writing at a table in the centre of the apartment. He seemed to take no notice of their approach, so absorbed was he in his work; not a movement escaped him beyond the manipulation of his pen, which was decidedly rapid, George thought, for an "uncivilized savage."

The prisoner had time to note the long sword hanging at the man's side, and also the sinister projecting butt of a revolver from his belt, but beyond this there was nothing to mark him out as anything much above the rest of the rebels he had seen.

George and his guide halted in front of the table, and the officer with a movement of irritation threw down his pen and looked up. There was a momentary silence, and the two men exchanged glances of mutual defiance and hatred. Then, with an unpleasant smiling curl of the lip, the latter said—

"So, George Helmar, we meet again!"

It was Mark Arden. Helmar had not been altogether unprepared for this meeting. Mark, he knew, was in the neighbourhood, but he had not been certain he was to be the arbitrator of his fate. He thought swiftly, and quickly realized that no feelings of similar nationality and education would help to save him from this villain's vengeance. He therefore determined to put on the boldest face possible, and meet defiance with defiance, hatred with contempt, and let his captor understand that he did not care a jot for anything that he could do to him.

"You escaped me before, but I thought it would not be long before I should again get hold of you. That was a smart trick you served me at Port Said, and I haven't forgotten it."

George smiled, as he thought how easily he had outwitted this man before, and wondered if there were no possibility of repeating the operation. Mark seemed to read his thoughts.

"No, my friend, it will not happen again; I will see to that. I have you more fully in my power now, and I can assure you I have no intention of letting you again slip through my fingers."

"That remains to be seen," replied George, coolly. "But you haven't paid me that money yet, and I shall be glad of it just now."

This was only said out of bravado, and had its effect. Mark could not refrain from smiling as he replied—

"What, still harping on the old theme? Ah, well, you always were a cool fellow, but I'm afraid your coolness will avail you little now. I gave you a chance at Port Said, for old acquaintance' sake, a chance which you wantonly threw away in a manner little calculated to enlist my sympathy; and now, nothing I can do will save you," and he grinned fiendishly at the irony of his own words.

George was not in the least taken in by them; he knew full well that this man would stop at nothing to injure him, so he treated his words with contempt.

"Ah, you do not believe me," Mark went on, observing the look of disdain on George's face.

"But you will soon see. Listen to this," and he read from what he had written on the paper in front of him.

"I am sending down a man captured, by my command, in the act of spying our works here. He is an interpreter to the enemy, and therefore a man to be feared. I refrain from sentencing him here, as a spy is always a useful subject for interrogation for the authorities, and if he receives his punishment here, of course that will all be lost."

"That is my dispatch to Arabi, Helmar, as far as you are concerned. Doubtless you can draw your own conclusions as to its meaning."

"Yes," replied George, "I can. It means that you are asking to have me shot, probably tortured first to extract information from me which I do not possess. Bah! you are a cowardly hound!"

"Exactly. For the sake of Auld Lang Syne," he replied coldly. "I do not care to have your execution on my hands. But I have no intention of letting you escape. Now you understand what I meant when I said that nothing could save you."

As he finished speaking, he again bent over his writing. George watched him as his pen flew rapidly over the paper; he had nothing that he cared to say to such a despicable hound. He was simply raging with indignation at the traitor, and his fingers twitched longingly to get to the man's throat. However, he restrained himself, and waited for anything further that he had to say. Presently he looked up.

"Well, is there anything I can still do for you?" he asked, in a sneering tone. "Although your fate has been decided, and I know that in less than a week you will be dead, I do not wish to deny you any comfort that my camp can provide."

His words came short and sharp, and their tone was in no wise calculated to bring any relief to George's pent-up feelings, but rather aggravated them.

"If you have finished all you have to say," he said sternly, "I shall be glad to return to my prison."

Arden laughed coarsely at Helmar's indifference, and yet, while the smile was still on his lips, a look of anxiety came into his eyes as the calm demeanour of his former friend struck a latent chord of fear in his black heart. It passed, however, as quickly as it came, and angry that even for one moment he should have feared this man, he burst on him with a torrent of invective.

"Leave me at once," he cried, pointing to the door; "go back to your kennel, you cur! If you stay here another minute I shall forget that I said I would not be responsible for your sentence! Here, guards, seize him and take him away!" He paused for a moment as the two soldiers obeyed, and then in cooler tones gave one parting shot. "When next we meet, Helmar, I shall pay my debts!"

"When next we meet, you can have no choice: you shall pay them in full," rejoined Helmar quietly, as the guards marched him off.

George breathed more freely when he found himself once more out in the brilliant sunlight. The atmosphere of that house had to him been unbearable, the presence of the villain Arden had taxed his feelings and temper to their utmost, and it was with a sense of intense relief that he surveyed again the mud huts and the lazy soldiers outside.

The bright, hot sun, the fresh, sweet air quickly restored his mental balance, and he glanced at the many faces of the men lying about as he slowly sauntered, under the escort of his guards, towards his prison. He had not gone many paces when his attention was attracted towards a man who, just as he came abreast of where he was lying, turned over and grabbed at the air with his hand as though to catch some flying insect. The fellow's action was so out of keeping with the laziness of his attitude that Helmar glanced more keenly at him, and was astonished to see him looking hard at him.

Immediately it flashed across his mind that he had seen the man before, but where he could not say. However, the recognition seemed mutual, for as the soldier lay back again, there was an unmistakable smile on his face, and Helmar went on towards his hut wondering.

As soon as he arrived there, George stepped in and the door was closed upon him. While he had been away an aperture in the wall had been uncovered, and the miserable room was well lit up. He walked over to the opening and found that it was a small window, or rather square hole in the wall evidently used for that purpose. Carefully set in the centre of the floor was some rough food and a pitcher of water, and as he gazed at it, he thought that, uninviting as it looked, he could have done with quite double the quantity; however, satisfied that they did not intend to starve him, he fell to with a keen relish, and felt all the better when he had finished.

Notwithstanding the prospect of immediate death, he was in no wise disturbed, and, as he leaned back against the wall after his repast was finished, his mind centred on the familiar face he had just seen, and he wondered again and again where he had seen it before.

With tantalizing persistency the recollection stuck to him, and, equally tantalizingly, he was unable to recall his previous acquaintance with it. At last his thoughts began to drift, and he reviewed the events of his life since he had landed in Egypt.

An hour passed in this way, when suddenly he started up with an exclamation.

"Of course, what a fool I am!" he muttered. "He is the mate of Naoum's dahabîeh. I remember distinctly now. I wonder how he got here; he seemed a decent sort of nigger, too! I wonder if he were forced into Arabi's service against his will? I must find out; if so, he may be of use to me." Joy came into his heart, and he laughed aloud.

He already began to picture himself fooling Arden for the second time, although how was not quite plain even to himself. Still, as a drowning man will cling to a straw, George grasped at this one gleam of hope, and it brought him a peace of mind that he had not felt since he was captured the night before.

The day dragged wearily on. At short intervals his guards would look in to see that he was not attempting to escape, and, satisfied with their inspection, would prop themselves in a sitting posture outside the door against the wall, and to all appearance sleep.

Towards sundown food was again brought to him, and at the same time his guard was changed. While he was yet eating his unsavoury meal one of the new men entered—it was the man he had recognized.

Glancing furtively at his fellow-guard outside, he advanced to the centre of the room, and with a smile that displayed a row of brilliant teeth, said—

"You remember, eh, de dahabîeh?"

Helmar glanced up with a smile.

"Yes, you helped us to beat off the rebels, I remember. I saw you this morning. But how came you here?"

For reply, the man put his finger to his lips and glanced towards the door; then, as if expecting a spy, stepped over to the window and looked out. Satisfied with his inspection, he came back, and, squatting himself down on the floor, looked for a moment at his prisoner.

"I come because I cannot stay," he replied in fairly good French. "They come to de dahabîeh—Arabi's men—and they say I must go with them, so I am here, but I not like."

"Ah, I see, you were pressed into the service," said Helmar, "and you are here against your will."

The man nodded, then again glancing suspiciously round, said—

"But you, they kill you—Arabi shoot you when you get to Damanhour."

"I'm afraid that is their idea," replied George, with a rueful face, "unless I can escape, and that doesn't seem very likely."

"Naoum is at Damanhour," said the man thoughtfully. "If he know you here, he no let them kill you. You go from here at sunrise to-morrow, I am to be one of your guard."

George was on the alert in an instant. He could see that this man wanted to help him if he could only find a way. Apparently the fellow was not very resourceful, so he determined that he must suggest something himself.

"You say that Naoum is at Damanhour, and you are to be one of my escort— well, look here. Do you think you could manage to give him a note from me when we arrive? He will pay you well."

"Me want no pay. Naoum is a good master, and I am his servant. I do all you want. Naoum knows his servant. I come again at dark, and you have your letter written, and I take it."

Without waiting for anything further, the man sprang to his feet and joined his companion outside. There was such an air of sincerity about the fellow

- 113 -

that Helmar at once felt he could trust him, so without hesitation he set about writing the note. He found a pencil in his pocket, and using the inside of an envelope, gave a brief outline of what had befallen him, addressed it to Naoum, and then set himself to await the coming of his guard. Just as it was getting dark, the fellow again entered the prison, and without a word, took the note and departed. As soon as he had gone, George stretched himself out on the rough, sandy floor, and prepared to take as good a night's rest as possible. He felt convinced in his own mind that the means of escape had been found, and was now content to wait the outcome without apprehension. It was indeed a relief to him that he had found a friend in this hornet's nest of cut-throats, and he hoped sincerely that the man's honest intentions might not miscarry.

With his mind still dwelling on thoughts such as these he fell asleep, and, rough and hard as was his couch, his sleep was calm and peaceful; as the other guard looked in and listened to his regular breathing, his conscience was at rest when, later on, he followed his prisoner's example.

CHAPTER XVII

HAKESH THE PRIEST

As the guard had said, at sunrise the next morning the order was given for George to be conducted to Arabi's head-quarters. After the prisoner had been served with his rough breakfast, his horse was brought to him. His guard assembled, no less than six men, to form his escort, and he was ordered to mount. Just as they were about to start, Mark Arden made his appearance.

"So you are off on your long journey, Helmar?" he said, in tones that plainly implied his meaning. "Sorry I shall not be able to travel with you, but I have no doubt Arabi will know how to treat you *properly*. I have pointed out to him many salient points in your character, that I know will appeal to him—don't you wish you were back at Königsberg?" And he broke off with a taunting laugh.

"There's a good old adage that it would be as well for you to remember, Arden," replied George; "'There's many a slip,' etc. It's a favourite one of mine. And just by way of a piece of advice, don't forget the British advance, they'll give you but short shrift."

"You needn't worry about me, I know all their doings, and by the time their slow movements bring them near enough to do me any harm, my plans will all be complete, and I shall be miles away." He paused for a moment, and a shadow passed over his face; then he suddenly burst out, "Helmar, you are a great fool. Why don't you join me? I have power, you are a German, the British are our enemies—there is yet time. Say the word, and I will free you—we will blot out old scores, and work together."

George gave the man one look of withering scorn.

"You think to coerce me!" he cried with flashing eyes. "You think that I am made of the same currish clay as yourself, and because I am in your power, and you intend to have me wantonly murdered, that I will accept any means of saving my life! But you are wrong! The British are not my enemies, if they are yours. They have stood my friends ever since I came to this country, and, in return, I cannot do less than be faithful to their interests. Rather than associate myself with you, I would be blown from a cannon's mouth—that will show my opinion of you; and now let us get on with the journey—the very sight of you makes me sick."

"So be it! Go! Go to your doom, you fool!"

Arden gave the order to march, and the little party moved off. As they made their way out of the camp, Helmar could not help feeling pleased that he had had another opportunity of letting Mark know what he thought of him, it added to his sense of elation at the prospect which had been opened up to him, of a possible means of escape; he had that feeling which comes to all men after having performed an action that redounds credit to their moral character. So that when the little French-speaking soldier, who had first conducted him to Arden's presence, approached and bullyingly told him that any attempt to escape on his part would bring about immediate death to himself, he only smiled, and replied very cheerfully—

"All right, my friend, if I attempt to do so, I am quite willing to stand the consequences. But if I may be allowed to know—where am I being taken to?"

"The great Pasha is now at Damanhour, whither we go. If when we come there he is gone, we shall follow. My orders are to deliver you to him and no one else."

"Good!" replied Helmar. "I would sooner be sentenced by this great rebel than by any subordinate. I am more likely to be treated fairly decently."

Helmar was not in any way bound; he was given free use of his hands, but the bridle of his horse was secured to that of one of his guard's horses, and even if he had wished to do so, there was but little chance of getting away. However, he had not the least intention of attempting any such mad enterprise, infinitely preferring to trust to the man who carried his note to Naoum.

They were to reach Damanhour that night, the distance was about twenty miles, and they intended to travel only in the cool of the day. After about an hour's journey, the guard halted at a clump of bush, the horses were off-saddled, and the little party prepared to rest until evening. The heat was intense, and the welcome shade of the trees was like water to the thirsty rider in the desert. To Helmar, unaccustomed to this mode of travelling, it was an indescribable relief to sit down on the sandy soil, with his back propped against his saddle, and watch the shimmering haze of heat across the sun-scorched plains. It made him think of the stories he had heard of the weary traveller lost in the desert, no water with which to moisten his parching throat, his tongue swollen, black, and immovable in his mouth, with already the first signs of delirium and insanity showing in his erratic and aimless actions. He shuddered as the picture presented itself, and thanked his stars that he was seated, though a prisoner, beneath such a deliciously refreshing shade.

His escort distributed themselves under the various low bushes around, one man only, his little guide of the day before, sitting by his side to guard him. In a few minutes, with this one exception, they were all asleep. It seemed to George that these men could sleep at all hours of the day or night; in fact, as far as he could see, it was their one pastime. Work and watchfulness, except when compulsory, seemed to be quite out of the native ken.

Hours passed, and at last one by one the men awoke, a fire was kindled, and food, in a careless, lazy sort of way, was prepared. After the meal was finished, they again slept, and Helmar was once more left to his own reflections. The sun was already past the meridian, and getting well down towards the horizon, but the heat was still too great for travelling. The little Egyptian again sat silently beside his charge.

Suddenly, George caught sight of the figure of an Arab approaching. He was some distance off, and as yet the one wakeful guard had not seen him. Helmar eyed the stranger keenly as he approached, wondering who he could be travelling in that intense heat, on foot, in a country infested with lawless soldiery. The stranger came steadily on, and as he drew near, Helmar noticed that, although dressed in flowing Eastern garb, he was a white man, and of patriarchal age. He had a snow-white beard, that reached to his waist, and his figure was tall, lean, attenuated, and tottering. Altogether his appearance was so fascinating that George drew his guard's attention to it.

"Who can that old man be, coming along there on foot?" he asked, in French. "And what on earth is a tottering old fellow like him doing about by himself in such a place?"

The guard looked in the direction indicated, and a peculiar expression passed over his face as his eyes rested on the stranger. Without a word of reply the man jumped up and roused his comrades, and a conversation in Arabic ensued. Helmar listened intently.

"See, see," cried the little man. "It is that madman, Hakesh, the Christian, the priest who goes about calling down the wrath of Allah on our beloved leader. See, he comes from the direction of Mishish, where he has been stirring up the people against Arabi, calling on them to assist the dogs of Christians."

A whispered conversation followed, the purport of which George could not catch, but evidently there appeared to be a divided opinion in the discussion. The friendly mate from the dahabîeh seemed to be strongly opposed to some plan the little man was laying before them, and his eyes were flashing ominously. Suddenly the Arab who had first spoken raised his voice.

"You are no good believer, Belbeis," he cried, in angry tones. "This dog of a priest is harmful. If our master knew what you say, you would rot in prison. No, he must die—nobody will be the wiser, and we shall get reward. Think, the great Pasha will make us all rich, and Allah will be pleased."

The Egyptian's words struck on Helmar's heart with a cold chill. The old man, Hakesh, was approaching feebly yet fearlessly, perhaps not even knowing the danger that awaited him, and that these fiends in human form were about to murder him in cold blood. The thought was too awful, and George looked about helplessly for a means to thwart them. He might call out and warn the approaching patriarch, but this, he knew, would be useless, for then the five men would fire a volley of bullets into his poor withered old body. No, that would not do. Just then George caught the sound of Belbeis's voice protesting loudly.

"You are a fool, Abdu, you are like all the rest. Does Hakesh not look to all the sick? does he not help the poor?—besides, no Egyptian takes notice of his words, no true believer will follow his guidance, for he is mad. See, if anything is to be done, take him in as a prisoner to the Pasha, but do not kill him or evil will overtake you. He is insane!"

The old man had now sighted the occupants of the bush, and increased his pace. He was only a few steps off, and George could see the benevolent expression of the kind face, and the determined light in the dark, steel-blue eyes, which not even the man's great age could dim.

The discussion amongst the guard had now ceased, and they stood looking on as the old man came up. The little Abdu stood out ahead of his companions, aggressively eyeing the stranger as he came up.

"Peace be with you, my children!" said Hakesh, in a thin, quavering voice, as he stood in front of the party. "You are resting on your weary journey, I see. I will rest with you, for the sun is hot; I have walked far, and am weary too."

The old man made as though to walk over to a bush and sit down, but Abdu intercepted him.

"No, no, you cannot rest here, we are all true believers, and you are no friend of the Pasha's. You preach against him, and call upon all men to take up arms with the dogs of Christians. You cannot take rest with men of the true faith," and he barred the old man's way threateningly.

One or two of the other men backed their leader up, but Belbeis hung back with a look on his face that boded no good to Abdu. Helmar saw the look and had risen to his feet quietly, so as not to attract the attention of the soldiers, but Hakesh caught sight of his white face, and a smile came into his eyes.

"Ah," he said, addressing Helmar in English, "you can speak for me. I cannot make these people understand that I am a man of peace, and would rest."

Abdu did not understand what he said, but seeing him address Helmar, quickly interposed.

"He cannot assist you, he is a prisoner, therefore do not waste words with him. He is a dog of a Christian, too!"

"Peace to your revilings!" answered Hakesh, in a tone of irritation. "Because you are not of our religion, it is no reason to call us dogs. Stand aside, I am weary and must rest."

Either he did not understand that the soldiers were threatening, or he refused to let him see that he did, for he put out one trembling hand and endeavoured to push the little wretch on one side. The moment his hand touched Abdu, the match was set to the train and the explosion followed.

"You would dare to lay a hand on a true believer!" he cried, in his high-pitched voice, his small, wicked eyes glittering with the lust for vengeance. "Dog, you are in my power, you have roused the people against Arabi, you shall go with us, a prisoner to the great Pasha—we shall see! Seize him!" he shouted to the others. "Lash him to a tree and we will flog him!"

Four of the men advanced to do his bidding. Belbeis had not moved. The old man looked round helplessly, not knowing what to expect. Then as the men caught hold of him he struggled feebly. Abdu had stood by, but the moment he saw Hakesh struggle he drew a knife. Helmar, who had not taken his eyes off the man for a moment, saw this. The old man continued his struggle, and Abdu, with murder written on his face, edged round behind him.

Without a word of warning, Helmar with the agility of a tiger darted forward, and with one terrific blow felled the Egyptian to the ground.

"Murder him, would you! You miserable hound! I'll give you a lesson!"

He was about to continue his chastisement, when he found himself surrounded by the rest of the guard. He saw the flash of steel, and then jumping back beside the old man, he faced the infuriated men. As they were about to attack, Belbeis sprang into their midst, and, shouting at them, forced them aside.

For a moment the men paused, and Belbeis at once got the hearing he wanted.

"You fools! What would you do? Kill our prisoner, for the sake of this tottering old man? Out upon you for a flock of foolish vultures! If the white man is harmed we shall lose our heads when the Pasha hears of it."

He spoke quickly and with force, and the ignorant soldiers were quick to see the importance of his arguments, but their thirst for blood was great and they were loth to give up the hated Christian.

Abdu had recovered and sat up, with a huge lump on his forehead where Helmar had struck him.

"Why do you not kill him?" he shouted. "You stand there skulking, while he murders me. Seize him, and let him see what it means to strike one of the faithful."

Belbeis raised his hand.

"Peace," said he, "you brought it on yourself. You would have murdered the old man while we made him prisoner. You may be glad that the Christian stayed your hand, or our lives would have paid the forfeit."

"I care not!" cried Abdu, foaming with rage. "You shall obey me! I am your officer! Kill him, I say!"

"You may not care, but we do," answered Belbeis, calmly. "You may say and do as you like, but we will not let your doings bring the Pasha's wrath on our heads."

The little man still raged, but had to be content, and a compromise was brought about between Belbeis and the others, to the effect that Helmar's hands should be bound and the old man taken on to Damanhour a prisoner. As soon as this was settled, the party once more saddled up and continued their journey.

Hakesh was made to mount behind Helmar's saddle, and in this uncomfortable position the poor old man clung to him for support.

"I can never thank you sufficiently for saving my life," said he, as they rode slowly along. "True, I am so old that it does not much matter, but my work is not yet done, and I would live to see it finished."

"There is no need of thanks," replied George. "I am glad to have helped you. However, our troubles are not yet ended. Abdu won't soon forget that cuff I gave him—we have yet much to fear from his spite."

The old man's attention was now entirely taken up with clinging on to his position, and he relapsed into silence. Helmar was occupied with thoughts of escape, so nothing more was said until the town of Damanhour was reached.

CHAPTER XVIII

BEHIND PRISON BARS

On his arrival at Damanhour George was conducted by his guards straight to the prison where he was to be confined. The gaol was one of the many ramshackle buildings which the village was comprised of. As the little party slowly made their way through the unpaved streets, they were intently watched by crowds of men, women, and children; the men were principally rebel soldiers, mixed with a smattering of insurgent townspeople, the women and children—creatures of all sorts—from the village folk to the common ruck which follows a native army. Many were picturesque, but others looked like the drainings of the slums of larger cities. There was no doubt as to the sentiments they entertained for the white people, for, as they caught sight of Helmar's face, under escort of rebel soldiers, unmistakable signs of rejoicing were shown, and more than once the threatening attitude of the mob made Helmar wonder if he would reach his destination alive.

As they neared the centre of the town, Hakesh drew his companion's attention to a building surrounded by high walls.

"That, I expect, is where they will imprison us. It is the town gaol, and since Arabi has been here they have used it for military purposes. It is a filthy den."

"I expect so," replied George. "From what little I know of these people, I should hardly expect cleanliness to be amongst their virtues. What do you think they will do to us?"

"That, my son, I cannot say," he replied, with his eyes fixed on the mud walls of the prison. "Arabi is not likely to kill us, I think; but should he be away we may be at the mercy of some subordinate officer who, as likely as not, may wish to get rid of us to curry favour with his chief. It is as well to be prepared for the worst."

Helmar remained silent, he was thinking of Naoum and the letter which the man, Belbeis, was carrying to him. Belbeis had told him that Naoum was here. Well, if that were the case, all might yet be well; but, on the other hand, if Arabi should have left, possibly Naoum had done the same. The predicament in which he found himself was one of great danger. He did not mind facing death, but he felt that he would like to outwit Arden.

The gaol was at last reached in safety, although not without some trouble. Abdu, with villainous intent, made known along the road the fact that his prisoner was a spy, with the result that stones were frequently thrown, and in many instances George narrowly missed being struck; it was with a sigh of relief that he passed through the crazy old gateway of the prison-yard.

Abdu, with his wicked eyes shining triumphantly, ordered him to dismount, and, as he reached the ground, George, with solicitous care, helped his companion from his uncomfortable position.

Primitive and unsafe as the outer wall had looked, the gaol itself appeared to be strong enough. All the windows were heavily barred, and the doors looked as if they were capable of withstanding a siege. The place was constructed largely of wood, and, thinking of Hakesh's words, George felt sure that a place so constructed was more than likely to be decidedly unclean.

He was not given much time to view his surroundings, for Abdu had him hustled into the building with as little delay as possible. Two of the soldiers seized him by the shoulders and pushed him in with scant ceremony. Just as he passed through the door of the room where he was to be confined, one of the men had to drop back to let him pass, and he entered with only one of his guards holding him.

"Naoum not here, I go find him," whispered the man as he released his hold.

Turning, George noticed what he had not seen before—Belbeis was the man who had come in with him. There was no time for conversation, but the man's words had a reassuring effect.

"Beware of Abdu!" whispered Belbeis, as he turned to leave, and then, exchanging a look of intelligence with his prisoner, he joined the other guard and the two men went out. The door was closed and securely bolted.

Left to himself, Helmar surveyed his prison. There was not a particle of furniture in the place, and the only means of light and fresh air entering was through a small, narrow, heavily-barred window. George looked at this with thoughts of escape in his mind, but the prospect was dim and uninviting; even if the bars could be removed he doubted the possibility of forcing himself through the aperture. He next turned his attention to the floor; it was the rough earth covered with filth; portions of food lay about in a rotting condition. The smell that emanated from them nearly made him sick. With feelings of despair he wondered how long he was to be confined in the loathsome hole.

Selecting a spot somewhat cleaner than the rest, he was about to seat himself, when happening to glance more closely, he sprang back with a horrified exclamation. Again he looked at the window and again he turned away in despair.

Night had closed in, and George made up his mind to a night of wakefulness rather than seat himself on that filthy ground. Round and round, backwards and forwards, he walked, wondering when some one would come who could give him something to sit upon.

Hours passed, but no one came. The time dragged so slowly that the night seemed never-ending. He began to feel hungry in spite of his sickening surroundings, and with his hunger came vain imaginings. He pictured all sorts of horrible torturings to which his savage captors might subject him. He wondered if he would be beheaded, or whether he would be shot; he would much prefer the latter, it seemed a cleaner way of dying and more in keeping with his calling. He laughed, as he pictured the rebels aiming at him and repeatedly missing their target, through bad marksmanship. Then he began to wonder what his companions would say when they heard of his end.

He stopped in front of the window and looked up at the sky. He stretched his arms and took hold of the two iron bars and shook them repeatedly, but they seemed quite firm and immovable. Several times he tried them, but each attempt left him more convinced than before that efforts in this direction were futile.

At last, utterly worn out and sick at heart, he leant against the wall and involuntarily his eyes closed; several times, as he dozed off, his knees gave way under him, and he narrowly escaped falling to the ground. Again he roused himself and started to walk.

He had not taken more than half-a-dozen steps when a hissing, crackling sound caught his ear and he paused to listen. What could it be? He went to the door from whence the sound proceeded. As he did so he noticed an unmistakable smell of burning.

He rushed to the window and looked out. The sky was clear and brilliantly illuminated with stars. Here the air was sweet and fresh. Turning again to the door, he noticed that the smell of burning had increased and the crackling was still going on. The truth flashed on him suddenly!

The gaol was on fire!

"So they would roast me alive, the scoundrels!" he muttered, as he stood hesitating as to what he should do.

"Pull and shake as he would, the iron seemed to remain firm in its socket." p. 211

Glancing first at the door, then at the window, he quickly made up his mind as to the best course to adopt. Smoke was already penetrating the cracks of the doorway. If he were to escape, it must be through the window. At that instant he thought of poor old Hakesh, and wondered what was happening to him. Where was he? Did they intend to roast him too?

"The inhuman devils!" he cried, as these thoughts flashed through his mind. He forgot about his own safety for the moment, as his mind wandered to the old priest. A flash of light through the crack of the door brought him back to his own position, and seizing the iron bars of the window with both hands he heaved and shook at them till the wall rocked, but they gave not an inch.

Gasping for breath, his hands sore with his terrible grip on the iron, he paused for a moment and cast about in his mind for a new idea. No other means of escape presented itself, so with the energy of despair he flung himself again on the rough iron. The room was rapidly filling with smoke, and he already found difficulty in breathing.

Pull and shake as he would, the iron seemed to remain firm in its socket, and he was about to cease his efforts, when he noticed that the mud wall that held it was cracked, and hope again filled him.

Leaving the bars for a moment he picked up a narrow piece of wood and jammed it as far as possible into the crack, then seizing the bar with one hand, he drew himself up and, placing his feet against the wall, pulled with all his strength. The wall opened out, and he drove the wedge far into the crack with his disengaged hand, and once more dropped to the ground.

The fire was rapidly increasing, the room was filled with blinding, choking smoke, and he became at once convinced that he had not many moments to spare before the fire would be upon him. One thing seemed certain, that, whoever had set light to the place must have been ignorant of his whereabouts in the building, or they intended to let the process of cooking him be slow. To what refinement had they brought their art of torture!

Seizing the iron bars again, he set to work. The wood he had inserted held the crack open, and the bar, now under the terrific power he used, began to move about. For two minutes he worked incessantly, every moment bringing the chance of escape nearer. With feverish anxiety he watched the loosening bar. Once he looked round; the flames were lapping the door, and the hissing, crackling of the fire sounded in every direction.

Again turning to his work, he gave one supreme wrench at the obstinate iron, and with a crack it yielded, flinging him to the floor. A lot of the brickwork had come away with the bar, and, as he sprang to his feet, he saw that in releasing one of the iron bars he had torn away sufficient of the wall to free the others. He tore them from their place in a flash, and at last the window was clear of obstruction.

Taking one of the iron bars with him, he climbed up to the aperture, but found the process of squeezing himself through was no easy one; cheered on by hope, and with fear of the fire behind, he at last succeeded, and dropped to the ground outside, only to find that the high wall surrounding the prison barred his way.

At least he had escaped the fire, but now, how to get out of the yard? He ran round the burning building in the hopes of finding an outlet, expecting every moment to fall in with some of the guard, but to his astonishment not a soul was about. At first this seemed strange, but as he realized that the building had been set on fire purposely, the desertion of it was quickly accounted for.

The only means of escape that now presented itself was a small outhouse built against the wall. This he clambered on to, and then, by the aid of some loose planks in the roof, succeeded in reaching the top of the wall.

The moment he looked over he cursed himself bitterly for not having waited until the house had burnt itself out before attempting to go further, for then, no doubt, thinking him dead, the crowd would have deserted the place. As it was, he saw a cluster of rebels standing watching the fire carry out its fell work.

He withdrew his head the instant he saw the murderous-looking mob. To expose himself on the top of the wall was merely to make a target of his body for a dozen rifles to "pot" at, and so nullify all he had accomplished. Yet how was he to get over on to the other side without being observed? If he could but alight on firm ground safely, he could then make a rush for it, and trust to the luck which, so far, had been on his side. He thought of the shadow cast by the wall, owing to the brilliant light of the burning prison behind, and he determined to try this one chance of escape.

In the excitement of the leap from the window he dropped his weapon, and only just discovered the fact. Scrambling back, he soon found it, and climbing once more on to the outhouse, without further hesitation he gradually rolled himself full length on to the top of the wall, slid his legs over, and letting himself down to arms' length, dropped to the ground. The wall was nearly fifteen feet high, so that he had dropped about seven. The moment he landed he recovered himself and ran for dear life, not knowing in the least where he was going.

At first he thought he had escaped notice, but it was not so, for scarcely had his brain formed the hope than one wild shout went up from the rebels, and the next instant he found himself closely followed by a hooting, murderous mob.

CHAPTER XIX

THE ESCAPE

The moment George realized he had been discovered, the spirit of "do or die" entered into his soul, and he flew along at the utmost speed at his command. He did not even check his hope that the race would end in his favour; he did not pause to wonder where he was going, or how he would elude his pursuers. He had got a short start of them which he meant to keep, and, if possible, increase. He could hear the gibbering of the mob gradually getting louder and louder as the crowd gathered up fresh recruits and surged along in pursuit of him. The distant burr increased to yells and shouts, and the clatter of fire-arms became so loud that George began to fear that his attempt at escape was quite futile. He never lost heart, however, and raced on and on at a pace surprising even to himself.

A man never learns what is possible until he is placed in a position that requires the apparently impossible. This was the situation George was now in. If he had stopped to ask himself the question, "Can I do it?" he probably would have been forced to answer it in the negative. As it was, he paid no heed to the danger behind, and thought only of the safety in front, if he could but keep up his speed long enough.

The infuriated rebels finding themselves unable with even their greatest efforts to come up with their prey, now began to fire at him, but, as their shots were not those of very expert marksmen, George became more amused than frightened as the bullets dropped either short of him or flew far above his head.

He was now getting into the inhabited part of the town, and tried to elude the pursuers by turning abrupt corners, but there was little chance of success in these tactics, for the "blackies" knew more about the place than he was ever likely to, and kept cutting him off in an alarming manner.

The day was beginning to break, and George felt that he must soon give in. As he was making a rapid turn in his path a well-aimed nabout came most uncomfortably close to his head. This incited him to greater effort, not so much from fear of being hit, as from the knowledge of the nearness of his pursuers.

Breathless, and with the life almost run out of him, he continued his mad career, the hue and cry of the mob goading him on and lending wings to his feet. Swift of foot as the blacks had been, they had shown themselves no match so far for the trained athlete they were pursuing. But there comes a time when even the best man must give in, and that time George felt was rapidly approaching. He had been running now for a long time, and had traversed a lot of ground. However, he was not done yet, and he still kept on, although in what direction he knew not. The street he was now in looked like one of the principal thoroughfares, and, as he was nearing the end of it, he saw, to his horror, another crowd ahead, running towards him.

Instinctively he turned into a bye-way, and darted along in the shadow of the buildings. The turning proved fatal—it was a blind court, and ended in a small paved square, hemmed in on all sides by the best class houses. Seeing the mistake he had made, George paused for a moment to glance round. The mob were tearing down the court, their cries filling the air and making the calm morning hideous with discord.

Seeing no means of escape, Helmar made up his mind to sell his life as dearly as possible, and, rushing into the porch of the biggest house he saw, put his back to the wall and waited the oncoming mob.

Headed by a dozen or more soldiers, he saw the crowd enter the square. At sight of him standing at bay a loud, exultant cry went up, and they dashed towards him. He was fairly trapped now, and he knew it; with his iron bar upraised he awaited the leaders, determined that three or four should not escape him before he was done to death. At this instant he heard a sound beside him, and glancing in the direction, saw a door suddenly thrown open.

With instinct of self-preservation, he ran to it, and, without waiting to see who was inside, rushed in, and immediately the door was closed with a slam.

He had not the faintest idea where he was, and, for all he knew, might have fallen into a worse trap than before; but the opportunity had been too good for him to refuse to accept, and, as he paused in the dim hall, ready to strike down any one who attempted any violence, he was surprised to find it deserted.

Outside, the disappointed fanatics beat and hammered at the door, and every moment Helmar expected to see it forced in. He scarcely knew what to do. Suddenly he noticed in front of him a curtained archway; he ran towards it, and flinging back the heavy tapestry he started back as if he had been struck—he stood face to face with a smiling countenance. He dropped his weapon and rushed forward with hands outstretched, crying—

"Naoum! Friend Naoum! Thank God!"

"Luck is with you, friend Helmar," said the Arab quietly. "Allah is great! Allah is good! He has brought you to me in your extremity. But come in here, I must quiet the children of darkness."

He led the way in, and George found himself in a room of great splendour, arranged in Eastern style. Turning to his old friend he was about to speak, but the latter interrupted him.

"No, no, wait. There is danger; I must go and speak to the rebels," and he turned swiftly and left the room.

In a few moments the hammering and noise ceased, and presently Naoum returned.

"Now tell me what all this means," he said, glancing at George's dishevelled appearance, and doubtfully eyeing the torn clothes and the worried face in front of him.

"It simply means that they wanted to murder me by roasting me alive, and, failing that, with knives and clubs."

Helmar then recounted all that had happened to him from the time he had left Alexandria with the patrol. When he had finished, Naoum looked thoughtful.

"So you are an escaped prisoner of Arabi's," he said at last; "that is not good. It makes my task harder, but you must be saved somehow," and he relapsed into deep thought, drumming on the side of a cabinet which he leant against. "Just now I am very powerful with Arabi, he has forced me into service, with the alternative of confiscating my property. I am now one of his means of raising money, and as my fortune is considerable, he cannot quarrel with me, but——"

"Surely," broke in George, "you are not fighting on his side?"

"No, but you do not understand. I am in his hands, and for the sake of the result of my life's work, I cannot defy him. I take no active part with him in this war, but I have no other alternative than to supply him with money on purely business securities, the same as I would to anybody else. I am, as you well know, against him in all my feelings. If I refused to do as he requires, I should forfeit everything; so you see I am compelled. Being with him, I save my property, and can prevent much mischief by using my influence over him."

"I see," exclaimed George, heartily, "you are right. It would be folly to do otherwise. Well, returning to the awkward predicament I have placed you in, what is best to be done?"

"I heard during the night that trouble had befallen you. In fact, this note in your writing was brought to me by Belbeis, one of my men, just as I returned here from Cairo," he went on, producing a bundle of papers. "I had intended to intercede for you this morning, but now the situation is more complicated. However," with a smile of meaning, "I think you can safely leave it to me. For the time being you are free from the man Abdu, and are, at present, out of reach of your enemy Arden, so you can take some rest here. Food shall be brought you at once, and I will go and see what can be done."

George thanked his friend and threw himself on a divan, while his host started on his errand of mercy.

Good luck, as Naoum had said, was undoubtedly with him, and, as he lay back, with his weary, tired eyes closed from the bright light of the rising sun, he felt that Providence had been indeed good. He shuddered again and again as he went over, in thought, the exciting events of the night, and wondered what awful fate would have been his if he had chanced to take refuge in front of any of the other houses in the square. Naoum he knew would help him to the full extent of his power, and that seemed to be considerable, judging from the manner in which he had quieted the mob outside. It was too good to hope that he would be able to get him released altogether, but, probably, he would manage to secure for him a fairly comfortable prison and save his life.

His thoughts were interrupted by the entrance of a servant with food, and, as soon as the man had retired, he set to ravenously. The food was of the most luxurious description, and Helmar marvelled the more at the mysterious man who had provided it. Who was he in reality? Naoum he knew was his name, and he had hitherto only taken him for a successful trader; but apparently he was a man of great fortune and power, or how could he supply money to the extent he appeared to be doing?

After finishing his repast, George lay back on the comfortable cushions of the divan. He was tired and worn out, his whole body ached with his efforts of the night before, and the sleep that he so badly needed was not long before it overtook him. How long he lay unconscious of his surroundings he did not know; when he awoke it was night, and the rays of a small lamp lit the chamber he was in. For a moment or two he looked about him and tried to recall what had happened. At first it seemed like some horrid nightmare, but when he stood up and stretched himself he knew that it was all reality. He was greatly refreshed with his sleep, and now awaited eagerly the return of Naoum.

Before his host re-appeared food was again brought to him, and this, with the aid of soap and water, made him ready to face the world again. A few minutes later Naoum came in.

"I have been more fortunate than I had anticipated. Arabi, who fortunately chanced to return here from Cairo this afternoon whilst you slept, has promised me at least to spare your life; but, on the other hand, he will not hear of your being released. This, however, is quite a secondary affair and a matter which we can ourselves attend to later on," and he chuckled softly. "In the meantime," he went on, "I expect you will be taken to Cairo. This he gave me to understand without actually saying so."

"Well, beggars mustn't be choosers," said George, resignedly, "and glad enough am I that I am to escape with my life."

"You may well say that," answered Naoum. "From what I can gather, this man Arden, who appears to hate you so cordially, is very powerful and enjoys Arabi's complete confidence. In fact I was shown a dispatch from that worthy recommending you to be *interrogated*; I dare say you know what that means. I had great difficulty to dissuade him from acting on the man's advice. Even now, notwithstanding I have his promise, your position is anything but safe, and we shall have to keep a watchful eye on them all."

"What! do you think Arabi can be persuaded to go back on his promise?" asked George.

Naoum smiled deprecatingly.

"Go back, you call it. You mean break his word, I suppose. Well, I would not like to say, but if I am not about at the time there may be trouble."

"Then the understanding is that I go to Cairo—when?"

"When he sends word. In the meantime you will see him. He intends to—how you call it—interview you; I shall dispatch some of my men to Cairo, and also write to Mariam Abagi my mother, that she may know what to do when you arrive there. So now you can rest comfortable and wait for what the future has in store for you. I shall look after you."

George thanked him for his words, and then Naoum went on—

"I must go now, for I have much work and many things to do before morning. If there is anything you want, touch this gong, and my servants will wait on you—and now, good-night."

Naoum went away and Helmar was again left to speculate and wonder.

CHAPTER XX

ARABI PASHA

The next morning Naoum brought word that George was to start immediately for Cairo.

"Arabi intends mobilizing all his forces to the eastward, probably at Tel-el-Kebir or Kassassin. My men have brought me word that the British advance will be from the Suez Canal, which they have seized, towards Cairo. The rebels, indeed, have already been driven out of their position near the canal. This place is of no particular importance, and to all intents and purposes will be evacuated at once, so that you, in consequence, will have to be moved."

"And is all this to take place immediately?" asked George.

"Yes, immediately. The British have been landing a large army at Port Said, and if I am any judge, the days of the rebellion are numbered. If Arabi would only be advised by me, he would abandon his mad scheme."

"You are right," replied Helmar; "he little knows the people he is fighting or he would soon give it up. But how do you think this will affect me?"

Naoum paused for a moment before answering the question, and when he spoke, it was as if weighing each word before he uttered it.

"That is hard to say as yet. Toulba Pasha is in temporary command at Cairo, and he is a hard man. I understand your friend," with emphasis on the word, "Arden is to be sent down there to relieve him."

George made a grimace as Naoum uttered these words. He saw, in fancy, a busy time ahead of him. With this man Abdu, a renowned villain, to watch him at the instigation of his most bitter enemy there didn't seem to him to be much hope left.

Naoum stepped up to his side and seated himself on the divan. Leaning over, he said in impressive tones—

"My plans are complete. By the time you reach Cairo, Mariam, my mother, will know of your coming and be ready for any emergency. Before you leave here I will give you a sign by which you may know your friends. But more of this when the word comes for you to start, and, in the meantime, Arabi intends coming here to see you himself."

George started up.

"What! Coming to see me? Why?"

"Ah, that is the point I cannot myself understand. As I said, I do not trust him. But he dare not play me false," he added, thoughtfully. "It is bad, though, for there must be something in his mind. This man Arden is very powerful."

For some moments the two remained silent. Each was wrapped in his own thoughts. Naoum was endeavouring to solve the mystery of Arabi's intended visit to his prisoner. It seemed to him so unnecessary. Helmar was not a man of great importance, in fact, very much the contrary. Somehow he fancied that the man Arden must have sent another dispatch, privately, with reference to Helmar, making him appear to be in possession of information necessary for the rebel chief to acquire. If this were so, then it opened up a much wider field of danger. Altogether he did not like the trend of affairs at all. Helmar, on the other hand, saw no danger in this visit. It seemed to him that he would now have a chance of proving to Arabi that he—Helmar— was only a very small man on the British side, and that he was no spy at all, but merely a paid interpreter. Such being the case, there was no reason why he should be shot, for it was against the ethics of warfare. Consequently he was delighted at the prospect, and told Naoum so.

"It seems to me the best thing that could happen, Naoum. Why, I shall be able to explain away all that the wretch Arden has told him, and, very likely, bring Arabi's wrath down on his own head. It's splendid!"

Naoum watched the animated, hopeful face, smiling indulgently. The young man pleased him greatly; his sturdy hopefulness, his bright way of facing troubles, his general optimism, all combined to make the older man admire him. But, with better practical experience of the East, he did not share Helmar's view of the matter; he looked upon the Pasha's visit as of evil omen, to be treated with suspicion—to be watched with a lynx eye, and combatted with all the subtle means so dear to the Eastern heart. He vowed that if aught of evil befell his friend and *protégé*, some one should pay dearly for it.

Instead of replying to George's words Naoum turned the subject.

"I have found out," he said, "that the priest you befriended has been released, and that he has already disappeared."

"Then he was not in the prison from which I escaped?"

"No, he was never placed in it. There is a superstition regarding that man, and even the worst fanatics would not harm him, so he was set free, and the man Abdu has been reprimanded for interfering with him."

"And a good thing too, it will perhaps be a lesson to him and——"

"Make him hate you the more."

"Why hate me the more? He ought to thank me that I have saved him from murdering the poor old man."

"Ah, you don't understand the Eastern mind. That would be a strong reason for Abdu's hatred of you, you baulked him in his villainies—it is enough."

After a little more conversation Naoum left the room to prepare for the coming of the rebel Pasha. He paused before he went, however, to give some parting advice.

"When Arabi speaks, answer boldly. Say what your good sense prompts, but do not let him think you fear him. Arabi admires a bold man. Though clever, he is weak, and can easily be influenced by boldness. If he thinks you fear him, it will make your escape all the harder to accomplish, for he is in the power of his subordinates and will do as they bid him."

This was indeed news to Helmar; he had believed that Arabi, the man who could have brought about this terrible rebellion, must be a man of indomitable character, and here he was told that such was not the case. He was truly living and learning. Now he began to understand how Mark had attained a position of so much power in such a short time; now he could understand how that worthy had been able to promise him a speedy execution by the Pasha's orders—evidently he relied upon his influence, the influence of a bold, unscrupulous villain over a weaker man.

The time passed slowly after Naoum had left him, and George's patience was sorely tried as he waited for the great rebel. At last he heard a commotion in the hall, the clatter of arms and babel of voices telling him that at last Arabi Pasha had arrived. With beating heart and ever-increasing excitement, he waited for the summons that seemed so long in coming, but at length, after what seemed an endless period, a servant entered and signified that his presence was required.

Hastily smoothing out his worn and tattered clothes, George, with a slight touch of vanity, peered into a mirror and then followed his guide from the room. He hoped that the interview was to be a private one, with perhaps only Naoum present. He felt under those circumstances that he would then have less hesitation in speaking his mind. He feared nothing, convinced as he was that anything he could say could not possibly make his position worse. Naoum would not fail him, and he would rely on his power for protection.

His guide led him upstairs to a curtained doorway, guarded by two sentries, in front of whom he paused. At a sign from the former, one of the men disappeared behind the curtain, and the next moment Naoum appeared in the doorway. Waving the guide back he signed to George to enter, and a moment later Helmar stood in front of the great man.

Arabi was seated on a big lounging chair, dressed in the uniform of the Egyptian army. His face was turned away as the prisoner entered, so that George was unable to realize all that Naoum had told him; but no time was given him to speculate, for Naoum broke the silence at once. With an easiness that astonished Helmar, he addressed the Pasha as though talking to his equal. There was no cringing in his manner, and at times George thought he even detected a slight tone of command in his voice.

"This is the prisoner of whom I spoke," he said in Arabic; "he is not a British subject, but comes from Germany."

Arabi lazily turned his head in Helmar's direction, and without changing the position of his body slowly eyed him from head to foot. The face that was thus revealed was a blank to George; he had expected to see one of strong character, or to discern in it indications at least of great intelligence. One of the greatest characteristics apparent was of intense indolence, whilst the shifty eyes pointed to a nature vacillating almost to weakness. Whether this really were his true character, or whether it were simply a mask used to cover the inner workings of this remarkable man's mind, George did not know; at any rate, it was sufficient, after what he had heard, to make him dislike and distrust him.

"You are a spy!" said the Pasha, in Arabic, shifting his glance away from the prisoner.

"I am no spy," replied George, haughtily, "I am merely an interpreter employed by the British Government."

"How came you to be spying out our defences then, when you were captured?" asked he, sternly, looking up sharply at the tone of George's reply.

"I accompanied the patrol in my official capacity."

"Which means, I understand, that you were there to elicit information from any natives whom you chanced to meet."

"Not at all—simply to translate into English whatever they had to say. The officer was there to gather information."

A faint flicker of a smile passed over Arabi's face at Helmar's ready replies, and he exchanged a few words with Naoum in an undertone. Presently he turned again to his prisoner—

"Then by your own showing you were simply an accomplice of spies."

"A patrol on scouting duty is a legitimate tactic of warfare, therefore those who accompanied it were not spies, and I am entitled to be treated simply as a prisoner of war, not as prey for the rabble of the town to wreak their vengeance on by roasting alive!"

Again the Pasha eyed his man. George felt that his words were bold, even to being dictatorial, but he remembered Naoum's words and was determined to act as he had directed. With his eyes still fixed upon his interrogator he waited for him to speak.

The effect of the line of conduct he had taken up was apparent when next Arabi spoke.

"Then you think I have no right to have you shot! What do you expect?"

"You have less right to shoot me than the British have to shoot you, when they have destroyed your army. You cannot do more than keep me prisoner, and then you must treat me well, or you will have to answer for it later on. There are those in your employ, I know, who would willingly do me harm and resort to any base subterfuge to attain their ends. Doubtless you have been told many lies about me already, but if you listen to them you will regret it."

"So, you would dictate to me the course of action I am to adopt? You forget," Arabi went on, with an ominous pucker of his brows, "that this war is a war of extermination. We have been too long under the ban of European influence. The sons of the West have no right in the country of the ancient Egyptians, whose prosperity dates back to far before the Western countries were ever thought of. If Egyptians are not to be allowed their own country, if we cannot be allowed to rule according to our own traditions, who then is to dictate to us? Because your arms are powerful and other nations have joined in the task of conquest, do you think that there is the faintest semblance of right in the crime you would perpetrate? You speak of Egypt having no right to deal with you as it likes; it has all the right to do so, that you people of the West have to come and wrest our country from us. Your talk is not sound, and you cannot think well. I shall order for you as I think fit!"

"Very well," replied George, as the momentary fire in the indolent man before him died out, "but remember my words, there are those who will avenge me, should you choose to betray the trust that is placed in you as head of the opposing army. Murder is punished with death, and if you choose to commit it, you are no more free from its consequences than the commonest of criminals."

Helmar had become angry. The Pasha's words, so full of arrogance, had stung him, and he was not slow to answer him in like manner. He felt that in doing so he was jeopardizing himself, but for the life of him he could not stop, and he was almost sorry when, as he finished speaking, Arabi's face cleared and he smiled condescending approval at his bold words.

Naoum caught George's flashing eye, and a look of intelligence passed between the two men. Quick as lightning Helmar's equanimity was restored, and he waited to see what was next to happen.

"Spy or no spy," said the Pasha, "you are a brave man to dare me to my face. One word from me and you would be torn limb from limb, but I do not intend to utter it. For the present you will be sent to Cairo as a prisoner; you will be safely guarded and in decent quarters. Later on it may be necessary to obtain information that you are believed to possess. If you are a wise man, as well as a brave, you will not hesitate to give it."

As he finished speaking he turned to Naoum, whose stolid face had shown no variation of expression during the interview. He whispered a few words to him and then again spoke to Helmar.

"You can now go. Remember, until you leave here our friend Naoum is responsible for your safe-keeping."

Waving his hand in sign of having closed the interview, Arabi leant back in the chair, from which in his excitement he had sat bolt up straight, his eyes following the prisoner until he left the room.

Once outside George was again conducted to his luxurious prison, where an excellent repast awaited him. The effect of the interview in no way deterred his appetite, and he occupied his time, waiting for his benefactor, by doing ample justice to the luxuries placed temptingly before him.

CHAPTER XXI

TO CAIRO AGAIN

It was some time before Naoum joined his *protégé*. George finished his meal and waited impatiently for his coming, but an hour passed without any sign. At last he heard again, outside in the hall, a bustle and noise similar to that which had occurred at Arabi's arrival, and he knew that at last the rebel chief was taking his departure.

After a while the noise died away and Naoum appeared. His face was calm, but George noticed a something in his look that seemed foreign to it, and a presentiment that he was about to hear bad news took possession of him. As Naoum came forward, our hero greeted him anxiously.

"Well, what news? Nothing bad, I hope?"

Naoum turned his eyes away, and the strange look deepened on his face. George was quick to notice it.

"Yes, there is, I see it in your face. Tell me, I don't mind; it can't be worse than death, and I have already faced that often."

"Arabi is a strange man," replied Naoum, as though thinking aloud. "He appears to have no will of his own. This man Arden has him under his thumb. Death," he went on, turning his strong face towards his companion, "would be a blessing to that which I am afraid will be your lot, unless——"

"Unless what?" eagerly demanded Helmar.

"Unless we can prevent it," replied Naoum slowly.

"What is this dreadful fate you anticipate?" asked George with a sinking heart, as his friend's ominous words fell on his ears.

"After you had gone I endeavoured to draw from him what he intended doing with you. I felt convinced that some plans were revolving in his mind, and I wished, for our guidance, to discover them. In this conviction I am certain I was right. He assured me that he had no intention of having you executed, but he hung so persistently on the fact that you possessed information of the plans of the British Commander, that I knew he intended to force you to speak. Your enemy Arden has done his work well, for, with all the persuasion in my power, I could not move this foolish man in his belief. I fear that he intends to have you 'interrogated' at Cairo."

"Tortured, do you mean?" asked George in dismay.

"Yes, that is what it means, I fear. The barbarity of these inhuman creatures is frightful, and they carry out the rites of the Inquisition to the full extent of its cruelty. However," he went on, his face clearing a little, "although I tried to dissuade him, I was not altogether unprepared for this development, and you can rely on me not to lose a point in your favour. We must outwit these men somehow."

Naoum relapsed into thoughtful silence; his face was heavy with anxiety; George could almost hear the throbbings of his own heart, the silence seemed so profound, and it was with a sense of relief that he heard his companion again talking in his slow, measured tones.

"The sign by which you will know your friends in Cairo is the word 'Amman!' Your answer to it will be, 'Allah is good!' To which the friend will reply, 'And ever watchful!' To any one coming to you in this way you can give any message, or follow any instructions he or she may give. You can trust me that never for one moment will our watchfulness be relaxed, and, in times of your greatest danger, help will be near."

George repeated the sign so as to be sure he had made no mistake, then, infinitely relieved, he asked—

"And when do I start for my new prison?"

"To-night. You will go by train. Arabi will have gone before you. He also leaves to-night. I shall go and discover what news my men have brought in."

He turned, as he spoke, and left the room.

So after all he was to be the victim of Arden's cruel machinations, thought George, when he found himself alone. In spite of all Naoum's power he was unable to stay the hand of this ruthless enemy. Torture! The word was one of terrible significance; death was child's play compared with it. Pondering for a few moments on Arden's treacheries, his thoughts going back to the little petty theft at Constantinople, he tried to account for it all, but only came to the conclusion that it was inherent wickedness and villainy. George had outwitted and defied him at Port Said. To a man of Mark's cruel and villainous disposition this was sufficient, and he had made up his mind to leave no stone unturned to humble and ruin his former friend. Well, time would show if he were to succeed.

As these thoughts passed through Helmar's mind, a grim, set look of determination came into the young man's handsome face, that boded ill for the success of his enemy's plans.

The sun had set, and night had closed in when Naoum again came to George to notify him that the guard awaited to take him to Cairo.

"The little wretch Abdu is to be in charge of you, Helmar," said he, after informing him of the presence of the guard. "How this comes to be arranged,

I do not know, but there is evidently some purpose in it. Be prepared for anything, and do not forget what I have told you; above all, do not let anything your guard can say to you rouse you to anger—it is a favourite way of obtaining an excuse for getting rid of prisoners. And now, good-bye!"

George bade his kind host and protector good-bye, and with a haughty appearance of indifference, he accompanied Abdu and two soldiers to the station. If he had had any idea that he was to travel comfortably he was quickly undeceived, for the train, which was waiting, consisted of nothing but goods wagons; into one of these he was unceremoniously hustled and the doors firmly bolted. One source of comfort to him, at this treatment, was the fact that Abdu and his two guards had to travel in the same compartment.

The moment the doors were closed his hands and feet were securely bound.

"What is this for?" asked George, as in obedience to the little wretch's orders he submitted to the indignity.

"In order that you cannot play any more tricks upon us," replied Abdu in French. "I haven't forgotten what you did on the way to Damanhour—we have not that fool Belbeis with us now—heh!"

Helmar objected, and refused to allow the guards to bind his feet. Immediately Abdu's eyes flashed, and he drew a long, keen blade from his belt.

"Would you?" he cried between his teeth; "this knife is sharp, so——" And he pricked George's hands.

Feeling the uselessness of resistance, George allowed the little black wretch to secure his feet, and as it was complete, stooped to sit down. With a fiendish look on his face, the Egyptian raised his foot and gave him a vicious kick in the chest. Losing his balance, Helmar fell heavily to the floor, striking his head with great force against the side of the van.

Blind with fury at such inhuman treatment, George struggled to release his hands from the rope which held them, but his efforts were useless and only roused the soldiers to merriment. Suddenly, as if believing that his prisoner was succeeding in freeing himself, Abdu leaped upon him, and flourishing his long knife, pricked him several times in the body with it; with a brutal laugh he then kicked him again and rejoined his companions at the other end of the car.

Helmar now understood the reason this brute was sent in charge of him, and he knew that his journey was to be one of insufferable agony. Oh, for one moment of freedom again! If it cost him his life he would exterminate the hound.

After his last onslaught, Abdu left him alone for a while, and Helmar's anger began to cool down. He thought of Naoum's words, and realized how truly he had spoken. No, he must remain quiet, and then even Abdu could not be barbarous enough to murder him. It was one thing to come to such a determination and another to carry it out; alternately he was a prey to violent thoughts of revenge and the calmness of philosophy. In the latter intervals he wondered how long the train would take to reach its destination, he had not been in it half-an-hour, and yet it seemed to him an eternity.

The guards were talking in low tones; every now and then Helmar caught a word of Arabic, but they had taken the precaution to seat themselves so far from him that he could not hear what they talked about. The misery of his uncomfortable position and surroundings gave him little desire to interest himself with them.

About an hour after they had started, Abdu left his companions and came and sat beside him. Helmar knew this was the prelude to some fiendish cruelty, but what he did not know. He was not long left in doubt.

The train was bumping terrifically, the metals over which it was running being very uneven. For a few moments Abdu watched the motion of a piece of iron chain, hanging through a ring in the side of the car, then, having evolved some plan, he turned to his prisoner with a leer on his face.

"You see this," he said, tapping the place where Helmar had struck him in the face; "Abdu hasn't forgotten, but he is kind and forgives easily. You are a prisoner, and must be made comfortable."

As he said this he sprang up, and going over to where the chain was hanging, took it from its place, and coiling it up into a knot, returned to George's side. The chain was made of large iron links, with several sharp, square swivels in it, and these Abdu so placed that they projected from the rest. Having arranged it to his fancy, he seized his prisoner's hair, and raising his head by it, placed the bunch of chain beneath it, and then, with brutal force, pushed him back on to the sharp, rusty iron.

"You must have a pillow," he laughed, as he saw George wince with pain.

The moment Abdu had released his head, Helmar raised it from the cruel iron and moved himself away, but the Egyptian was ready in a moment; the knife flashed, and George felt its keen point prick through his clothes.

"Ah! you would refuse my kindness, would you? This must not be," and he pushed the chain again beneath the prisoner's head. "So, if you move again the knife will go farther in next time."

George now found himself compelled to remain with the chain under his head. Strain as he would, to keep from resting upon it, the motion and jolting of the train made it pummel the back of his skull, until he felt that he should soon go mad. Once or twice, in desperation, he moved, but the wretch was as good as his word, and the point of his knife was dug into his legs and arms until his clothes were covered with blood.

After half-an-hour of this Abdu seemed to have had enough of the pastime, and with a sneering laugh removed the chain, and then returned to his companions at the end of the car.

Helmar all this time had not uttered one word. Notwithstanding the agony he had endured, and the pain of the wounds Abdu had inflicted upon him, he had not allowed a single sound to escape him, but it was with a sigh of intense relief that he saw the little monster rejoin his friends.

The guards, for a time, now seemed to ignore the presence of their prisoner and spoke in louder tones. Possibly Abdu was not aware that his prisoner could speak Arabic, for they conversed quite freely, and George distinctly heard every word they said. Abdu was the man his attention was mainly fixed upon.

"No, no," he was saying, "the officer Arden has been fooled by this Naoum. Arabi would have killed him at once but for the money-man Naoum. I tell you he is his friend, and we will have no power to harm him."

"But Arden is powerful, and while Naoum is away, will be able to do as he likes," replied one of the men, in a tone of conviction.

"You are a fool, and cannot see before your nose," cried Abdu, irritably. "Arabi dare not quarrel with Naoum; the other is only powerful in favour, he does not wield the hold over our master. No, Arden will work his end, but not through his master, it will be in the way he ordered the prison to be fired."

Helmar listened to every word they were talking of him.

"So it was Arden that had the prison set alight," thought he; "evidently he would stop at nothing. Would his influence extend to Cairo?"

"Who says that Arden had the prison burnt?" said one of the men. "More likely that you did it, Abdu, because the Christian dog struck you."

All three laughed, and George shuddered as he realized what it meant to be in the power of such creatures.

"Whoever did it, it was good," said Abdu; "the dogs must die, or the true believers will be driven from their own land. I would that I were allowed, yonder dog should never leave this train alive, and his body should rot on the plains, and feed the vultures."

"You are a great man, Abdu," said one of his companions, sneeringly, "and very brave. Go and cut yonder dog's ropes and see how you will fare! Allah! but he would eat you, knife and all!"

Abdu was stung to the quick, and retorted hotly—

"Have a care; I have dealt with him before, and if he hurt me it was because I was not aware; but I am here in front of you, and by the Prophet's beard, I fear you not," and he showed his glittering white teeth.

Helmar was in hopes that they would start to fight amongst themselves, and he felt convinced that if they did so, they would not bother any more about troubling him.

"Allah! but you think because you are the son of a great man that I fear to speak," retorted the other. "Shoo! I fear you so little that I spit in your face!"

The man suited the action to the word, and immediately sprang to his feet. Abdu promptly followed suit, as did the third man. The little officer's eyes were blazing with rage, and he rushed, with upraised knife, on the man who had insulted him. Instantly the two men locked, and a struggle to the death ensued. Their knives gleamed and flashed in the dim light of the car as each tried to bury his weapon in his opponent's vitals.

So interested was Helmar in what was going on that he forgot his pain and the torture to which he had been subjected, and laughed and cheered Abdu's assailant on with an enthusiasm that astonished even himself.

The third man of his guard seemed in some magic way to have disappeared, but George had not thought about him, so busily occupied was he with the combatants. To and fro they swayed; now Abdu seemed to be getting the best of it, and now the other appeared to be forcing the little man back. It was most exciting, and George struggled to a sitting posture, the better to follow their movements.

Suddenly a whispered tone reached his ear; some one close beside him uttered the word "Amman!"

CHAPTER XXII

HORROR

Turning in the direction the sound came from, George saw it was the third man close by him who had whispered the word. Here was a surprise; but a light began to dawn on him as he answered with alacrity—

"Allah is good!"

"And ever watchful!" said the man at once.

So Naoum's power was already working. Evidently this fight was a planned affair between these two men, and Helmar waited wonderingly for what was to happen next.

The moment the fellow had given the sign he stooped down and quickly cut the ropes from the prisoner's feet and hands, and whispered, "Come! we will stay this Abdu's hand and give him a lesson!"

George sprang to his feet instantly, and the two men dashed at the struggling pair. Abdu's assailant, doubtless prepared for this, at once relaxed his hold and, before the enraged little officer could deliver a home thrust with his knife, he was seized by Helmar and his friend, and the weapon wrenched from his grasp.

The two guards now seemed inclined to leave the affair in the white man's hands, for the moment Helmar had got a firm grip on Abdu they fell back.

"So, traitors," screamed the maddened little man, bursting with fury, "you have turned on me and released your prisoner! By Allah! I swear you shall pay for this! You are in league against the great Pasha Arabi, and your lives shall pay the forfeit!"

All the answer he got to his ravings was a stolid smile of triumph from both men, and, to stay his tongue, Helmar gripped his throat until he almost choked with a spluttering cough.

"Never mind about traitors," said Helmar, in Arabic. "We are just going to read you a lesson; retribution has come to you sooner than you expected. See!" he went on, turning to the others, "pass that rope along and we will bind him!"

The two men did as they were bid, and together they secured the officer in no very gentle manner. His hands were folded behind his back and bound in that position, so that when his feet had been secured also, he looked like a trussed fowl.

"I'll be more merciful than you were," said Helmar, laughing, as he forced him to lie full length on the floor. "I will not provide you with a pillow—but," as Abdu opened his mouth to speak, "if you utter a sound unbidden, I will fasten you to that chain and let you hang outside the door for the rest of the journey."

Abdu ground his teeth with rage, but kept silent. His eyes gleamed murder at the two men who had sold him and released his prisoner. This, however, in no way seemed to trouble them, for they only grinned defiance; whilst one of them drew his knife and felt its sharp point, as if meditating giving the little wretch a taste of it.

The humour of the situation appealed to George; all thoughts of revenge had gone, and he merely intended to keep the little man a prisoner in punishment for what he had done to him. After watching the contortions of his captive's face for a few moments, George turned to the two men.

"Well, what do you think is best to do?" he asked, wishing to find out what their instructions were. "I suppose it is no use to attempt escape. If we were to manage to jump from the train, it could only end in disaster."

"No, no," said one of the men. "There can be no escape. Abdu would have killed you had we not interfered. Our orders were to see that no harm befell you by the way, so while he sat beside you, we planned that little affair."

"And very well done it was," replied George, laughing. "But what will happen when we reach Cairo? You will be shot!"

"No," said the man, complacently. "It is all arranged. Abdu is a servant of Arden's, and although the master has ordered that you shall not be killed, yet has Arden ordered differently, and appointed Abdu to carry out his orders for him. Therefore, what we have done will bring us in favour with our chief, and Abdu will be punished—probably hanged," he added in a loud tone so that the prisoner could hear.

"Oh, I see," replied Helmar. "Then you will take him where you take me, and hand him over as a prisoner too, for attempting to murder me against Arabi's wish. That is decidedly smart. Do you hear, Abdu?"

All three men laughed, but the victim of their plans gave no sign. George was astonished at the workings of Naoum's power. He had already established a safeguard for him, even on the short journey to Cairo; what then would he do when at that place where Mariam Abagi was? The feeling of relief at this fresh instance of his protector's watchfulness filled him with a sense of security that he had not yet felt, and he blessed the man who was so kindly disposed towards him.

The rest of the journey passed uneventfully, and, as the train pulled up at its destination and Helmar and his guards alighted on the platform, he was glad to leave the stuffy, heated atmosphere of the place in which he had had such an exciting time.

Abdu and he marched from the station side by side. The difference between them was that Abdu's hands still remained bound, while he was allowed to walk unfettered. His guards hailed a conveyance, and the four were immediately taken to the prison.

This precaution was necessary, as Helmar soon discovered, for as they passed along the thoroughfares he saw that the whole city was in a ferment. The streets were thronged with a shouting cosmopolitan mob even at that early hour of the morning. Armed rebels were parading the streets, jostling and hustling any with whom they came into contact. There was not the slightest doubt that his white face would have served as a red rag to a bull in that mixed assembly, and he would never have reached his destination alive.

He remarked on this to his guards, and his surmise was at once confirmed.

"Your life would not be worth a minute's purchase exposed to view," replied the man he addressed. "For that matter, even natives have to be most careful, the place is almost in a state of riot. Egypt cannot last like this, we shall eat ourselves up."

Abdu was furtively watching the seething thoroughfare from the window, and, as the man finished speaking, he endeavoured to attract some one's attention outside by holding up his bound hands. The instant he did so, the guard flung himself upon him and forced him down; but it was too late, the mischief was done. With a cry, two or three of the crowd elbowed their way, at a run, towards the hack. Helmar glanced with apprehension at his guards, and noted the fear expressed in their faces, while Abdu was grinning with the most intense malice.

The driver evidently saw danger threatening his vehicle and whipped his horses up, but apparently some signal had been passed along the road, for the number of pursuers was momentarily increasing to a howling crowd.

What the issue would have been it is doubtful to say, but just at that moment they reached the citadel, parts of which were being used as prison cells, and, with intense relief, Helmar heard the gates of the courtyard close behind them.

The moment he alighted he was conducted by two evil-looking warders to his cell, whilst the guards, with Abdu, were taken to an office.

As soon as he found himself alone, Helmar looked round his prison. It was a decidedly uninviting place. Although much cleaner than the one in which he had been confined at Damanhour, it was bare of all furniture, except a sort of wooden trestle, evidently intended for his bed. This occupied one side of the room, which was a narrow apartment, about eight feet long by five in width. A dim light was allowed to penetrate into this dismal hole through a heavily-grated window high up in the wall. As George surveyed the place he came to the conclusion, from the solid construction of the walls, that he was in no ramshackle makeshift. There was none of the filth and dirt of his previous experience, and he felt that here at least he could lie down on the hard and uncomfortable boards without being eaten alive by loathsome insects.

He felt tired after his long journey, and his appetite was keen. He fancied that no matter what his diet might be, he could do ample justice to it when it should be brought along.

Using his coat as a pillow, he stretched himself out on his trestle and waited patiently for some one to come. Every now and then he burst out laughing, as his thoughts went back to the journey to Cairo.

What stunning fellows those two guards had proved themselves—and how smartly they had fooled Abdu! He wondered where they were, and if they would be allowed to look after him. Such luck, he was afraid, could not be. No, he would probably be waited upon by one of those two surly fellows who had conducted him to his present abode.

An hour passed, and at last he heard a footstep outside; he wondered if it was the much-desired breakfast, or a summons before Arabi's tribunal. The steps came nearer, and a key was placed in the lock of his door. A moment later a warder entered with some bread and coffee.

The man silently advanced. Helmar's eyes watched his movements closely; he set the tin of coffee on the floor and the bread beside it, and thus, without a word, turned to depart.

"I say," cried George, as the man neared the door, "is this all a hungry man is to have? Why, hang it all, I was treated better by Arden!"

George had spoken in English, thinking it wisest not to air his Arabic before this man.

The warder only shook his head, to signify that he did not understand.

George then tried him in French, but with no better success. At last, seeing that his chance of a better breakfast was slipping from him, he repeated his remarks in Arabic.

"Bread and coffee is too good for a dog of an unbeliever," replied the warder, in a surly tone, "better food is only for the sons of the Prophet. The white dog will soon not need anything in Egypt."

As he finished speaking he left the cell, slamming the door behind him, as if to emphasize his disgust at waiting on a white man.

"The surly pig," muttered Helmar, when the man had gone. "It's scant favour I shall get from him. Heigho! my troubles seem never-ending, but there—upon my word, I am getting used to them now. Bread, eh?" he went on, picking up the hunk of stale, black, husky-looking stuff before him. "I could make better bread myself out of bran."

He picked up the tin of coffee and tasted it.

"Ah, that's a bit better. I must say they do understand making coffee." Without more ado he ate his bread ravenously, and, in spite of its blackness and heaviness, felt very much refreshed when he had finished. The coffee was certainly good, and George drank it sparingly, lest it should be long before he got any more.

After this he lay down to take a nap. Sleep was not long in overtaking him, and despite his troubles, despite his hard uncomfortable bed, he slumbered peacefully.

It seemed to him he had not slept five minutes when he was rudely awakened by some one pulling at his leg. It was his gaoler.

"Come on, you're wanted," he said, with an unpleasant smile; "they're going to ask you some questions."

"Eh, what? Who's going to ask me some questions?" said George, sitting up and rubbing his eyes. "Eh?" as he looked at his gaoler in great surprise. "Oh yes, I remember now—all right, lead on, I'm with you."

He sprang from his hard couch, and stretched himself as he spoke. He had not yet had time to think or he would scarcely have answered as cheerily; neither had he seen the unpleasant look on the man's face, which portended anything but something pleasant awaiting him. However, he followed his guide, who led him out of the building across the courtyard he had entered in the morning, to a sort of miniature tower standing alone. The place was of peculiar structure, and there was no doubt that it was not built by European hands. So interested was he in the place that he drew the warder's attention to it.

"What place is this? part of the prison?"

"Ay, it's part of the prison, but a part not much used—until now," and he turned to the door, fumbling with a great key in the lock.

Helmar's curiosity was still further aroused. The man's words conveyed hidden meaning.

"Yes, but what is it for? Does it contain another series of cells?"

"You will soon find out what it is for unless you are sensible, and it certainly contains another series of cells," replied the man, flinging back the heavy iron-studded door, which creaked and groaned as if it hadn't been opened for years.

Without another word the warder led the way in. The air was musty and dark, and George shuddered as he stepped into the dark passage that lay before him. As soon as he had passed in the gaoler turned and closed the door, and then proceeded to guide our hero to the head of a flight of stone steps. Here he took a lighted lantern from the wall, and together they descended into the depths below.

The moment he put his foot on the first step of the stairway, George remembered Naoum's words. Was this the place in which the *interrogation* was to be carried out! The very thought of it sent a cold shiver of terror down his back, but he knew that it would be worse than useless to fight against the inevitable; even if he refused to go farther his retreat was entirely cut off, and doubtless his gaoler could summon aid to force him to the tribunal. No, he would endeavour to put a bold face upon it, and trust to circumstances and Naoum's help to see him through. Keeping close to his guide he steadily descended. The staircase wound round and round, and as they got lower and lower the steps became more and more damp and slippery, until at last he had to cling to a sort of rough wooden balustrade for support. At last the end of what seemed an interminable journey was reached, and the two men stood in front of an iron door. This, with some difficulty, the gaoler opened, and proceeded along a short narrow passage which ended in an archway covered by some rough damp fabric. Pulling this aside, the man led the way.

Helmar stood where he was, just inside the archway, while his guide proceeded to light several lanterns which hung round the walls.

As the light spread over the room, a frenzy of terror seized Helmar, and he stood rooted to the spot.

CHAPTER XXIII

IN THE HANDS OF THE PHILISTINES

The feeling of terror passed off as quickly as it had come. As the light spread luridly over the dismal room it exposed to our hero's gaze the unmistakable signs that the place was to be used for the administration of tortures. Instruments and tools of all sorts lay about in every direction, bottles were stored on a shelf in one corner, whether containing medical material, or stuff of a more deadly nature, George had no means of discovering. In another corner of the dungeon stood a brick forge, with various irons scattered about on it, which were doubtless used for branding purposes. His attention was drawn to a pile of manacles and chains, amongst which he detected iron collars, anklets, iron bars of enormous weight, all cruel-looking and of dreadful portent.

In one wall was placed a series of rings with ropes attached, while close by lay a heavy thonged lash; the nature of these things left him in no doubt concerning their use.

As his eyes rested on them in turn, George again felt the terror coming on him; involuntarily he trembled, and it was only by a supreme effort he was able to cast it from him. The tension of his feeling was so great that to relieve it he turned to his gaoler.

"But why am I brought here? They cannot torture a prisoner of war!" he exclaimed. "But perhaps," as an idea struck him, "they intend to frighten me."

The gaoler guffawed in a sepulchral manner at what he considered his prisoner's simplicity; he did not understand that George was trying to convince himself against his own better judgment.

"Frighten, eh?" he said at last, when his gruesome merriment had ceased, "they'll not waste their time in trying to frighten a Christian dog! These things are not for show, but use. Since the white people came to this country, this place," he went on, with a comprehensive sweep of his hands, "has not been used, but kept more as a curiosity than anything else; now the Egyptians again rule, they will once more adopt the methods of our forefathers."

"Oh, yes," replied George, with growing irritation at the man's undisguised hatred for the white people in general, and himself in particular, "I know all about the *mighty* Egyptians and their forefathers. I've heard all about that before, but it has nothing to do with bringing me down here. What I want to know is, why I'm brought here."

At the sneering tone George used when speaking of the Egyptians the expression of the gaoler's face lowered and his eyes shot fire, and as he ceased speaking the man turned away, and busied himself with setting a great arm-chair in position in the centre of the room.

"You know a great deal about Egypt besides," he said in slow, measured tones, wiping cobwebs from a cumbersome piece of furniture, "and that is the reason you are brought here. Those who will not speak must be made to speak."

"I am ready to tell them all I know, and I can assure you it isn't much."

"About the British troops and their Commander's plans?" asked the man, with a stolid look of surprise.

Helmar burst out into a laugh, although he felt anything but like doing so.

"Why, man, how should I know anything about it—I am not an officer!"

The gaoler smiled grimly. He had expected this, and refrained from comment, contenting himself with shrugging his shoulders in an approved Eastern style.

Seeing that nothing further was to be gained from this unintelligent pig, Helmar gave up the attempt, and examined more closely the instruments of torture, wondering in a hopeless sort of way what was to be his fate. Unable to come to any decision, he flung himself into the chair his gaoler had set in the centre of the room, a prey to a horrible despair.

He had hardly seated himself when he became aware of the sound of approaching footsteps. They did not come from the passage by which he had entered, but from the opposite side of the room. At that moment the gaoler approached, and, seizing him roughly by the shoulder, attempted to hustle him from his seat.

"This is for another; we will find something less comfortable for you."

Helmar detested being pushed about, and as he expected to be handled badly later on, he determined to put up with none of it now. He sprang in a bound from his seat and, turning, dealt the great Egyptian a smashing blow on the face, and was about to follow it up with another, when a door, which he had not seen, suddenly opened, and a procession of dusky figures entered. Instantly two of the new-comers sprang forward and, before George could continue his chastisement, had him securely pinioned, his flashing eyes indicating the storm of rage that was going on within him.

Realizing that now, if ever, he must be calm, he stifled back his feelings, and waited for the next act in the horrible drama. Six men had entered, and one of them seated himself at once in the arm-chair George had vacated. He was a powerful, thick-set fellow and evidently, by the deference the others paid him, a man of considerable importance. His expression was one of fixed malignity, and George rightly surmised that he need look for no mercy from this individual. He wondered who and what he was. Was he a magistrate, or some potentate of Arabi's army? He did not give him the idea of being a military man. His costume was decidedly that of the native civilian, and yet there was an air of stern command about the man that puzzled him.

At a sign from the new-comer, the two men who held him proceeded to divest Helmar of his coat and shirt. This done, his hands and feet were fastened, and he was then thrown on the floor face downwards, while the bigger of his two custodians stood by, handling the deadly kourbash.

There was no mistaking their vile intentions; he was to be interrogated with a vengeance, and George eyed the cruel thong as it lay idly resting on the ground beside the great Arab. The horrors it conjured up in his mind were too appalling for words. Already in fancy he could feel its relentless blows on his bared back, and he shuddered again and again. He shut his teeth and, to use his own phraseology, determined to "die hard." He would show these inhuman monsters that a white man could stand without a sign anything they could think of to reduce him to submission. In bitterness he felt that this mockery of interrogation was only an excuse to vent their hatred of the European, and that in reality they did not hope to discover anything from him, and, in fact, knew that he had no information to give.

The dreaded kourbash, he was determined, should do its fell work with no response from him, terrible as he knew that punishment would be; they might kill him, they might flay him alive, but they could not reduce his stubborn pride as no doubt they hoped to do. This spirit bore him through those few moments that preceded the first words of his mock interrogation, but he felt himself shrink on the floor when he saw the slightest movement on the part of his executioner. The torture of that short period was the refinement of cruelty, but never for one moment did he waver from his fixed determination to face his inquisitors like a man and a son of his fatherland.

At last the man in the chair spoke; his tones were calm and dispassionate, but there rang in them an undercurrent of intensity that warned George, whose mental faculties were painfully acute, that the latent feeling of racial hatred was only held in check by the power of an iron will, and that like a boiling volcano it needed but the faintest extra aggravation to make it burst forth and overwhelm its surroundings. The man's words fell on his ears like the knell of doom, and ere he replied he braced himself for the inevitable result of his answer.

"Being a secret agent of the British, you possess information that will be of use to the great Pasha now ruling the land of the faithful!"

Though the words were an assertion, the tones in which they were delivered were undoubtedly those of a question. While yet considering his reply, George saw out of the corner of his eye the fearful kourbash raised from the ground. Quickly making up his mind that no subterfuge would hold him, Helmar replied—

"I am not a secret agent, neither do I possess any information whatsoever of the British movements. How should I? Have I not been a captive ever since Arabi was expelled from Alexandria?"

Notwithstanding the fearful position in which he stood, George could not resist this little bit of sarcasm at the expense of Arabi's prowess. Apparently his interrogator had no sense of humour, for although Helmar could not see the man he was convinced that he gave some sign. There was a horrid swish in the air, and the kourbash fell across his bare shoulders with ruthless force, and a great wale was raised where it struck. George uttered no sound, but, bursting with indignation and in great pain, waited for the next question.

It came quickly, and in the same even tones.

"Your retort is untimely, and will bring retribution upon you. The faithful require no comments from the Christian dog. Answer the questions put to you, simply, that your punishment may be less severe. We would mercifully save you more pain than is necessary. It is known that you are aware of the point at which the forces of the great Pasha are to be attacked. The English dogs are slow, but they are cunning. Where will their men-of-war be concentrated?"

"How can I tell you that—I don't know," replied Helmar irritably.

The last words were scarcely out his mouth when the kourbash again fell with terrific force on his flesh, this time twice in rapid succession. The pain was intense, and as each blow fell George hollowed his back involuntarily as if by doing so he would lessen the force of the dreaded thong. His back was scalding, and the sting of the cruel lash pervaded his whole body, but he only shut his teeth the harder and waited for what next was to come.

"Where will the concentration take place?"

The words came like the knell of doom, the monotony of their tone was appalling.

"I do not know," replied George again.

Again the lash fell, with another cut added—again he writhed in pain, pain that was anguish of mind as well as of body. He felt as if his brain was bursting with the dreadful slowness of the proceedings. It seemed to him that if he were to receive a hundred lashes in quick succession he could easily stand it, but the torture of the delay was fearful.

Again the fiendish inquisitor asked his question, and again our hero replied in the negative. Four more frightful cuts of the inexorable kourbash fell on his rapidly-scarring back. The torture he endured was frightful, not a single blow from the raw-hide thong but was timed to produce the utmost effect; his back was waled in large ridges, and with a fiendish cruelty the inhuman executioner with unfailing aim had smote and re-smote him in the same place. Already he could feel that the skin had burst, and it came almost as a relief as he felt the flow of blood down his back. Again and again the malignant man in the chair asked his question. Again and again the answer came from our hero, followed quickly by the increased number of lashes from his executioner.

The terrible punishment was beginning to tell; already George had passed from the defiant stage to one of patient endurance. As the torture continued his body began to feel numbed, and he became light-headed; he caught himself counting in a foolish manner the number of strokes he had received, and as each one fell, he would add two or three according to whether he felt it more or less than its predecessor. Once he even laughed as the man struck him on a part of his body that was clothed, with the effect that the executioner, enraged at the levity, redoubled his merciless attack.

The light-headed stage passed off and was replaced by a feeling of horrible despair. He wondered when these monsters would have vented their spite sufficiently; he wondered if he would be alive at the end of the castigation, or if they would flay the flesh from his body. He thought of the ignominious ending it would be to his brief career with the fighting line.

[Transcriber's note: Illustration not available.
Caption: "He was already beyond crying out. All sense of feeling had left him!"]

His head was buried in his arms, and he was becoming indifferent to how frequently the kourbash fell on his shoulders. Had he but known it, it was the beginning of unconsciousness; he uttered no sound, he cared nothing for what was going on; he no longer, as the blows were rained on him, shut his teeth to bear the pain—it was not necessary, he was already beyond crying out. All sense of feeling had left him.

Now and again he could hear, as if a long way off, the voice of the inquisitor repeating his question, but it had no meaning for him, the words were blurred and indistinct to his mental faculties, and he made no attempt to answer.

Presently the blows ceased to fall; his body lost all feeling as his legs became cramped, and he fell into unconsciousness. Suddenly he was aroused from his torpor by angry voices. Far away they sounded, but still they penetrated to his dulled and aching brain. He could hear a high-pitched, shrill, screaming sound that struck on his almost senseless nerves with a shock.

Vaguely he became aware that his flogging had ceased, and that something had gone wrong with his persecutors.

With a supreme effort he roused himself, but he was too weak and feeble to be able to grasp the meaning of what he heard, and quickly sank down to full length again, as he felt a warm touch on his hands.

CHAPTER XXIV

A FRIEND INDEED

The oblivion into which our hero had fallen did not last long, the suspension of brain-power was but passing and soon gave place to dreams. With that extraordinary irony of reduced mental power these dreams were of the most beautiful description; all the agony he had suffered had passed away, and he dreamt that he was in a gorgeous garden on the banks of his beloved Danube; all around him the most beautiful fountains played, and people were wandering about terraces and lawns dressed in lovely white flowing robes. Many of the faces he saw about him were those of the friends of his earlier associations, and they smiled and bowed to him as they passed by where he was reclining. No one seemed to speak, and a silence too peaceful and delightful for words reigned everywhere.

In the distance beyond the limits of this perfect place, he saw many dark shadows, in each of which he could distinctly trace the figures of dusky Egyptians vainly endeavouring to reach him, but, as each one made the attempt, he was beaten back by the heavy fall of some terrible weapon. Suddenly the scene changed and he was seated on a throne. On every side the white-robed figures stood waiting for him to speak; this he was vainly attempting to do, but at each effort a terrible pain passed over him and the words remained unuttered. At last a big fountain began to play in front of where he sat, and the spray, in falling, played over his throne, saturating him and every one around; then his tongue seemed released, and he suddenly awoke to find himself lying upon a comfortable bed, with Mariam Abagi stooping over him bathing his back. The moment he regained consciousness the agony of his position burst upon him with terrible force. Racking pains shot all through his body, until he felt that he must shriek aloud; he could move neither hand nor foot, for, at each effort, his pain was redoubled, and he lay still, moaning piteously.

At last the bathing that Mariam was administering began to soothe him, he felt easier, and his moans lessened. As time went on they ceased altogether, and the bathing was at once discontinued.

He was now aware of everything that had happened, and longed to ask his nurse to tell him all that had occurred after the flogging had ceased. Once he made an effort to speak, but Mariam restrained him by giving him something to drink. After that he slept.

When next he awoke there were several people in the room. Mariam was seated at his side, and Naoum stood near, while several dusky figures were waiting in the background. He found that he had been turned on to his back, and he felt very little pain until he attempted to move, when he at once realized that he had better make no further effort in that direction.

"Where am I, Mariam? In prison still?" he asked in feeble tones.

The old woman's face relaxed from its stern expression and became wreathed in a wrinkled smile, which set George's heart at rest before she uttered a word.

"Yes, my son, still in prison, but with those around you who will no more allow harm to reach you. We only found you out just in time, or you would have seen the light of day no more. Your enemies were clever, and attacked you quickly to prevent our interference, but the news was brought to us and we hurried to your assistance. You are now in safety."

George thought for a moment, his eyes resting on Naoum's face, everything became quite clear to him, and he remembered, though indistinctly, the angry tones he had heard before he became unconscious, and was wondering if they were Mariam's.

"Did you come yourself?" he next asked her. "Ah," as she nodded, "I remember your voice."

"Yes, I was indeed angry, and had to exert all my power before the wretched Pasha would release you."

The old woman's look as she uttered these words was one of intense hatred, and boded, as George thought, but little mercy should ever opportunity arise for the man who had attempted to defy her. Again he caught himself wondering at the power of these two strange people. His reflections were put a stop to as the sound of Naoum's voice fell on his ear.

"I will leave you, mother; he will recover now, and, under your administering, rapidly. See that you tell him the news I have brought you. There is much work for us all, and his share of it will require a healthy body."

As he finished speaking, Naoum turned and left the room, followed by the rest of his onlookers, whom Helmar quickly surmised were servants.

Mariam alone remained, intent upon the care of her patient. Her eyes never for one moment left the thin and drawn face on the pillow before her, anticipating, with the solicitous care of a mother, every need for his comfort.

"How long do you think it will be before I can get up?" asked George suddenly, after a long pause. "My back feels much better already. To-morrow?"

"No, no, my son. Not to-morrow or the day after, neither will you get up for some days to come," replied the old woman, shaking her head. "You have been injured almost unto death, and your recovery must surely be slow. As Naoum said, there is work to be done in which you will have to bear your part, and, to that end, we must take the greatest care of you. Now, listen, to-night I shall come again, when I shall have news of the greatest importance to communicate to you; by that time you will be sufficiently refreshed to listen, and for the while you must sleep."

She then administered an opiate and left him. In a few moments he was again buried in profound slumber. It was not until the morrow that he awoke; it was broad daylight when he did so, and while he waited for the coming of Mariam he scanned the apartment in which he was a prisoner. Evidently it was a room unused for the retention of people in custody, for it was fitted up in luxurious style. The walls were hung with heavy tapestries, and the floor was carpeted with Eastern rugs. The window he observed was unbarred, and this alone brought him a sense of comfort and repose that he could never have felt, in spite of Mariam's assurances, had the ominous gratings obtruded their sinister presence. The window was sheltered from the intense rays of the burning sun outside by a protecting lattice, and this kept the atmosphere pleasantly cool within; he sighed as he mentally thanked his kindly friends for their goodness to him—a stranger. Several times his thoughts reverted to the wretches who had so cruelly flogged him, and vividly he traced his arch-enemy Arden's hand in all his sufferings; he was too weak to rouse himself to indignation, but he could not forget his inhuman treatment.

Presently his nurse entered, and his wounds were at once attended to. After submitting to the process he felt much relieved, and lay back, prepared to listen to the promised news, when his protectress should be disposed to deliver it.

"And now, Mariam, what about the news you have to tell me? I am quite strong enough to listen."

"Yes, I think I can safely tell you. You must not let anything I have to say excite you." She paused for a moment, as if to think how best to express herself, but, as she observed her patient's growing irritation at the delay, plunged into the subject at once.

"The information you were supposed to possess has already been communicated to Arabi. The silence and apparent inactivity of the British Commanders have now taken the form of a definite plan, and the Pasha is aware that they intend advancing against him from the direction of Port Said, through Ismalia on the canal. Against this Arabi will bring his army to meet them at some place on the railway, in the hopes of driving them back to the Suez. If this succeeds he will then destroy the canal, the further to hamper their movements."

"Yes, but is he aware of his opponent's strength? Surely they would not advance unless in overwhelming numbers?" George broke in. "Psha! The man must be mad to hope for success!"

"That of course remains to be seen," said Mariam slowly. "Naoum's people bring us word that soldiers have been landing ever since the beginning of the war, but Arabi's people, probably to encourage the rebellion, say no, that the British army is but a puny affair."

"What fools!" said Helmar. "They'll find out their mistake before long, and get such a smashing up that they won't forget in a hurry."

"Yes," said the old woman, "that we know, but all this will take a long time, and by the time the blow is ready to fall, I must get you well enough for the work before you."

Mariam paused, as if weighing her words. George was at once all interest. Something was coming, he felt sure, that was of even greater importance than the conflict and probable overthrow of Arabi. Mariam, he knew, never spoke lightly, and when she hinted at work that, apparently, could only be carried out by himself, it must indeed be of an urgent character.

"But what is this work you speak of in such solemn tones? Surely, it cannot be as important as the downfall of this arch-rebel, Arabi?"

"Listen, and I will tell you; then you can judge for yourself as to its importance. Naoum's people have discovered a cruel plot. Arabi, influenced by his wicked advisers, has arranged that, should he fail in his campaign against the British, should he receive one overwhelming defeat, then, to avenge himself upon his conquerors, at a word from him, Cairo will be burned to the ground."

"The villain!" exclaimed George. "He would ruin thousands of his own people for the sake of revenge on others! And this is the man to whom the misguided Arabs trust the emancipation of their country!"

"You must not excite yourself, my son," said Mariam, alarmed at the effect of her words on the invalid. "What I have said is the truth, but the scheme can be stayed through you. Naoum and I, whose interests do not entirely lie in this city, intend to thwart him for the sake of humanity, but without you our object will be difficult to accomplish."

"Yes, yes," said George, impatiently. "But how can I stop it? I am at best but one man, and a prisoner, and," ruefully glancing at his nurse, "by the present signs, not likely to be able to get about for a month."

"All that we have taken into consideration," replied Mariam, calmly. "Your help in our plans will not be needed for some days yet, and by that time I hope to have you well and strong; but, in the meantime, we cannot care for you too well, for your enemies are powerful, and Naoum will have to keep an impenetrable shield over you while you lie here on a bed of sickness."

Helmar remained silent, thinking of the deep significance of Mariam's words. Evidently, he gathered from them, there was some very desperate enterprise in which they required him to take part. What was the nature of a scheme that could require such a solemn preamble?

"And what is required of me?" he asked, presently.

Mariam smiled, with a look of maternal affection in her calm, hollow eyes.

"In the first place to get well as soon as possible. Do not delay that desired end by worrying about the future. Everything that can be done by us for your safety will be attended to, and when the time comes, you shall be acquainted with what is required of you. You must rest content with what I have told you. The reason for telling you so much and no more is that you must see the importance of getting well as soon as possible."

George had to be content; no persuasion could draw from her anything more of the scheme with which she and her son determined to thwart Arabi. Many times he tried to get her to speak, but she would only shake her head and refuse to reply, so at last he gave it up and devoted himself to recovering from the effects of his flogging.

His recovery, despite the unremitting attention of his nurse, was somewhat slow; the frightful mauling he had received from the cruel kourbash had done its work well, but at last his terrible lacerations began to heal. His constitution did wonders for him; he was young and of strong vitality, and this, aided by Mariam's wonderful skill, brought him to the turning-point, and finally safety was reached.

It was some days, however, ere he rose from that bed of sickness, and when he did, the stalwart young athlete was hardly recognizable when he staggered from his bed to a chair. Notwithstanding his stern old nurse's fortitude, there was no mistaking the look of relief in her worn face when that day arrived. All her patience, all her untiring energy had not been in vain, she had helped to save his life, as she hoped to save, through him, the lives of thousands of poor souls in the beautiful city of Cairo.

George's strength came apace; every day saw him nearer the desired end. His bones, which at first had been almost bursting through his skin, quickly regained their wonted appearance, and he began to feel now that if there was any work for him to do there must be no further delay.

One evening he was seated beside the open window, Mariam was busying herself with arranging his supper, when he broached the subject that was ever in his thoughts.

"Mariam," he said, without turning his head, "tell me about the work that you and Naoum require of me. Is there yet time, or has my recovery been too long delayed?"

The old woman ceased in her preparations and came beside him. Just as she was about to speak a draught blew across her face, and she at once stepped to the window and closed it.

"The wind blows cold in the room to-night," she exclaimed, with a troubled look on her face. "I like it not. To-morrow we shall have you laid up again."

She looked round the room as she spoke, as if to discover where the draught came from. Failing to discover its source, she turned again to her companion.

"The time is even now at hand," she said, with deliberation. "To-morrow, Naoum will be here, when he will explain everything that you should know. Remember, every word that he speaks with you must be graven on your heart, nothing must be forgotten, for the lives of thousands of innocent souls depend upon your undertaking."

At this moment a sound attracted her attention and she turned round with a look of uneasiness in her eyes. Presently she continued—

"I ask not, in my own name, that you should do aught to show the gratitude you may feel for what has been done for you, but if you feel that gratitude you have so often expressed, show it by carrying out Naoum's instructions to you as if your life depended upon it, and the debt will be largely on our side."

Without waiting for reply, she left the room.

So engrossed were these two in the subject of their conversation, that neither observed the shaking tapestry on the wall, or the faint exclamation that proceeded from it, as Mariam took her departure.

CHAPTER XXV

NAOUM PLANS

The next morning, as Mariam had promised, Naoum presented himself. George had not seen him for many weeks, and was prepared for some slight change in his appearance; he knew that Naoum had much to trouble him, much opposition to contend with, and, consequently, expected that the serenity of his expression would bear traces of the mental strain of his position; but it was not so. The cheery, smiling face was the same as ever, and he greeted Helmar as if no matters of moment had ever weighed on his mind, the firm, set jaw and smooth forehead giving not the slightest indication of what was passing within.

"My mother tells me you are once more sound and well," he said, gazing admiringly at the straight, lithe figure in front of him. "It is good, for the time has now arrived for action."

He paused, and looked thoughtfully out of window. "Before I disclose my plan, there is one question I must ask you," he said at last. "Perhaps it will seem a strange one, but I have reasons."

"Go ahead," replied George, all anxiety to hear anything this man had to say.

"Have you had occasion to use the sign I gave you at Damanhour?"

"Only that once with your people in the railway train," replied George, at once.

"Has my mother spoken to you of the matter in hand when there has been any one near enough to have possibly overheard the conversation?"

"Decidedly not," was the prompt reply.

"Strange!" muttered Naoum. "However, it cannot now be helped. Somebody has got wind of our plans; I do not think to any damaging degree, but sufficiently to have me regarded with suspicion. Arden is in the city."

His words were uttered calmly, but they lost none of their significance by the tone. George started involuntarily at the mention of Arden's name, and a presentiment of evil at once took possession of him. What was he here for? What did his coming portend? Was it simply coincidence, or was it in reference to himself? These questions passed rapidly through his mind before he replied.

"You then anticipate something?"

Naoum smiled his calm, inscrutable smile.

"Not from him directly, but he has many friends, or paid servants, ready to carry out his orders. However, we must not seek trouble. In the meantime, I will tell you what I propose."

He stepped round the room, examining the tapestries, tapping the walls as he went; apparently satisfied with his inspection, he secured the door and returned to George.

"These precautions are necessary, for one word of what I have to say, overheard, would ruin everything and probably bring death upon us all. My mother, I understand, has already told you of the plot to burn the city to the ground. Very well," as George assented, "you must now understand Arabi's position. He has so far done little but spread sedition over the country. The British have forced him back step by step from Alexandria, until he anticipated a direct attack on Cairo from that direction; but suddenly your friends changed their tactics, and brought over a large force which they have landed at Port Said and Ismalia, whence a steady advance has been going on ever since. Arabi has summoned all his forces together, and mobilized them in the direction of Tel-el-Kebir, at which place he means to make a big stand. The position he has taken up is supposed to be impregnable, and success is anticipated by all his people. Personally, I am assured he must fail; there is too much lack of discipline, too much rivalry and disaffection in his ranks for him to stand against the well-drilled and splendidly-armed forces of a European Power; consequently, the inevitable is that he will be driven back on Cairo. The moment this happens, the place will be fired in every direction, and those who succeed in escaping the conflagration will be ruined and homeless. This must not be allowed, Cairo must be in the hands of the British before he can carry out his scheme, and you are the man to bring it about."

"I?" exclaimed George. "But how? I am a prisoner, and cannot hope to be released in time to reach the British lines!"

"Nevertheless, it must be so, the attempt must be made. My emissaries bring me word that the engagement at Tel-el-Kebir cannot take place for a few days; the British are not ready. That will give us time to effect your escape and for you to reach there."

A light began to dawn on Helmar, and he at last understood what Naoum was driving at; but how was the escape to be accomplished?

"I am ready and willing," said George, "but tell me how you hope to get me out of here."

"That will be simple enough. The part that is difficult will be the journey. From here to Tel-el-Kebir the country is covered by Arabi's men, besides which you do not know the route to be taken. There are many ways, of course, but the difficulties are stupendous, and to have any hope of success requires a man who knows every inch of the trails. However, I have discovered a route by which the journey may be accomplished in safety; but it will require all the ingenuity you may possess to bring it to a successful issue."

"When will the start be made?" asked George, with many misgivings, as he listened to Naoum's words.

"To-night," came the startling reply.

"To-night?" echoed George, in surprise. "But how?"

"I have arranged that Belbeis shall accompany you as guide; he is subtle and brave, and I can rely upon him as myself, besides which he has much love for you. From my mother's apartments in this place there is secret communication with the grounds, so that there will be little difficulty in leaving here. You will wait for a summons, which will occur late in the night; it will be a scratching sound on the door. Immediately afterwards, you will leave this room and follow the passage to the extreme end, then, without giving any sign, enter the door that you will find facing you. The moment you enter, a guide will give you the sign and then conduct you to where Belbeis is awaiting with horses."

"How about the news I am to convey? I require some proofs!"

"Exactly; this packet," said Naoum, holding out a small bundle of papers, "will convince the authorities of the truth of what you tell them. You can deliver them to whom you think best."

George's heart beat high with excitement and hope, as he carefully placed the packet in an inner pocket. The thought of once more being at liberty was indeed alluring, and he hoped and prayed that the attempt would be successful. True, he had little now to complain of since his rescue by Naoum and Mariam, but the love of liberty was strong upon him. He felt that to be so keen about it was almost like ingratitude to his two friends, but he could not control the feeling, and it showed plainly in his face. Naoum saw it, and smiled as he noted the bright, anxious expression of the young man.

"There is one thing you do not seem to have thought about, Helmar," he said, in his paternal fashion, "and that is—money. You will need some, and I do not suppose you have much of that necessary."

"Not a cent," answered George, suddenly brought to earth by this reminder.

"Ah, well, I will see to that," he replied, drawing forth a small bag of gold. "Here, take this, the contents will more than pay your expenses. No, you need have no scruples," as George drew back, hesitating to accept the money.

"This is my affair; you are doing this thing for me, and it is only right that I should pay all expenses."

"Yes, but I have received so much at your hands which I can never repay, Naoum. Do not make me increase the debt! I shall never be able to return the money."

"Neither is there the smallest need," said Naoum, quietly. "In this case you are my paid servant, or, at least, you must look upon yourself in that light. Come, do not be foolish! These Europeans are very proud," he went on, shaking his head.

Allowing himself to be convinced by his protector's words, George at length accepted the proffered money, and thus everything was settled. Naoum made him repeat his instructions to be assured that there was no mistake, and, having satisfied himself upon this point, he prepared to take his departure.

"One word, Naoum, before you go," said George. "I understand that I may not see you again before I depart———"

"Yes, yes," interrupted his companion, hastily. "I know what you would say, but it is unnecessary. The thanks must be on my side, and as for seeing you again, that is inevitable. Twice I have been able to assist you, rest assured I shall meet you a third time—it is fate. Allah will care for you by the way; your journey is in a good cause, and He will guide your steps. And now, farewell!"

At last the two friends parted; George felt it very much indeed. So long now had he known Naoum, and though he had not always been near him, his protection had been always felt, that the parting left him with a sense of loneliness which he had never before experienced, and for some time he was quite depressed. Realizing the folly of giving way to it, he at last pulled himself together and thought over the enterprise on which he was to embark.

He was thankful that his guide was to be Belbeis, for this man was well known to him, and he would be able to talk freely on matters which, with a stranger, he would have to avoid. Belbeis had long ago proved his fidelity, and as to his "subtleness," of which Naoum had spoken, that was beyond doubt. It was still quite early in the day, and George sat idly by his window, impatiently waiting for the approach of night. It seemed to him that the hours were of intolerable length, and would never pass. His excitement increased as the day wore on, till he hardly knew what to do with himself. Mariam came in with his mid-day meal, and he tried to detain her and discuss his prospects of success, but the old woman would not listen, and the moment he opened his mouth to speak, she placed her finger mysteriously upon her lips and hurried from the room.

There was no help for it, he must put up with his own thoughts and company, and bear the delay as best he could. The day dragged slowly on, and the sun began to set. With the approach of night his spirits rose, and he busied himself with plans of procedure for when he should find himself outside the grounds of his present prison.

Mariam brought in a light and his evening meal, and took her leave of him. The parting was a sad one. She treated him as a son, and could not have been more affected had she been saying good-bye to Naoum himself. George, on his part, was deeply touched by her solicitous care of him, but words did not come easily; yet his farewell lost nothing of its sincerity in the silence that accompanied it.

At last it was over, and he was left to himself for the few remaining hours before his departure.

It yet wanted at least a couple of hours to midnight. George had stretched himself out upon his couch, taking all the rest he could to prepare himself for his journey. He was buried in deep thought, and not a sound broke the stillness of the room; so profound was the silence that he gradually began to feel drowsy, and every now and then he found his eyelids closing involuntarily. He fought against this sleepiness for some time, but at last he fell into a light slumber.

Suddenly he was aroused by a gust of cool air passing over his face, and sitting bolt upright with a start, his eyes rested on the motionless figure of an Arab standing in the centre of the room, watching him.

George rubbed his eyes and stared again at the figure, hardly able to realize that it was a human being, and not a creature of his fancy. The sleepiness passed instantly, and his faculties became intensely acute. He sprang from his bed and stood confronting his visitor.

"Who are you, and what the deuce do you want here?" he asked sharply, eyeing the stranger from head to foot with a stern glance.

The man was dressed in the native costume of the lower class of Arab, and his features were peculiarly regular for the colour of his skin—details which George was not slow to note. The fellow was armed with the usual long knife stuck in his waist-cloth, and looked the picture of the unscrupulous mercenary so frequently found abroad at the time.

"I come as a messenger from Naoum," replied the stranger, in a peculiar, strained tone of voice. "I have matters of importance to communicate to you."

At the sound of the man's voice George eyed him keenly, then as the purport of his mission fell on his ears, the faintest suspicion of a smile passed over his face.

"Ah," he said, keeping his eyes steadily fixed on the man's face, "and what has Naoum to say to me?"

"Your escape cannot be attempted to-night. News has got abroad, and the guards are doubled. Your enemy, the officer Arden, has discovered your plans and will thwart them."

"Oh," said George, walking to the door and fastening it. "So our plans are frustrated? 'm! that's bad," he said thoughtfully. "Then what is to be done?"

As he spoke, he came close to the Arab, and peered steadily into his face. The man never for an instant flinched under the close scrutiny, but returned glance for glance. Suddenly, before the man could reply, George raised his hand and snatched at the fellow's head-gear, and pulling it from his head with a jerk, displayed a shock of brown hair.

"So, Mr. Mark Arden!" he said, in stern tones, "you think to play a trick on me! I recognized you the moment my eyes rested on your face, and I heard your feeble attempt at altering the tones of your voice. Now, what's your game?"

So sudden was George's movement that Arden had been unable to stay his hand and prevent his own unmasking. Consumed with fury, he replied through his clenched teeth.

"To prevent your escape! You fool!" he hissed. "Do you think that you are going to be allowed to get away from here to foil Arabi's plans? I tell you no! I have but to go from here and summon the guard, and you will never again see daylight!"

"'m! that certainly would be awkward," replied George, quietly. "But you have first got to leave this room. How do you propose doing that?" he added, with an ironical smile.

Arden grasped his meaning, and was at once ready with his retort.

"By the same way that I came. Yes, I am aware that you have secured that door, but," drawing the tapestry on one side, he disclosed, to Helmar's utter dismay, another door in the wall, "this is the way I entered," he said cunningly, "and by the aid of this door I discovered Naoum's treacherous plans. He shall pay for his double dealing, as shall you. Ostensibly Arabi's friend, he would betray him through you into the hands of his enemy; but I tell you it shall not be!"

"You are indeed the right person to speak of another's so-called treachery! But no matter. So you intend to prevent my escape? What if I prevent your leaving here—by force—how will you prevent that?"

"Try," was Arden's sneering response.

George was carefully calculating what this visit meant to him. Fortunately in giving him the details of his escape Naoum had spoken vaguely of the means by which he was to leave the palace, therefore, if he could reach Mariam's quarters, there might still be hope of success. There was to his mind only one thing to be done, and that was to keep Arden where he was, if possible, until his summons came, and then defy him. Let him call the guard, and the moment he had gone, dash down the passage to Mariam's quarters. It took him but an instant to decide on what to do, and, as Arden's sneering tones fell upon his ear, he burst out into a laugh.

"It is not worth my while to do so, or you may rest assured that long knife in your belt would not prevent me." To gain time he went on. "Now, what do you want me to do? Apparently the game is in your hands—doubtless you have some purpose beyond thwarting Naoum?"

The tone Helmar had adopted seemed to lull Arden's suspicions, for, as he put his question, the latter, before he replied, strode up to the bed and seated himself upon it, always, however, keeping his eyes upon his companion.

Arden seemed in no hurry to speak, he was endeavouring to penetrate George's innermost thoughts; when at last he did express himself it was as if weighing each word before he gave it utterance.

CHAPTER XXVI

A DASH FOR LIBERTY

"You are right, Helmar," he said, slowly. "I have another object in coming here." He paused for a moment, impatiently tugging at the fringe of his sash. "You remember I asked you at Port Said about joining Arabi?"

"I do—what about it?" said George, in tones of supreme indifference.

"That offer was made with the best of feeling towards you, and, as I thought, for your good. It would have brought you wealth, as it has me."

"And very nice comfortable means you adopted to attain my conversion, didn't you?" broke in Helmar, with upraised eyebrows.

"Well, perhaps the treatment was a little rough, but the intention was, nevertheless, sincere."

"Doubtless. Go on."

"Well," Mark went on, with eyes looking anywhere but at the man in front of him, "at that time I thought that Arabi would be bound to win the day, and *we*," with emphasis on the word, "should be made for life. But I was mistaken, and now it is plain to me that Arabi must fall."

Again he paused, as if waiting for comment from his companion, but none came, and he nervously continued, while Helmar kept his keen eyes fixed upon him.

"Of course I've made a pile of money," he went on, with a leer, "so that now I've only to get out of the country when the crash comes, and I can do anything I wish."

"Ah!" ejaculated Helmar, beginning to see through this man's scheming. "And you would get some one to help you do that, eh?" he added, unable to conceal his contempt, as he realized the sneaking character of this villain.

"Not necessarily," replied Arden, coldly. "I have in no way appeared in this Rebellion, and, therefore, nothing can be traced to my handiwork. The British cannot accuse me of having taken any part in the affair, and there is no one who can inform them of my share in it."

"But I could," said George sharply.

Arden smiled indulgently. He had no fear of Helmar; he considered him in his power.

"You cannot harm me, for you will never leave this place alive, unless— unless I choose."

"Well," said George, "granting that, what, then, do you propose? What is all this talk leading up to?"

"You, as you say, are the only man who is aware of the part I have played in this affair, except, perhaps, some of the men immediately under my control. Therefore I need not fear; but I should like to make doubly sure of my position against any accident. Although I can see no possibility of my share being known, I do not want to run any chances. Now, if I were to allow you to escape, I should have done you a good turn, for which, I have no doubt, you would be glad to make some return. This could be done by your statement to the British authorities of the assistance which I shall give you. Do you understand?"

"Yes; go on. Is that all?" And Helmar leant back in his chair, keenly listening for the sign from Naoum's agent.

"Yes, that is all. I offer you your release, with no possibility of re-capture or bodily harm, in return for which you will have to secure me immunity from the consequences of the part I have taken in the Rebellion. And a very fair offer I consider it, seeing that without my assistance you can never get away!"

As he ceased speaking George noted a slightly anxious expression on the man's face, but he said nothing. Waiting for a moment to see if Arden had anything further to say before he replied, he fancied he heard a light footfall outside the door. As his companion offered nothing further, he rose to his feet, and, with flashing eyes, gave him his answer.

"So, Mark Arden, you would again play the part of tempter, even in your last extremity, for notwithstanding your assertion to the contrary, I know that to be the state you are in. You cannot be other than a villain, you cannot even stand alone in your villainy, but must attempt to draw others into it. You try, with cunning purpose, to save yourself by forcing me, who have never done you harm, to become a participator in your crimes. You bid me lie to save you, you who have persecuted me from the moment of our meeting at Port Said until now, when you hold the threat of your vengeance over my head as an alternative to the non-compliance with your wishes. You dare to ask my assistance after the inhuman flogging you caused to be given me! You dare even to face me after such treatment! Liar! cheat! scoundrel that you are, I will be no party to your villainies! I have managed, with the help of those who are good and true, to save myself from the fate you would have wished for me. I have escaped from your toils thus far, I will now dare you to do your worst. If I am to die this time, it shall be fighting; no more imprisonment will I submit to, and least of all at your hands. Go!" he cried, his voice rising in anger, "go and call your guards! Bid them do the deed that you are too cowardly to perpetrate yourself! I care not that much for your power!" and he snapped his fingers in the air.

While he was still speaking Helmar had heard the scratching at the door—the signal was given. He now only waited for Arden to go and carry out his threat to call his guards. During his tirade the villain's face had shown the sneer so habitual to him, but, as Helmar's words gradually struck home, his expression changed to one of rage, and, as George ceased, Arden sprang up, and shaking his fist in his face, cried—

"You shall never live to see daylight! You have dared me to do this deed, and I will see that it is carried out! You have flouted my generosity and defied me, then your blood shall be on your own head," and striding to the wall, he disappeared through the secret door.

Helmar waited for the door to slam behind his retreating enemy, and then, dashing out into the passage, ran swiftly down it. A few moments sufficed to bring him to the door Naoum had told him of, and without hesitation he pushed it open and entered the room. As he passed in he heard the sound of the approaching guard, with Arden's voice excitedly urging them on.

He closed the door after him immediately, and as he did so he heard a voice close beside him from out of the darkness in which he found himself.

"Amman!" it said quickly.

"Allah is good!" replied George, without hesitation.

"And ever watchful!" was the instantaneous response.

Then, without another word, George felt himself seized by the arm, and unresistingly allowed himself to be led whither his guide pleased. A few steps, and the voice said—

"Bend low."

George complied, and passed through a narrow doorway. As he did so, he heard the door of the room he was leaving open and the guard rush in. The same instant the secret door, by which he was escaping, silently closed and the lock snapped to. No sooner had this occurred than his guide struck a light, and he found himself at the head of a flight of tiny, narrow, stone steps. Hurriedly they descended these, which seemed unending, and, before they reached the bottom, Helmar concluded they had passed down several hundreds of them.

The atmosphere became very damp and rank, all sound from above had died away, and for a while, at least, George thought they were safe. At the bottom they came to an earthen passage; along this they ran, the light from his guide's torch steering them through the many obstacles this apparently ancient and decayed passage presented. It was a weird flight, the ruddy glow on the broken and uneven walls and roof made the place very ghostly, while the flapping, whirring little bats shooting past their heads, often flying blindly into their faces, gave George a creepy sensation that was anything but pleasant.

At last they came to the end of the passage, and another flight of stone steps presented itself; this time they had to ascend. Half-way up they came to a solid stone wall, the sight of which filled George with dismay, but the guide, with perfectly assured action, stooped and in a moment touched a spring, and the solid mass revolved on a pivot, disclosing more steps. They passed through the opening, and the stone swung back into its original position as they hurried up the steps.

"We are quite safe from pursuit now," said the guide. "They cannot move that stone; only three persons know its secret—Naoum, Mariam, and I. We have nothing to fear until we reach the open air."

"When will that be?" asked Helmar, glad to think that they would at last leave this underground passage.

"At the top of these steps," replied the guide. "Then we shall have to reach a postern in the wall of the grounds. That is our greatest danger."

A few moments later they reached the end of the steps. A small wooden trap formed the outlet to this place. The guide raised it and looked out, then cautiously pushed his way up through it, and assisted Helmar to do the same; the trap was then replaced. As soon as he reached the open air George turned to see what outward sign of its presence the trap gave, and was surprised to see none. It was covered with a thin layer of soil, and, when replaced in its setting, a few scrapings of his guide's foot sufficed to obliterate all traces of it.

The place in which they now found themselves was the centre of a thick shrubbery, and before leaving it the guide went to reconnoitre. Presently he came back, having satisfied himself that the coast was clear.

"There is no sign of the guards," he explained, "but they cannot, I know, be far off. Come, we must run for it. There is no doubt that where they are, Naoum's men will be watching to help us."

Emerging from the thicket, the guide, followed by George, dashed across the open gardens towards another cluster of bushes. The night was one of supreme loveliness, the moon was up, and, though only in its first quarter, shone brilliantly. This was one of the dangers of their journey, but, even so, it assisted them as well, for if it was likely to betray the fugitives, it would also warn them of the approach of the enemy.

As they ran across the open, George could see the palace some distance off. The whole place was lit up, and the flashing lights warned him that his escape had brought about this activity so late at night.

At last they reached the thicket, and were congratulating themselves on their success when suddenly the guide seized Helmar's arm, and dragged him down under a bush.

"Hist! there is some one near us! Listen!"

George could not hear a sound, but the sharp ears of his guide had detected something which caused him alarm. Crouching down beneath the bush, they waited in silence; then, as nothing further occurred, the guide cautiously crept out and again listened. Apparently satisfied that the intruder, whoever he was, had gone, he signed to George, who immediately joined him.

Together they made their way stealthily to the outskirts of the bush, and prepared to make their final dash for the wall, which they now saw before them.

"It seems all right," said George in a whisper. "I can hear nothing."

"Yes," replied the guide slowly. "I think we are yet safe; Allah is with us. Yonder is the wall, and the gate is opposite us. The gate is an old one that has not been used for years. The guards will not think of it, for it has been heavily secured with bolts. But Naoum has had them removed to-night, and, in case of accidents, his men are stationed in hiding near by. Come!"

They were just about to rush across the intervening space to the wall, when, without the slightest warning, a small, dark figure sprang up at their very feet and barred the way. So sudden was the apparition that George almost fancied the figure had sprung out of the ground.

Quickly drawing back from the long, gleaming knife that flashed before their eyes, George and his guide stood for a second irresolute. The stranger at once spoke.

"Ha! you thought to escape, did you? You forgot that Abdu was still in Cairo. No, you don't, my friend; we will have you bowstrung at daylight."

Helmar made a dart at the little man. He saw in this one untoward incident the loss of all Naoum had planned for; he saw his liberty already slipping away from him, and the thoughts of Arden's villainous intent spurred him on. There was yet time; no alarm had been given. As he sprang forward, Abdu, with the agility of an ape, sprang out of reach, and, setting his fingers in his mouth, gave one prolonged whistle. Immediately it was answered in every direction.

All hope now seemed to be gone, and the two men prepared to fight to the end; his guide passed Helmar a long knife, and they backed up to a tree. Help, however, was nearer than they had expected.

Hardly had they taken up their position, when, with the sound of hurrying footsteps, came a long-drawn, hissing sound through the air. Before they had time to even conjecture its cause, they saw a knife strike Abdu in the breast, and he fell to the ground with a moan, the weapon still quivering in his body with the force of its flight.

Without waiting for anything further, the guide beckoned to his companion, and the two dashed for the wall. Directly they reached the open, they saw hurrying figures on all sides, who, the moment the fugitives appeared, set up a howl and gave chase.

George and his companion had a fair start of them, and, provided there was no delay at the postern, a chance of escape.

Running with all possible speed, they reached the gate in a few seconds—it was closed. Again their position seemed hopeless; but again, to their joy, Naoum's power was evidenced, and at their approach the gate was thrown open as if by magic.

Once outside, they found Belbeis waiting with three horses, ready saddled. They mounted in an instant, and, as the pursuing guards dashed through the gate, all three started away at a gallop.

CHAPTER XXVII

ACROSS THE DESERT

Casting one glance behind him George saw the crowd of soldiers pushing and jostling their way through the little gate. Those who had reached the outside opened fire on the fugitives, but their aim was hurried, and the darkness quickly hid the departing men from view. As a consequence their shots became erratic, whistling over the heads of George and his companions.

Belbeis drew alongside Helmar, his horse pulling at his bit and endeavouring to make a race of it.

"We have to skirt the south of the town," said he, when his horse had settled down. "It will be no use attempting to cut our way directly to the east; that course will take us through the heart of the city."

"Yes," replied George, as he leant well over his horse's neck to ease the animal, "that, of course, would entail much danger, but it would also save time."

"It would save time, I know," replied Belbeis, "but we could never get through, the town is alive with troops, and the alarm will have spread. No, my orders are to take this route, but even so, our danger will be great."

"How do you mean?" asked George, failing to understand the drift of his companion's thoughts.

"Our flight will cause us to circle the city," replied the Arab, "and, before we can strike the desert road to the east, we shall have to reach the eastern limits of the town. The officer Arden, who is cunning, and will understand that we are making for the British camp, will probably send out a party of horsemen in that direction to wait for us."

"Ah, I see, while we are making a circle they will take a short cut across and intercept us," answered George; "but I presume you have thought this out before?" he hazarded.

"Yes," replied Belbeis.

Then he turned to the man who had guided George from the palace, and held a low conversation with him. Presently he turned again to Helmar.

"With Allah's help we shall avoid them by striking the road at another point," he said, "but the chance is small, and we shall probably have to fight sooner or later; if they do not catch us on the outskirts of the city they will very likely do so where we cross the road to Suez, and before we reach the desert trail for Tel-el-Kebir."

The prospect was not alluring; Helmar was unarmed except for the knife his guide had given him, and this would be of little use to him. Belbeis seemed in no way disturbed, and kept his horse going steadily on, while his ever alert eye glanced from side to side of the route, watching for the slightest sign of anything that could obstruct their flight.

They were rapidly nearing the south-western limits of the city, and the streets were becoming more open. The fresh night air stimulated their spirited Arab horses, and they raced along the silent roads at a speed that would have made it difficult for Arden's men to overtake. As they reached the open, Belbeis turned his horse to the south-east, and, making a big *détour*, keeping the city in sight to their left, the three travelled rapidly over the open plain. They reached the railway in safety, and crossed it without an encounter of any sort; then, drawing rein, they breathed their horses, watching for daylight before beginning the great effort of their escape.

"Our horses must be fresh and ready for a hard gallop," said Belbeis, in answer to a question from Helmar. "If we are to be pursued, of which there is not the least doubt, we shall sight the enemy very soon. When that comes to pass we must try a race, and, if we fail to get away," he shrugged his shoulders, "well—then we will fight."

"Yes, but how?" asked George. "We have no arms, at least I have none."

"You have not yet examined your saddle," replied Belbeis, with a smile. "Naoum thinks of everything. You are equipped with pistols and a carbine, and your magazine is filled with cartridges."

The darkness had hidden these things from George's notice, but now, reaching his hand down beside his horse's flanks, he realized the truth of his companion's words, and a feeling of relief passed over him, as he thought that, at least, he could now give a good account of himself.

The slowness of their pace seemed to Helmar unnecessary. He turned to Belbeis, and for a moment watched his quick sharp face as it turned in this direction and that, nothing in sight escaping his eagle glance. A smile spread over George's face as he noticed the keen reliant countenance beside him.

"Upon my word, Belbeis, I really believe that you are hoping for a brush with the enemy, notwithstanding the size of our party."

Belbeis did not reply for a moment, then rousing himself as if from deep thought, said—

"I have many scores to wipe out with the officer Arden, and should be glad of a chance to do so;" then with a backward jerk of the head, in the direction of the guide riding behind, "You do not know that we have a man with us who is the greatest renowned fighter in the Egyptian army. He also hates this Arden."

"Good," replied George. "As far as I can see we are all of the same mind on that point, but, to satisfy our own personal grievances, we must not forget that we have a most important mission to fulfil. Cairo must be saved, no matter how much we want to pay off old scores."

Day was now beginning to break, and the first streaks of dawn were already shooting across the eastern horizon; in a few minutes the light would have spread, with the rapidity only to be found in tropical climates, and the morning twilight passed. The desert air was delicious as it swept with the light morning breeze into the faces of the fugitives, and though for only a period of short duration, was more than refreshing to both horse and rider. Soon the scorching sun would rise, and the stifling, burning, parching heat would take the place of this balmy atmosphere; then the endurance of the travellers would be taxed, and all their fortitude be required to reach their destination.

The city was still in sight, but rapidly sinking from view. George reckoned that they had already covered eight or nine miles.

"How far off is the road to Suez, where you expect to meet Arden's men?" asked our hero.

"Eight miles further on. We could strike the road sooner, but it is not good," Belbeis answered; "there is time enough."

"And how far is it to Tel-el-Kebir?"

"Fifty miles as the bird flies," he answered. "The way we go, about sixty. Ah!"

The exclamation was caused by the sight of a small cloud of dust to their left front. It was far in the distance, but in the broadening daylight plainly visible to the keen-eyed Belbeis. Pointing in the direction he drew Helmar's attention.

"See, there go the officer Arden's men. They are riding hard to overtake those who are behind them," he said, smiling grimly. "Their horses will soon tire. Good!"

George looked in the direction his companion indicated. No horsemen were visible to him, but the cloud of dust rolling along over the sandy plain showed the course that the party were taking.

"We will now change our course," said Belbeis, turning his horse's head towards the south as he spoke. "Those scoundrels will ride on to the first water and wait for us; we must get round them."

All three set off at a good pace, and soon the cloud of dust was lost to view. On they rode with all possible speed; their horses beginning to feel the effects of the now risen sun, settled down to a steady canter. The heat was already intense, and the barren, uninviting plain that lay before them seemed interminable. When they had made sufficient southing, Belbeis again headed for the Suez road, and after another two hours' ride this was reached without accident.

"They have gone further than I expected," said Belbeis, as he looked in vain for the pursuers. "See, the hoof-marks on the road are quite plain, they did not stop at the water."

He shook his head as he spoke, and his face assumed an anxious expression.

"And what of it?" said George. "As I understand we do not go by this road, there should be less to fear."

"No, no, not less," said Belbeis, "but more. The party are scouring this road only; there are evidently others in search of us; some have doubtless gone to the north."

The guide approached.

"It is plain as the daylight," he said. "Word has gone forward, and the soldiers between Cairo and Tel-el-Kebir will be warned, and our course will be watched by patrols the whole way. Allah, but we shall be kept busy," and the man grinned at the thought of fighting ahead of him.

"Yes, there are soldiers in El Menair, Abu Zabel, El Khankah, and many other villages along the fresh-water canal," said Belbeis. "They will all be warned, and the country will be scoured. We must not fear, but ride hard, keeping as far in the desert as possible."

They now pushed on again, and in a short time the disused railroad between Cairo and Suez was reached. Here the horses were watered and rested, whilst the riders partook of breakfast. After an hour's rest they again resumed their journey. The caravan road to Tel-el-Mahuta was reached, and for the present adopted as the best course to pursue.

This journey was very different from the one George had made to Damanhour; there it was through more or less cultivated land, and was done in the cool of the day, whilst now they were travelling rapidly, with the sun pouring its intense rays down upon them as they traversed the shelterless desert. It taxed the endurance of all three men to the utmost, the Arabs, who were used to the scorching sun, feeling it severely; so what must it have meant to Helmar, who had recently recovered from an illness? Still, with a determination to see his work through, he never for one minute allowed his spirits to flag. He had a duty to perform, and, if for nothing else, his gratitude to Naoum would not allow him to succumb to the trials of his undertaking. Belbeis and the guide rode on in stolid silence, evidently with no intention of allowing the effort of speech to increase their thirst. George, following their example, let his thoughts dwell upon the cool forests in the land of his birth, and longed ardently for a few minutes' shelter beneath one of the great elm trees that grew in the grounds of his father's house. The time passed on, and mile after mile was covered, until shortly after noon a watering-place was at length reached. Another short halt was called, and a rest taken before the last stage of the journey was begun. So far, only distant clouds of dust warned the travellers of the nearness of their enemies, and with the subtle intuition of Belbeis, they were skilfully avoided. Another twenty-five miles only remained before Tel-el-Kebir would be reached, and already Helmar was promising himself success.

Suddenly Belbeis roused himself from a light doze he had fallen into, and, glancing quickly round the horizon, called on his companions to saddle up their horses again.

"I see a party approaching from the north; we must hasten! I fear we shall be observed," he said, as he sprang into the saddle.

George and the guide quickly followed his example, and the party moved off with all possible haste. They had scarcely gone a quarter of a mile when George drew Belbeis's attention to another cloud of dust.

"See," he said, "there are some more ahead of us! It looks as if we are hemmed in on all sides. We cannot retreat—our horses will not last."

Belbeis gazed at the cloud George had drawn attention to, and then anxiously glanced at the one to the north.

"They are both coming towards us, but it looks as if some conveyance were with the one you have pointed out."

"Ah," said George, "and if so, what do you expect?"

"That I cannot say," replied Belbeis. "It might be one of Arabi's patrols, or it might be—no, it cannot be British, their patrols would never venture so far into the enemy's country, unless, of course, it was in a strong force, and that does not seem to me the case."

"Anyway," said George in determined tones, "we have come so far, there must be no turning back—we'll make a fight for it. They are not going to take me back to Cairo alive."

"Set your mind at rest on that point," said Belbeis quietly; "they will not attempt to do so. The moment we are seen they will swoop down on us and attempt to cut us up. Well, let them come!"

"So say I," answered Helmar, his eyes glittering with excitement as he spoke.

The rolls of dust were coming nearer; the party to the north was the one that occupied the fugitives' attention most. Already the figures of at least twenty horsemen were plainly discernible; the other cloud was still in the far distance.

"They must have already seen us," said Belbeis, with his eyes fixed on the northern party, "and cannot be more than two miles off. Come along, let us give them a race!"

As he spoke all three men urged their horses on, but the approaching party were travelling more rapidly than they, and every minute seemed to be coming nearer. At last Helmar said—

"Look here, Belbeis, it seems to me we are uselessly distressing our horses; let us slow down and wait until they come up. We may as well fight now as later on."

"Good," answered Belbeis, his eyes sparkling with pleasure; "my duty is to convey you safely to Tel-el-Kebir, and I thought there might just be a chance of avoiding the risk of a fight; but it is not to my liking, I would sooner fight."

"We shall get all we want of it, I expect," said Helmar, drawing his carbine from its bucket and examining the breech.

Since they had drawn rein the party of approaching horsemen neared rapidly; as they galloped over the plain George counted at least twenty mounted men, headed by one who rode by himself. The companions determined to save their ammunition until the enemy was at short range, which did not take long, the distance decreasing every instant.

"Our horses will stand fire," said Belbeis, "they are well trained, and we can shoot from their backs."

"Good," said George, "that will be in our favour. Now wait till I give the word to fire, and then take a steady aim at their horses."

The fight in the desert. p. 319

The three men sat keenly watching the advancing soldiers. They were plainly visible, and the uniform told our hero that they were Arabi's men. In five minutes' time Helmar turned with an exclamation to his companions.

"A white man leads them!" he cried, in excited tones. "Who can it be?"

Belbeis narrowly scrutinized the leader, then turning to George smiled grimly into his face.

"You will have the opportunity you wish for. Old scores can be wiped off before we are taken. The leader is your old enemy, the officer Arden himself!"

The foremost of the party were within eight hundred yards of the waiting trio; Helmar gave the word "Ready," and taking a careful aim, his companions waited for the word to fire. It came short and sharp, and the three carbines rang out. When the smoke had cleared away three horses were plunging, and a moment after, fell headlong to the ground. This for a moment checked the advance of the rebels, and Helmar saw several of them dismount.

Out rang the enemy's rifles, and a heavy volley of lead flew round the heads of the fugitives. Helmar gave the word, and again the carbines rang out, simultaneously several of the rebels' horses ran off riderless. The fight now waxed furious; the deadly aim of Helmar and his two friends was telling rapidly, whilst the rebels were shooting wildly.

This seemed to alarm Arden, and he immediately adopted different tactics. Instead of wasting his shot, he decided to advance, and galloped forward as hard as his horse could carry him, his men following his example. Helmar's party fired as rapidly as they could work the levers of their magazines; each one of that devoted little band realized that they must soon be overwhelmed, but still determined to sell their lives as dearly as possible.

Their rapid fire into the advancing enemy told its tale, and many saddles were emptied, but they were now nearly at close quarters. Helmar and his men clubbed their rifles and waited.

George's horse was struck and fell; its master extricated himself, and stood up ready to face the enemy to the last. On they came, tearing down on the little party like hawks on their prey. The suspense while they covered the intervening space, although only for a few seconds, was terrible and seemed as if it would never end.

Suddenly a rattle of musketry from behind drew Helmar's attention. Turning his head quickly he saw a large party of men approaching at a gallop, in skirmishing order. A Maxim gun was in position and belching forth a hail of lead.

There were others who had seen the same thing, and felt the deadly effects of the relentless Maxim. Arden pulled his horse up nearly on to its haunches. George, whose attention was again turned to the rebels, saw his old enemy reel in his saddle; then, throwing up his arms, he shouted to his men—

"Back, back for your lives!" and fell headlong to the ground.

CHAPTER XXVIII

MEETING OF FRIENDS AND CAPTURE OF ARDEN

The murderous fire continued, and the rebels, urged by their leader's words, turned like a flock of sheep worried by the herder's dog and fled precipitately; not one of that cowardly band waited to help their fallen chief, not one of them had any thought other than to save his own skin. Those who still remained in possession of their horses, scattered and galloped away in every direction, while those on foot threw down their arms and ran for their lives, pursued by the skirmishers who came galloping across the sandy plains.

George and his companions took in the situation at a glance, the uniform of the new-comers told its tale—the British soldiers had come to their rescue.

Helmar had no time to realize what this timely succour meant to him, and, for the present, he watched with interest the panic-stricken retreating rabble. He saw the sturdy horses of the honest English soldiers overtake one by one the flying Arabs, until at last the whole of that murderous band was in the hands of his friends. While he was still watching this interesting sight, three men rode up from behind, and a voice, sharp and clear, in tones of command addressed him.

"Who are you, and what does all this mean?"

George turned at the words and glanced at the man who had uttered them. He was tall and slight, with a thin aristocratic face, and, by the stars on his shoulders, Helmar knew him to be the officer in command. Without replying to the question, he said with heartfelt fervour—

"Thank God you came in time, you have accomplished more than you know of, sir!"

"Yes, yes, but answer my questions," the officer said impatiently.

"I am an escaped prisoner from Cairo, and bear dispatches of the utmost importance; on their instant delivery to the Commander of the British forces depends the lives of thousands."

"Eh, what?" ejaculated the officer. "How do you mean?"

Helmar then explained who and what he was, how he had escaped, and the facts of the mission on which he was now embarked. The officer listened with interest to all he had to say, the varying expression of his face betraying his feelings of surprise and disgust, horror and admiration as his story proceeded. At its conclusion he got off his horse and shook Helmar heartily by the hand.

"You are a brave man, and if the plot to destroy Cairo is as you say, and you bear the proofs with you, should we be in time to save it, you will have earned the nation's thanks, and any reward that Her Gracious Majesty can confer on you. But come, there is no time to be lost, we must return at once to camp."

As he finished speaking he turned away to give some orders; during the conversation the men not otherwise engaged had clustered round, standing at a respectful distance from their chief, eyeing George and his companions with curiosity. The moment the officer had moved off, one of the men rode up to George, and, glancing for one moment at the weary face before him, sprang from his horse and grasped him by the arm.

"What, George!" he cried. "I thought you were dead!" and the eager young face was wreathed in smiles, his eyes looking suspiciously watery as he gazed into the worn face of his friend.

"Charlie! Well, I never!" cried George in delight, as he grasped the fact it was his friend Osterberg in front of him. "Why, what are you doing here? This is nothing to do with banks!"

"And to think I should be with the party who has saved you," Osterberg rattled on, ignoring his friend's questions. "But, George, you are looking ill and not like your old self. What's the matter?"

Then Helmar went again through his story, and Osterberg, when it was finished, in his turn told him that the peaceful life at the bank had not suited him, so he had thrown it up and got employment with the British army, attached to the Engineers.

Before the two young men had finished exchanging confidences, the officer, having arranged the disposition of the prisoners, again approached. Seeing Osterberg in close conversation with his friend, he looked from one to the other, as if for explanation. Osterberg, understanding the look, promptly spoke up.

"Helmar is a very old friend of mine, sir. We came to this country together— in fact, we left the University for that purpose. I remember him being captured near Kafr Dowar; he was on patrol with an officer of the Engineers."

"Ah," replied the officer, "that is all the better. But we must start at once. You," he went on, turning to George, "had better take one of your men's horses and ride with me in advance of the rest of the party."

He was about to turn to his horse when, seeing Osterberg's speaking glance, he smiled and continued—

"Yes, you can accompany us, but hurry up!"

The young man, delighted at this extreme mark of favour, jumped on his horse, and Helmar, in obedience to the officer's instructions, took Belbeis's horse.

"It is good," said the Arab, "the master's work is now done. Be careful of him," he went on, handing over his sleek Arab charger. "He is Naoum's favourite steed, and will never fail you. I regret that he is wounded."

Belbeis and the guide now remained with the main body, whilst Helmar and Osterberg joined the officer, who, accompanied by an escort of four men, started at once for head-quarters.

"By the way," said the officer, after they had ridden a little way in silence, "the man who was leading the rebels is a prisoner—he is a white man. Do you know anything of him?"

George glanced at his young friend riding beside him.

"Do I know him, sir?" he said, repeating his superior's question. "There is a story of villainous treachery surrounding that man that will sound to you like fiction; if it will not weary you, as we have yet some miles to travel, I will tell it."

The officer expressed his willingness to listen, and George recounted to him all that had occurred from the time the three companions left Germany. The latter part of the story was new to Osterberg, and he exclaimed in horror and indignation at the villainous way Arden had persecuted his friend. When our hero came to the flogging, the officer's face became hard and stern.

"And you still bear the marks of that inhuman treatment?" he asked, when George had finished.

"That I do, sir," he replied, with a look of chagrin on his face. "My back is scored and lined like a ploughed field. I shall carry the marks to my grave, but, even so, I regret not one moment of the agony I have gone through so long as Cairo and the many hundreds of true men and women in it are saved. Had I not gone through this, had I not been a prisoner, I do not know who Naoum could have sent with the news. It is an ill wind that blows no one any good. Let us hope I am in time."

George's calm words, his lack of resentment at the treatment he had received from Mark Arden, touched a deep chord in the officer's nature, but he wondered at George's apparent unconcern.

"I should think considerably more of vengeance than you appear to do," he said, with an ominous glitter in his eyes; "prisoners, when left to the authorities, do not always get what they deserve."

"That may be, sir," replied George, "but time will show. Arden has lost his chance, the chance he wanted, of getting out of the country with his ill-gotten gains, therefore his rascality has brought him but little fortune. To my mind that is sufficient punishment, and, after all, revenge is but a small thing—he will be punished in some way."

"'m!" said the officer doubtfully. "I should want something more definite."

By sundown the British camp was in view, and, to Helmar at least, never was any sight more welcome. The heat of the sun, the excitement of the encounter with the rebels, the strain of the sixty miles' ride, all combined to weary him both mentally and bodily. The thought that after months of degrading captivity he was at last free was scarcely sufficient to raise his flagging spirits. As he saw the miles of white lines of tents stretching before him, a feeling of contentment gradually crept over his tired body, but there was none of the exhilaration he had anticipated; all he longed for was to fling himself from his horse and rest his weary bones. The watchful eye of young Osterberg had noted all this, and he anxiously looked over towards the camp as if expecting to see his friend give in before he reached it.

George, however, had no such intention; the sufferings he had gone through had hardened him to trials such as this, and though enthusiasm had gone from him to a great extent, he was nevertheless determined to see his duty through to the bitter end.

At last the outposts were reached, the countersign given, and they passed down the endless lines towards the Commander's quarters. After what seemed an interminable time, their destination was reached and the little party dismounted. Several *aides-de-camp* were about, and to one of these the officer explained his business; George, too weary to stand, seated himself on the ground and waited while the *aide* delivered the officer's message. In a few moments the man returned and said a few words to the officer and then returned to the hut. The officer approached Helmar.

"Brace yourself up," he said, in kindly tones, as he noted the weary expression of the young man's face. "Your work will soon be over, and you can take all the rest you need. You must come with me and see the Commander-in-Chief."

George sprang to his feet and followed his guide. He passed through a number of officers, who eyed his dishevelled appearance with curiosity, but they all made way for him, and at last he stood in the presence of the great man. Helmar waited in respectful silence until the Chief looked up. He found himself in the presence of a thin, wiry-looking man, with iron-grey hair, and a keen, sharp face, the aquiline features of which were lined from exposure and care. He spoke abruptly, and in the usual tone of an English military man.

"You have matters of importance to communicate?"

Helmar fumbled in his pocket, and produced the bundle of papers Naoum had given him.

"Yes, sir; these papers are the proof of what I have to say," he said, laying them on the desk in front of the Commander-in-Chief.

The officer unfastened them and glanced rapidly over the contents, then looked up.

"Well, what is your story?" he said, fixing a penetrating gaze on the young man's weary face.

George told his story as briefly as possible. During its narration the Commander kept his eyes on the papers, glancing up every now and then as something more astounding than the rest attracted his attention. When the story was finished he carefully folded up the documents and put them in a drawer.

"Thank you, my man," he said, in a dispassionate voice. "You have done well. The news you have brought through is of the utmost importance. Action will be taken at once. Your name is George Helmar, is it not?—good," he went on, writing it down on a tablet, then turning to the officer at his side, said, "Let this man be provided with quarters, and every comfort given him. This rebel officer, Captain, I believe you said was a prisoner. I shall want to see him in the morning. Er—that will do."

George knew this was his dismissal; but he hesitated as he turned to go, and the Commander was quick to notice it.

"Well, what is it?" he asked, without raising his eyes from his work in front of him. "Have you anything else to say?"

"Excuse me, sir, I do not wish to trouble you too much; but if any one is sent to Cairo," said Helmar, diffidently, "I should like to be allowed to go too—I know the best route to take."

The officer looked up, and scanned the drawn face before him.

"You look tired, my man, and I do not wonder at it. You must rest; but your orders will be given you later on. You can go now."

George was compelled to leave, and he did so reluctantly. He felt it was hard if a relieving force should be sent, and he not allowed to accompany it after all he had done. Still, he knew this man's word was absolute, and he must abide by his decision whatever it might be. With keen disappointment he left the room, accompanied by the officer who had been directed to see about quarters for him.

Once outside he was handed over to a subordinate, who carried him off to his tent. The man was a sergeant, and a good sort. After traversing the lines for a few minutes they stopped outside one of the many white tents.

"It's very late to see about quarters for you," said the man, "but this is my tent, and if you would like to share it with me to-night, I will see that you are made comfortable to-morrow. You'll find they are not so bad," he went on, throwing back the fastenings as he spoke. "There are plenty of blankets and some good grub."

"I shall be delighted," replied George quickly; "only let me sleep, the bare ground will do as well as anything else."

"Ah, well, you'll find my quarters better than that," said the sergeant, with a laugh, leading the way in.

Inside, George found as the man had said, and he quickly had a comfortable bed made on the ground.

"There you are, fling yourself on that while I go and get you some supper. Your horse has been put on our lines, and the men have attended to him, so you needn't bother. Your saddle shall be brought here."

The sergeant went out, and soon returned with the promised supper, and George fell to with an appetite in no way impaired by his fatigue. While he was in the middle of it, chatting away to his companion, an orderly strode up, and, putting his head in the doorway, said—

"Does the man named Helmar stop here, Sergeant Smith?"

"Yes, here I am," answered George, before the sergeant could reply.

"Good!" said the orderly. "You will hold yourself in readiness to leave at daybreak on special duty."

"Hurrah!" exclaimed Helmar. "I'm going to Cairo after all!"

"You, Sergeant," continued the man, "will have other work to do. The general assembly will sound at ten-thirty. Arabi's going to get fits to-night!" he added, as he went off, laughing.

CHAPTER XXIX

TO DEATH OR GLORY

History chronicles the events that followed on the night Helmar arrived at the British camp outside Tel-el-Kebir. It is therefore unnecessary to give here the details of how on that night, the thirteenth of September, the camp was struck at Kassassin Lock, with a few men only left to hold the place; how the whole force, consisting of about 14,000 men, marched out in the dead of night towards Arabi's entrenchments; how they bivouacked within a short distance of them until nearly morning; and how at length the order for attack was passed along the line, and the rebels, taken by surprise, utterly routed by this daring manœuvre. There is no need to dilate on the gallantry displayed by the Highland Brigade and the Royal Irish regiment on that occasion, all this is known with the rest of the history of the British nation's many great victories, and will remain until the day of doom graven on the pages of the military achievements of the English race.

But the events that resulted after the news of Arabi's intention to burn the beautiful city of Cairo to the ground reached the Commander-in-Chief, concern us most, for in their development Helmar was largely concerned.

After the orderly had warned him to hold himself in readiness, George, with the help of his new-found friend Sergeant Smith, set about collecting his accoutrements. His saddle was brought to the tent, and his horse placed where he could easily find it; this done, he lay down to snatch all the rest he could.

So weary and tired was he, that he failed to hear his companion leave the tent, when the troops moved to the attack. There was no noise in their leaving, and even had there been, it is doubtful if it would have roused him, so worn out was he with his day's work.

Towards daybreak he was awakened by one of the men left in camp, and he rose refreshed and ready for the journey that lay before him. A few minutes sufficed to devour a few mouthfuls of food, and then he saddled up his horse; by the time this was over he saw a large body of mounted men already assembling further down the lines. Mounting his sleek Arab steed he rode hastily over to them, and in a few minutes the whole body moved off.

As far as he could see there were about nine hundred men of various regiments, all mounted on horses in the pink of condition, the men themselves looking fit to undertake any work, no matter how arduous.

Before the party had proceeded far, an officer rode up to George.

"You are the man who came from Cairo yesterday, are you not?" he said, as he drew rein alongside.

"Yes, sir," George replied.

"Very well, your two men are on ahead acting as guides with the advanced guard; you will ride on and join them, and act under the orders of the officer in command of that party. Hurry up!"

Helmar at once started off, and in a few minutes caught them up. He found Belbeis and his guide of the previous day riding on the lead with the officer. Reporting himself, he was told to ride with them, and the journey began in deadly earnest.

"We are bound for Cairo," the officer explained, "and must reach there in the quickest possible time."

"Yes, sir; and which route is to be taken?" asked George.

"Via a little village called Belbeis, where we shall rest for the night."

"Belbeis," exclaimed Helmar, looking over at his faithful guide.

"Yes," replied the Arab, "I know, it is my native place, the village from which I take my name. It is on the fresh-water canal. We must take the desert route, and so avoid Arabi's entrenchments."

Turning to the officer, George interpreted what Belbeis had said, adding that he thought the suggestion the guide had made was the best plan possible.

"Very well, but there must be no mistake, for our work will admit of no delay. The man can be trusted, I hope."

"Without doubt," said George, at once. "He is absolutely faithful and trustworthy."

Considering the large number of men, the journey was most rapid, and, under the guidance of the trusty Belbeis, his native village was reached at sundown in safety. The journey was made in the heat of the day, and, notwithstanding the fortitude of both horses and men, was very trying. Even the guides and Helmar, after their terrible journey of the day before, were thankful when the little village was sighted, and the order for the bivouac was given. Many of the men lay down where they off-saddled, tired and worn out, and, after a frugal meal, slept where they were, without covering, and with only their saddles for a pillow.

George, after the wants of his horse were attended to, glanced round the scattered soldiers, and noting the worn-out condition, registered a mental wager that many of them would never be able to last till Cairo was reached.

At present only the shortest part of the journey had been traversed, how would they feel at the end of the next forty miles?

With many misgivings he found his two friends, and communicated his fears to them.

"Seems to me," he said, seating himself beside Belbeis, "many of those fellows will never reach Cairo."

Belbeis was thoughtfully smoking, squatting on his haunches in true Oriental fashion, his water-bottle lying beside him, and the remains of his supper scattered about on the ground; the other guide sat facing him.

"The children of the West," replied Belbeis, watching the puffs of smoke as he emitted them from his mouth, "are not used to the Egyptian sun and the sand of the desert. It is hard for them, but they are good men, their hearts are big. The horses are what I most fear."

"Yes," put in the guide, "the Arab courser is as the wind in the desert, he never tires, and nothing can travel like him."

"You are right," said George, gazing admiringly at his own mount, calmly feeding a little way off. "The desert has no terrors for the fleet-footed Arab, but I doubt if he would do as well in my country."

There was a short pause, and then Belbeis again spoke.

"What are we going to do when we reach Cairo?" he asked. "The way is long and we are but few."

"Going to take the city, I expect," replied George.

"But we are not a thousand fighting men," exclaimed the cautious Arab, "and there are at least twenty thousand rebels in the city. Poof, the English are mad, we shall die."

George burst into a laugh, and Belbeis looked disgusted.

"You do not understand our people, there is some trick on hand, they know their business; besides, if it came to a fight with such a number, I would not wager on the rebels."

"Allah is great," replied Belbeis solemnly, "His ways are mysterious, but I cannot understand."

"No," said George, smiling, "neither will Arabi, he does not know the sons of the West. They will dare anything."

"Allah is powerful," replied Belbeis, "and we are but His children."

Again a silence fell upon the little party, a silence only broken by the sound of the resting horses' movements and the buzzing of insects now abroad in the cooling air. On all sides, as far as the eye could reach in the darkening night, soldiers lay about in various attitudes of rest. Here and there, though infrequently, small groups sat smoking and talking, but mostly the weary men slept. One or two sentries, doing short reliefs of watch, hovered about, leaning for support on their carbines.

The scene was an impressive one, and, to Belbeis, who understood not the daring of a British soldier, it seemed a pity that so many men should be doomed on such a futile effort as Helmar had said. George sat scanning the scene with very different feelings. He knew the subtle strategy of the soldiers, and was convinced that the task in hand must be more than possible, or this small force would never have been sent on such an errand.

At last George and the guides curled themselves up and slept, the problem of the work in hand no longer interesting them. At last, after a period that seemed all too short to the weary men, came the first streak of dawn, and the guard walked among them, rousing each as he went for the beginning of the last stage of the journey. In a few minutes all was bustle and activity. The neigh of horses, the clatter of accoutrements, the voices of the men, resounded on all sides. With the trained discipline of soldiers, everything was in readiness before daylight, and, as the dawn began to broaden, the journey was resumed. On they rode, mile after mile, hour after hour; daylight gave place to sunrise, and with it the heat of the day once more brought streaming perspiration out on the horses and riders. None but those accustomed to the terrible heat of the tropics could understand the terrors of that journey to the Western-bred men. Every minute, every second of the day was a constant agony to man and beast, but still with indomitable pluck they kept on. At mid-day a halt was made and food partaken of; here many of the men had to fall out, their horses too exhausted to go further. The weary faces of the men told their tale, and the officer anxiously scanned the ranks in fear lest his troop would not be able to reach their destination.

It was an anxious time for the man in command, but, with set purpose and grim determination, no thought of retreat entered his mind. So long as horse could travel, so long must the journey be kept up.

George's horse seemed indefatigable, and still, at every halt, champed impatiently at its bit. Some of its spirit seemed to be communicated to its rider, for though absolutely worn out, he anxiously sought to hurry on.

This part of the route was less barren and dreary; their course lay fairly near the canal, and signs of agriculture appeared at intervals.

Again, with diminished ranks, the order of march was resumed. Horses floundered in the sand, too weary to lift their feet, others with drooping heads marched along in a dogged determined sort of way that betokened their condition. It was terrible.

The officer riding beside Helmar was well mounted, and his horse as yet showed no signs of giving in. Observing the freshness of Helmar's mount, he said—

"Your horse stands it well."

"Yes, he is one of the purest Arabs. He travelled over this journey the day before yesterday, and he is fresher now than any of them," replied George with pride.

"Marvellous! marvellous!" replied the officer. "What we shall be like when we reach Cairo I shudder to think; this journey is awful."

"The ranks are thinning," said Helmar, "our advanced guard can scarcely keep their seats. Heaven only knows what will happen if we are attacked!"

"Let us trust that nothing of the sort occurs," answered the officer. "Even as it is, I do not see that we can do anything to-night."

"What! is the attack on the city to be carried out to-night?" exclaimed George, incredulously.

"Those are the orders," replied his superior, simply.

George relapsed into silence, wondering even more at the ways of the Commander.

The sun was sinking, and they were now nearing their destination. Already in the distant haze they could see some of the spires of the city they were to take. Each man of that devoted little band realized that the critical moment was nearing, and each man braced himself for the effort that would be expected of him. The nightmare of it all was not yet passed, and the last stage, they knew, would be worse than its predecessors.

Six miles from the city a halt was made. The sun had already set, and the party that, at the start, had been a smart, compact, and fit body of troops, now trailed up to the halting-place in a scattered line, horses hardly able to put one foot before another, the men reeling and fainting with exhaustion in the saddle. It was a despairing sight to the officers in charge, with work to carry out that now seemed hopeless.

As each man rode up, the last flicker of discipline asserted itself, and they closed up their ranks in one long line, whilst the officer rode down inspecting them. After that the horses were off-saddled.

After a rest of two hours had been given, the men were called up and their Chief addressed them.

"It is," he said, "absolutely necessary to ride into Cairo to-night! Many men and horses are not fit to move, but the orders must be obeyed. I shall leave it to you yourselves to decide who can travel on. The officers will inspect their troops and assist in that decision."

After this, weary as they were, volunteers were not wanting, to a man they were all anxious; but on inspection it was found that one hundred and fifty only out of that nine hundred were fit to proceed further, and so it was decided that the gallant Major Watson should march in at the head of this infinitesimal force and demand the surrender of twenty thousand armed rebels.

The task seemed utter madness, even to Helmar, whose adventurous spirit had made him one of the first to volunteer. Directly darkness closed in, the advance was made; one hundred and fifty tired but desperate men started on that fateful mission. George never expected to come out of it alive, and many and varied were his thoughts as the little band made its way towards the town. The one thing that he regretted most was, that he had not been able to see Osterberg before he left Tel-el-Kebir. He had been too tired to seek him out after his interview with the Commander-in-Chief in that labyrinth of tents, and by the time he left in the morning, doubtless the boy was with the fighting line at the trenches. Well, it couldn't be helped now; if George survived this night's work he would see him again some day, and if not——

Here his reflections were broken in upon by the word being passed down the line to urge their horses into a trot, but with strict injunctions to keep together. Helmar was still on the lead, accompanied by Belbeis and the officer.

"Four more miles and then we are in for it," said the latter, as his horse quickened his pace.

"Yes, sir," replied Helmar, "four more miles and then—Death or Glory."

"They rode straight for the citadel." p. 344

Nothing further was said, and in grim silence the march was continued. Major Watson now headed his men, and the outskirts of the town were reached. Without hesitation the gallant Major rode straight for the citadel. The clatter of mounted men in the streets alarmed the natives, but the darkness kept the numbers of the invaders covered, and it was believed the British were upon them. Hundreds flung down their arms and grovelled in the dust, as this victorious little army galloped on. At length the city itself was entered. Each man of the one hundred and fifty sat on his horse with his arms ready for use, prepared to fight to the last. But no opposition was offered them.

Natives kept behind their doors in fear and trembling, thinking that the rest of the army was following, ready to adopt their own barbarous methods and massacre every one they came across. Panic had seized the city, and every one waited the catastrophe that each felt was about to fall upon them.

On rode Major Watson towards the eminence on which stood the citadel; as they came to it the poor worn beasts could scarcely carry themselves up the hill. By superhuman efforts at last the gates were reached. The crucial point had come.

CHAPTER XXX

CAIRO SAVED AND HELMAR'S REWARD

As they arrived outside the citadel of Mehemet Ali, Helmar looked up at the frowning wall of the great fortress. Here he was at the place where he had received his inhuman treatment; this was the place where he had been found by his friends and rescued when in dire extremity. Under what different circumstances was he now returning to it. No longer to be a place for the perpetration of atrocities, they had come to demand its surrender, and, with that surrender, the capitulation of the town. And how was this done? By the daring of a devoted little band of a hundred and fifty exhausted, though determined, men!

Twenty thousand fanatics in the city and ten thousand troops in the citadel— was there any limit to the daring recklessness of the British soldier? After this exhibition, George thought not, and waited to see what next this brave little band was capable of.

During the short pause while the garrison was being summoned, the men, with stern, set faces, gripped their weapons ready for any emergency. As Helmar glanced at the faces of those nearest him, the expressions he saw written upon their features put all doubt as to their intentions at rest. He had said truly on his journey to Cairo that they were marching to "Death or Glory!"

At last the gates were flung open and Major Watson's summons answered. The troops marched in, and to their utter surprise found the commandant willing and ready to yield up his sword. After that, the whole of the garrison laid down their arms like a flock of sheep. Without a blow, without any resistance whatsoever, one hundred and fifty thirsty, hungry, exhausted men had captured Cairo, with its enormous garrison of nearly thirty thousand rebels! The feat was one unprecedented in history, and though it reflected little credit on the sagacity of the leaders of the campaign, it at least was a tribute to the commander's knowledge of the peculiarities of the Eastern character, and the reckless devotion to duty of the men under his command.

The work of receiving the submission of the troops seemed as if it would never end, and Helmar, wearied beyond words with the work, felt that he was at the limit of bodily endurance. At last it was over, and he was at liberty to take his rest.

He sought out his two friends, who had been occupied in a similar manner, and the three men set out in search of quarters. There was no fear from attack by the populace. Terror had been struck into their hearts, and they hugged their dwellings, fearful that to show their faces abroad would bring down summary chastisement upon them.

With this knowledge of security, they prepared to take their hard-earned rest. After a little trouble, quarters were found.

"Well, Belbeis," exclaimed Helmar, with a triumphant smile, "what do you think of it now? We are not going to die, as you prophesied!"

Belbeis seated himself preparatory to enjoying a comfortable smoke, smiling benignly on his two companions the while.

"Allah is great, and Mahomet is His prophet. The English are a brave race."

"You've about struck it there," answered George, yawning and stretching himself out on a heap of rugs. "To use an expression of your own—it is Kismet. I wonder what will happen next?"

"Sleep," replied the Oriental, laconically.

"Yes, and not before we need it. I suppose you will stick to the English now?"

"If the work of their servant is good in their eyes, I am content. Naoum is my master, and he knows what is best for Belbeis. I like the children of the West, they do not beat the faithful."

"I never came across a man with so much sense as you have, Belbeis," said George. "You always seem to understand intuitively."

"My life is for peace," replied the Arab. "Where I get that best, there is my heart, I am no soldier!"

"But a jolly good imitation of one, then," exclaimed George, laughing. "Why, man, you have the heart of a lion?"

"That I cannot help," he replied, with a look of pleasure in his eyes at his companion's words. "It is no doing of mine, circumstances make it so."

"Well, it's a good thing for us there are not many of your countrymen as brave," said George, sleepily. "Well," yawning again, "here goes for a little 'shut-eye.'"

In a few minutes Belbeis and the guide followed George's example, and the room in which they lay resounded with their stertorous breathing. At daybreak they awoke refreshed and once more ready for the day's work. After they had foraged for and devoured breakfast, the little force were paraded prior to manning the forts. An hour later the remainder of the nine hundred rode into the city and joined them.

Cairo was quite quiet and orderly. Patrols were sent out to prevent any riotousness on the part of the fanatics, and in this manner they awaited the arrival of the rest of the army.

During the afternoon, the Commander-in-Chief, with a large force, marched into the city from Zag-a-zig. He was met with acclamation by the entire populace, and received from the officer in command of the party to which our hero belonged the surrender of Arabi and Toulba Pashas; thus the war of rebellion, which had threatened to overwhelm the land of the Pharaohs and exterminate the domination of the Khedive's rule, was at an end.

Helmar saw now that his career with the British army would soon be at an end. He had done his duty, and, by his timely arrival at Tel-el-Kebir, had prevented the razing to the ground of the ancient capital. What now remained to him? As he looked these facts in the face, he realized that after about six months of hardships, misfortunes, and privations he was no better off than when he started; whatever he had done seemed now entirely forgotten.

Consulting Belbeis upon the matter that evening, he received the good fellow's opinion and advice.

"You do not know what to do?" replied the Arab, with a look of unusual surprise on his impassive face. "How can that be? You have not yet seen the master; he loves you, and you have done that which he wished for most, you have conveyed his papers to the General. Go to him, he will tell you that which you should do."

"That is all very well, Belbeis," said George, simply, "but I did it for my own benefit as well, and, besides, I owe him more than I can repay already."

Belbeis only smiled in answer, and, after a moment's pause, went on—

"We shall see, there is yet time for thought of the future. Allah will provide!"

After that, he left the citadel, and George was left to the companionship of his own thoughts. They were not very pleasant, and he put them from him and went out in search of his friend, Charlie Osterberg. He had not the least notion of where to find him. He knew the Engineers had arrived, but he was not aware of where they were quartered. However, a soldier whom he met told him they were outside the western gate of the city.

With this information he made his way through the slums until he came to the Governmental portion of the town. This he passed through, and at length reached the west gate. On making inquiries there, he was directed to the camp he sought, and with some difficulty discovered that Osterberg was with the troops. At last he found him in a tent with two or three other civilians attached to the force in a similar capacity to himself.

Charlie greeted his old friend and companion with open arms.

"Thank goodness, you are all right, George," he exclaimed, the moment our hero appeared in the doorway. "I was wondering when I should find you. I have only just been relieved from duty, or I should have been in search of you now."

"It's a good thing that it happened so," replied George, "or we should have both been searching in different directions, and so missed each other. Now tell me of all that has happened to you, we only had such a short time to talk when I saw you on the way to Tel-el-Kebir, that there must be still much to talk about."

Osterberg's career had been so uneventful after they parted at Alexandria that his story was soon disposed of, and then George consulted him on matters concerning the future.

"What do you intend doing, Charlie," he said, "now that the war is practically over?"

"Why, go back to the bank, of course—what did you expect? You see, I made that arrangement with my employers, and they gladly consented to it. Of course, business was at a standstill while the war was on, and they were glad to dispose of their clerks; but now it is over they'll want us back again. But you—how do you intend going on? Shall you still remain with the Government authorities as interpreter?"

"I can't say, I'm sure. Perhaps they won't want me," replied George, in tones that betrayed his reluctance to leave the service. "However, I expect they will soon enlighten us on that point."

"Why, George, you are a bigger stupid than I took you for! Do you think they are going to discharge the man who made that magnificent ride to save Cairo?"

"And himself!" put in George, in disgust. "There, for goodness sake, don't harp on that! Belbeis has just reminded me of it—it was nothing!"

"That may be so," replied Charlie, "but anyway all the troops seem to have got hold of the story, and do nothing but talk about it—they can't say too much for you. It isn't likely the Government will forget you."

"Oh, by the way," exclaimed George, to change the subject, "what is to be done with Arden? I suppose you haven't heard?"

"Yes, I have. He's to be tried along with other leaders of the revolt. The probability is that he'll get a heavy sentence and no doubt be banished from the country."

"Poor devil!" exclaimed George. "His ill-gotten wealth won't have done him much good. I doubt if he'll ever be able to touch a penny of it."

"'M! I'm not so sure. Mark is a cunning fellow, and probably has sent it all out of the country to some safe place where he can get at it again. For my part, I am not in the least sorry for him. Hanging would be a too merciful sentence for such a villain."

"Well, I have no doubt that all he deserves will fall to his lot. I bear him no malice; he is in trouble enough now; let us hope it will be a lesson to him."

"No fear," exclaimed Charlie, with a hard look on his boyish face. "Nothing will ever be a lesson to him; villainy was born in him, and if ever he escapes, mark my word, the authorities will hear of him again, or I am much mistaken."

His tone of conviction impressed his companion, and he looked sharply at him.

"Why, what do you think he will do—raise another rebellion?" he asked, incredulously.

"Stranger things have happened. We shall see. I am going to walk back to the city with you," he went on, as George rose to go. "A little fresh air will do me good."

The two friends linked arms and strolled back to Cairo. The night was deliciously cool, and each had much to talk about, going over and over again through the many incidents that had occurred since their arrival in Egypt. At last the citadel was reached, and George, to his great surprise, found Belbeis anxiously awaiting his return.

"My master, Naoum, bade me deliver this note," said he, directly our hero came up. "He wishes to see you to-night. He had not anticipated that you would return so soon."

"Good!" exclaimed George, scanning the contents of the missive. "Now you shall see my benefactor, Charlie. Come, Belbeis, conduct us to him, that is, if I may bring my friend."

"Your words are law to my master's servant," replied Belbeis; "to refuse you would be to cross the wishes of Naoum, and that cannot be."

Without waiting for a reply, Belbeis led the companions down to the best part of the city. Stopping at one of the smaller Oriental palaces, he disappeared, asking George to await his return. In a few moments he came back, and led the way into the great entrance hall, where they found Naoum waiting to receive them.

He greeted our hero with affection, and looked in surprise at Charlie. Helmar was quick to interpret the glance, and hastened to set his mind at rest.

"This is my greatest German friend, Naoum," he said, "and I brought him with me that he might meet the man who has done so much for a stranger in a strange land; his name is Charlie Osterberg."

Naoum acknowledged the introduction cordially, and begged them to rest.

"I was surprised when Belbeis told me that you had returned to Cairo again so quickly. Had I known it before, I should have sought you earlier," he said, in his well-known kindly tones. "There are many things I would say to you, but time presses, and no doubt you would return to rest."

The two young men shook their heads, and declared their willingness to hear all he had to say.

"I have been thinking of your future," he said, looking keenly at George. "We have so long been associated that it seems as if Allah had woven our lives together. I am unwilling that we should now part. The war is over, therefore the Government will have little for you to do."

George waited. Evidently Naoum had some proposition to make for his good. Somehow he did not like the thought of accepting more from this man who had done so much for him already, and yet he felt he had no right to refuse anything he might offer.

"As you know," resumed Naoum, as if afraid to come too bluntly to the point, "I am wealthy beyond the knowledge of your people. I do not rest, my money begets money, and I trade and traffic always—it is my pleasure. I have caravans all over the Soudan and Upper Egypt, bringing in the wealth of produce of the scattered tribes in that country, therefore I employ many to do my work."

He paused again, and a look of anxiety came into his eyes. He was fearful that Helmar might refuse what he was about to suggest.

"I would not ask you to be my servant, but I would give you caravans that you may go and trade for yourself. There is wealth beyond your dreams in the enterprise. I have no children of my own, my mother is old, and she is all I have in the world to care for. If you will accept what I offer you, you shall, when Allah brings my work to a close, succeed me in my business. Say, shall it be so?"

George did not answer at once, and Naoum waited patiently for him to speak. The generosity of this man knew no bounds; his offer was princely, and George hardly knew what to say. He hated to refuse this thing, for Naoum's heart was evidently set upon it, and yet he could not accept. The peaceful life of a trader, or at least the peaceful life he imagined it to be, had no attraction for him, despite the wealth accruing to it, and yet how could he make this good man understand? Naoum was still awaiting his reply, and George felt that he must not delay in giving his answer; perhaps if he could gain time he might see his way to doing as his protector wished, although, at present, he did not see how. Stepping over to the good man, he wrung him by the hand.

"Naoum, you are all too good to me—you overwhelm me with your generosity. At present I cannot give you a definite answer, you must give me time to consider. You know, at heart I am a soldier, and I would that my life ran in that groove; therefore I must think carefully before I decide. You will not think me ungrateful, I'm sure, for you know me well. To-morrow evening I will see you again, and give you my answer."

"Be it so, my son," answered Naoum, indulgently. "It is well to think. May Allah guide your thoughts into the right course! Go, and sleep well!"

The two young men left Naoum's house and hurried back to the citadel; here Osterberg said good-night, and went back to his own quarters.

That night Helmar did not sleep much, over and over again he thought of Naoum's offer, but with each attempt he failed to come to any decision. Wealth was not his main object; that, of course, had its attraction, but he wished to live the life of his choice; he had started as a soldier, and he wished to remain one, so that wealth sank into insignificance in his thoughts. He could not decide. For the first time in his life he failed to make up his mind.

With daylight he awoke from the broken slumber that had, at last, overtaken him. Already Belbeis was awake, and preparing breakfast. George sprang up to assist him. During the meal Helmar was unusually silent. The doubts of over-night were still upon him, and made him irritable. Belbeis noticed these signs, and refrained wisely from breaking in on his thoughts.

After breakfast Helmar went for a stroll round the fortress; the place was alive with troops, all the work of the day was carried out at this early hour, so that, when the heat of the day came on, the soldiers could rest. He was nearing the officers' quarters when a sergeant came out and walked quickly towards him.

"Ah," he said, as he came up, "I was just coming to look for you. You are wanted at once at the office—you had better come with me now."

George followed his guide without demur, and was conducted to the orderly room. After a short wait, he was shown in. A colonel was seated at the table, dictating a letter to his clerk. When our hero appeared he ceased, and, turning to a pile of papers, selected one from among the rest.

"I have just received this from the Commander-in-Chief. It is the result of the excellent way in which you assisted in saving this city from destruction. Listen!"

He then read out the following order—

"In consequence of the gallant conduct of Interpreter Helmar in conveying the information of the rebels' intention to destroy the city of Cairo by fire, his Highness the Khedive of Egypt has been pleased to appoint him to a responsible office in the Intelligence Department. The appointment will carry with it the honorary rank and pay of Lieutenant in the Egyptian army. Interpreter Helmar's acceptance of the post must be forwarded to the Commander-in-Chief without delay."

"I congratulate you, Lieutenant Helmar, on the result of your distinguished services," said the Colonel, breaking through his official iciness. "I hope what has gone before may be but the precursor of many such services in the future," and he shook our astonished hero by the hand.

"But, sir——"

"Tut, tut, man! I suppose I can reply to that letter in the affirmative? Such opportunities and promotion come but rarely. Good luck to you!"

Helmar signified his intention of accepting his good fortune at once, and with his head in a whirl of excitement, he left the orderly room in search of Naoum.

Hurrying down town, he found his benefactor, and explained what had happened.

"You see, Naoum, all my aspirations are for a soldier's life, and last night, when you made me that generous offer, I felt it impossible to tell you so; events that have happened since have made it impossible for me to longer conceal from you that a civil life would be distasteful to me. I beg that you will not be hurt at my refusal, and will understand my motives."

Naoum smiled at the young man's earnest manner, but the smile did not for a moment conceal from Helmar his deep disappointment that the decision was unfavourable to his offer.

"I am glad that you are pleased, my son, but it would be idle to disguise my disappointment. I had hoped that you would have been a son to me upon whom I might lavish all my wealth, but it is not to be. You must make your own way. You are young and independent, your brave heart is unquestionable, do as it dictates. I am your friend always. Allah is good and great—may He watch over you!"

After his conversation with Naoum, George had an interview with Mariam, and then sought out Charlie. He found him in his tent, getting ready to leave for Alexandria.

"I have just received my discharge," he said, directly George entered, "and am now off back to the bank. What are you going to do?"

Helmar seated himself on a flour barrel, and Charlie propped himself on an ammunition box.

"Do?" our hero exclaimed, bursting to recount his good fortune; "why, stay here, of course! I am now Lieutenant Helmar of the Egyptian army, with a post in the Intelligence Department! Well," he added, laughing at Charlie's astonished face, "why don't you salute me?"

And so, after months of hardships and failures, George Helmar had at last found what he sought. He reasonably considered that he had made a record in his search for fortune. An assured position in the walk of life he preferred, a liberal salary, and the prospect of heaps of adventure in the future. What more could he desire? Was there anything? Yes, there was. He wanted news of all in Germany. During the excitement of the last few months he had thought little of his friends and relatives in the Fatherland. Now that peace reigned, and he began to settle down in his new occupation, he longed to hear what had happened to them. As nobody, excepting friend Osterberg and foe Arden, knew of his whereabouts or what he was doing, he determined to write to his father and describe the adventurous time he had had, and tell him of the reward the end had brought him.

After a few weeks' interval he received what he wanted—a long letter in return. The item of news which pleased him most was that telling of the safe recovery of Landauer, his opponent in the duel.

"Thank God!" he exclaimed fervently. "My prayer was answered."

THE END